ALSO BY PATTY RICE

Somethin' Extra

REINVENTING THE WOMAN

A Novel

❧❧❧

PATTY RICE

SIMON & SCHUSTER

New York   London   Toronto   Sydney   Singapore

SIMON & SCHUSTER
Rockefeller Center
1230 Avenue of the Americas
New York, NY 10020

SIMON & SCHUSTER and colophon are registered
trademarks of Simon & Schuster, Inc.

Designed by Leslie Phillips
Manufactured in the United States of America

1   3   5   7   9   10   8   6   4   2

LIBRARY OF CONGRESS CATALOGING-IN-PUBLICATION DATA
Rice, Patty.
    Reinventing the Woman : a novel / Patty Rice.
        p. cm.
    1. Self-actualization (Psychology)—Fiction.
    2. Young women—Fiction. I. Title.
PS3568.I2927 R45 2001
813'.54—dc21   00-050471
ISBN 0-684-85341-8

ACKNOWLEDGMENTS

Commit thy works unto the Lord, and thy thoughts shall be established. Jesus, this work, I commit to you. Perhaps these fictional thoughts will establish the unthinkable . . . a multitude of women everywhere who, no matter what, realize they are beautiful, special, intelligent, and deserving of abundant life because you made them!

During this process there were many to lean on. Always, my family is at the foremost of my heart, especially my sister, Jan, and my brother, Mike. You two have no idea how much I needed you to be my friends and you've filled that prescription without question.

My husband, Tyuan . . . You have adapted to all of my many reinventions. Thank you for taking this journey with me.

Tonja and Pamela, you are the children I prayed for and I hope you grow to understand that a woman can do anything her heart desires. No apologies, no excuses.

Daddy, who just like the undertaker, is the last man to ever let me down. This reinvented woman will always be your little girl.

Dr. Ronald Frazier—chosen by God for many things; thankfully, one of those is to be my pastor and advising angel.

My editor, Dominick, you are the coolest, and somehow you always know the right things to say to this emotional being.

Catherine Hurst—I named a character for you, girl. I wish you well.

ACKNOWLEDGMENTS

Megan Bradley—your tireless effort is the greatest gift. In return, I wish for you the gift of every sweet dream you hold.

Neil Halliday—your patient spirit and endearing warmth are never forgotten; this project would not have been if not for you. I love you truly.

Jonathan Woodfork, my spiritual friend and a true angel—diamonds cannot compare to the jewels of wisdom you gave me.

John Inscoe—I pray your path runs smooth and well always. Let's keep kicking the big steel door. One day they'll forget to lock it and we will run free in the land of Oz that is fame and fortune.

Sandra Price—as usual, you are part of that glue that holds me together.

Sharon Conn—our friendship is ageless, boundless, bottomless.

Ronald Rice—my deepest respect belongs to you.

Oprah Winfrey—you taught me to remember my spirit and in doing so, unwittingly helped me write this book.

For Betty Massey and
Guiniviere Rice, who sacrificed,
and for Tiffany Griggs,
who did not . . .

Looking back to what has been
I understand that transformation is eternal
The woman stands, always almost formed
The Sculptor is forever molding, shaving, chipping
Forever uncovering new dimensions
That I could not have imagined exist inside of me

PATTY RICE, *Mosaic*

REINVENTING
THE WOMAN

1

*R*EINVENTING RULE ONE: *Don't be the wheel!*
Observe, take stock of your life. Then DECIDE
that you must change it.

A STORM WAS BREWING. The air had smelled of rain all day.
The sky was pitch black at a time when dregs of daylight
should have still been present. That meant the rain would
come any minute.

That morning, Camille had opened the dining room windows because the carpet was somewhat old and made the
room musty. Fresh air hadn't helped. The day had been too
stifling. But now a steady breeze whipped through the screen
of the long window, swelling the heavy rose drapes and rocking the vinyl vertical blinds like wind chimes. Outside, tree
leaves rustled in the wind, and there was thunder.

Inside, the lights were low, the table was set with fine china

15

and a good dinner. A Barry White CD played. It should have been a perfect evening. But there was spilled chardonnay on the table, flowing out of an overturned crystal wine glass that had chipped at the rim when it hit the table. Evan was angry.

"I asked you a question, woman," he said. "Why the hell were you gone so long?"

His perfect teeth were clenched, and Camille cringed, saying nothing. It wasn't a question, but an accusation. The keen nostrils of his blunt, straight nose were violently flared. He stroked his neat, dark goatee thoughtfully as he leaned across the table to look at Camille up close, ignoring the spilled wine. Then he moved away. Camille audibly sighed. She watched him begin to pace, stalking the room. Evan was a big man, six feet three inches, but lean and knobby, giving his movements a kind of sleek glide. He had a generous forehead and abundant black brows shadowing bronze eyes that were cold and clear. Despite his clean-cut appearance—a close cut, clean shave, and natty clothes from the men's shop where he worked in sales—those eyes were dangerous.

She knew what this was really about: Evan's promotion at work hadn't come through. It always began like this. Out of nowhere. One moment he was calm and laughing. In the next minute he would be furious, flexing his hands as if he wanted to tear something apart. Shaking his head as if he was locked in a battle with his own thoughts. Nothing could reach him when things got that far.

Camille stared at her food, her whole body drawn into a

single knot, and whispered, "Evan, please." Tears fell into her plate. She had held onto so much hope lately. Four months had gone by since the last incident—enough time to make her think that things would work out finally. That she wouldn't have to leave Evan.

"Please. That all you got to say for yourself? I know you been creeping! Out with some punk!" A vein in Evan's neck stood out like barbed wire.

Camille measured out her words. "I went across town," she said. It was so hard to force the words out that she had to clear her throat and sip some wine. Her hand shook, and some wine slid down the side of the glass onto her palm.

"I went to that bakery you like so much. It was rush hour. Traffic was bad." She remembered to be careful with her tone.

"Is he better than me, Camille? Is that it? Some high-on-the-hog dude from work, I bet! Wearing expensive suits. Pushing a Benz. You like that kind of shit, don't you? 'Cause he can afford you and your expensive ass taste! Limoges, my ass!"

She watched in shock as the new dishes crashed against the wall and broke apart. Fettucini mingled with flakes of leftover caesar salad and a wedge of uneaten garlic bread, and dribbled down the wall.

"Evan, please don't do this. Please." Lightheaded with fear, she slid her chair out from the table.

A sharp line of lightning etched the sky, and the lights flickered. Camille thought about her purse near the front door where she always left it, just in case. Thankfully her keys were in her left pocket. She'd put them there when she had struggled with the shopping bags out of the car.

"Tell me his name, Camille. What he look like?" Evan's face was contorted. His brilliant brown eyes were narrowed to slits. Brow furrowed. Mouth tight. Chest heaving. He was ready to lash out.

Camille did the only thing she knew how to do. She tried to reason with him. Reassure him. Sometimes it worked, sometimes not. When it didn't she ended up bloody and once in the emergency room lying about how her nose had been broken.

"Evan, you know how much I love you. I swear, I would never—"

In a swift moment she was blinded with a vicious slap and wrenched by the wrist from her chair. Her glasses struck the floor and a lens cracked. The room blurred somewhat. If she could get to her car, she could get her extra pair of eyeglasses and get away, but right now Evan was gripping her and yelling.

A flash of lightning whipped across the sky, snuffing out the electricity. The lights and music went dead. A blast of thunder followed. Evan was surprised enough to loosen his hold. Camille was quick enough to dash away from him. Her shoes were slippery from the pasta she'd stepped over in the dining room. She tripped by the coffee table in the living room and found herself flat on her stomach on the hardwood floor. For a second she was panicked and disoriented. The fall hurt. It almost knocked the wind out of her, but she forced herself to move and shimmied like a rabbit beneath the long sofa while she caught her breath and held her stomach in anguish.

No one who knew her would ever guess that this happened to her. But it was as if when he beat her, she became someone else. It was almost as if she could channel a different Camille. Out of fear, she scaled down to the lowest denominator of a human, a kind of weak prey whose only thought was movement and whose single instinct was survival. She never fought back. She didn't dare. She struggled. She cried out. She pleaded. She protected her breasts, her neck, her face. Or she hid. Like now.

The house was completely dark, though intermittent streaks of lightning threw spools of brightness through the living room window. It wasn't raining yet, but it was on the verge. The tree leaves still rustled furiously in the wind, and thunder grumbled low.

"Woman, bring your ass out here! Now!"

Camille cringed. A splinter of wood from the floor poked through her sweater. The side of her face and mouth stung where he'd slapped her. She could taste blood in her mouth and from the throbbing in her cheek and eye, knew that her face would swell. Her wrist hurt terribly, and she thought it might be sprained. It was hard not to cry out. She was scared, sure that he would eventually smell her hiding place as he had before. But she'd never thought of the sofa before.

Camille wished she could see, but there was no light anywhere. She concentrated on trying to determine where Evan was. His footsteps resounded on the hardwood floor.

"I mean it, Camille," he said.

The calmness of his voice was a warning. The last time he sounded like this he'd rushed the locked bathroom door to get to her and had broken her nose. If she could just get enough time to slide out from her hiding place and get to the door, she could probably make it to her car. A loud crash almost brought her out from beneath the sofa.

Jesus, make this stop, she prayed silently.

"Shit." He had probably hurt himself somehow.

Things were being thrown.

"When I get my hands on you, girl . . ."

The rain started. It was hard, angry. Camille felt the bulge of her car keys in her pocket pressing uncomfortably against her thigh. Sweat caused her scalp to tingle. If she was careful, she could get to the front door now. With the rain, he wouldn't be able to distinguish the sound of her movements, especially since the windows were open. She inched. Evan was pounding toward the bedroom, raging.

With one hand, Camille pulled herself, sliding across the waxed floor. And she ran. Without looking back, she charged full force toward the door and tore it open. She ignored the cold tingle of wild rain pounding her flesh and melting into the fibers of her clothing. She barely heard Evan screaming her name and never turned to see him racing behind her. All she knew was that she had made a promise to herself three months before and that somehow, she had to survive. So she ran. She ran for her life.

⊰⊱

ON THE DRIVE HOME, on the drive back to Maryland from New Jersey, Camille drank warm soda to wash down Advils for a throbbing headache. She talked to herself about what she was doing, gassed up the car once, fished out toll money, listened to a motivational tape, and thought.

Her clothes had the feel of damp, excess skin. She had wrung out her thick, wet hair in the gas station lot, found a scrunchy in the glove compartment to make a ponytail with, and turned the defrost up high to warm herself and erase the white glaze from her car windows.

The rain fell in ragged sheets. The car wipers swung furiously across the windshield, and Camille drove at snail's pace. It was difficult to distinguish the lanes, so managing her black Saab carefully across the highway, she stuck close to a tan Voyager in front of her.

Normally, she would have been afraid of all the rain and would have pulled over to wait it out. But tonight she thanked God for its cover; it helped her feel safe. Besides, she was too deep in thought to worry about the rain. She sifted through the past seven years of her life trying to understand what went wrong. Why it had to end with her leaving like this when their life together had begun with promise.

Camille thought back to the warm fall day she'd met Evan.

She had been a senior at Columbia. Back then the only things that fazed her were getting good grades, trying to fit in, and the pull of Manhattan. There was life being lived in New York City. People roaming the streets on their way to somewhere fast. Gritty sidewalks. Other languages. Pungent smells of foods and car perfumes. Showy buildings. Noise. But most of all the people.

Camille liked to sit and watch them. She often sat near Rockefeller Center with a yellow legal pad and pen and wrote out details about what the people might be like—their backgrounds. She wasn't sure at the time what she would do with her degree when she finished school and hadn't quite made up her mind about graduate school.

She met Evan on a Friday. He was drinking a Coke and loafing with four other boys. He was cute. Cool. Tall. A lemon brown. Bowlegged. Wearing khaki shorts and an Eddie Bauer T-shirt. She couldn't see his eyes because of his black Ray-Bans.

"What you looking at?" His smile was devastating. She hadn't known teeth could be so white. When he smiled like that, his friends faded into the background, and it made her bold enough to tell him, "You."

When he lowered his shades, she saw that his eyes were like a cat's. She wanted him to push his shades back above his nose because that way he looked less intimidating. She felt plain in his presence. No guy that attractive had ever paid her any attention.

"You from around here? What you writing?"

"I'm in school," is all she said.

"An educated woman. I like that. Where you go?" He sat next to her, folding his arms.

"I'm in my last year at Columbia. I might stay and do my master's. I'm not sure yet. Are you from New York?" she asked.

"Jersey. What's your name?"

"Camille."

"Pretty. It suits you. Camille what?"

She was so flattered she could barely regulate her intense smile.

"Foster." She uncrossed her legs and her pen fell on the ground. As they both reached to pick it up, his lean fingers touched hers. A swift, fluttery feeling lurched in her stomach.

"I'm Evan. You like buffalo wings?"

The question made her scrunch her nose. "What?"

"I don't have a lot of money to take a girl to dinner, but I got enough for some wings and something to drink at TGI Fridays. It's walking distance." Camille liked the way he talked with his hands.

He ate most of the wings because Camille was too nervous to eat. But they talked nonstop. When he dropped her off at her dorm, she knew that he was the eldest of four boys. He had told her that he had been raised by his mother and stepfather after his father died from a heart attack. That he had dropped out of high school in the eleventh grade, had gotten his GED at twenty, and was working as a sales associate at a men's clothing store. He'd just started. Commission was a bitch, he'd said.

She knew too that Evan was immature, but in a sweet, sincere way. He asked her if she wouldn't mind if he joined her to people-watch on Saturday, and when she said yes, he kissed her hand.

What followed were nights when they sat in greasy spoon restaurants thick with frying food smells, drinking hot Lipton tea with milk from paper cups (Evan was convinced that coffee was as bad as cigarettes), and eating chicken wings most often (Evan's favorite). They'd sit, sharing the same side of the booth, their eyes on each other shyly while they talked about her classes, his job, their outlooks on life, places they'd been, and everything they hoped to do and see.

Then they'd walk around the city silently, her slim brown hand pocketed into his firm one. Camille would squeeze his hand, pressing her palm close against the calluses he'd gotten over the summer while helping unload ships, and a satisfied lightness would warm her in the crisp fall air lurking in the dark streets.

On a particular night, a month after they had been meeting nearly every evening, Camille told Evan she loved him. She remembered it so clearly now that she could have been watching a movie of her life play out on the rain-whipped windshield of her car. She remembered saying it to herself in her room first before telling him. *I love you, Evan.* A whisper made under her breath. She lay awake half that night saying it. Smiling. Saying it again, then shifting beneath the covers with a sigh, anxious and happy. There had begun an ache in her to tell Evan how she felt, coupled with worry she had lived with for days that kept her from studying for a poli sci exam.

That special night they went to Rita's Place, a lights-down-low kind of place with candles in the centers of the tables in red globes with white netting basketing the globes. Evan had reached for her hand across the table. Fed her a smile. And then she was saying it, telling him she loved him in a voice so soft that he almost didn't hear it because of the Eckstine mood music lifting out of wall speakers hanging on the bark brown paneling. Evan started to laugh—not in an amused way but a shy one. He'd stirred milk into his tea with his butter knife. "I love you too, honey babe," he'd said. "I love you, too."

At that moment when he'd loved her, she had felt alive and powerful. As if nothing on earth could break her stride.

Camille flexed the fingers of her right hand, then gripped the wheel again. Her wrist still hurt. She tapped the brake as she reached a toll booth and asked herself, *When did it change? When did I change?* Somewhere along the way, she had fallen asleep in her life. That brought tears. She took deep breaths to ward them off. She couldn't afford to cry again right now. She had a few more hours of hard driving to do. Her face still throbbed and the Advil hadn't quite dulled the pain behind her eyes. She flipped exact change into the toll basket and sped off when the signal turned green.

Camille caught her reflection in the rearview mirror. It was terrible. Her distended cheek and her lip were scarred from Evan's ring. Her eyes were deerlike and lost. *Don't think about it.* She needed a diversion. A little music might help. Something light and carefree. She ejected the motivational tape and pressed the Seek button. An oldies station played a Motown song. One of her favorites. She liked movie soundtracks. It was Diana Ross singing "Baby Love" in an offbeat nasal whine.

If she had to make a clear determination of when things went wrong, her automatic answer would have been that the spiral started the first time Evan struck her. At the time, they had been dating for a good year. Her virginity was gone. She'd visited the clinic for pills and condoms during their second month together, when the kissing got so overwhelming that whenever they'd stop long enough for her to open her eyes and breathe a moment, another article of clothing would have amazingly disappeared.

She had graduated from college by this time, come back from a trip to Europe, and found a tiny apartment to share with two other women. She was preparing to enter grad school too. She and Evan were like twins, joined at the hip, because he didn't like her to be out of his sight for long. All of his big plans had not come to fruition over the summer. Not yet, he would say repeatedly, then tell her more of his dreams. She later realized that Evan was just a talker. Sheer laziness and procrastination always got the better of him.

Camille paid for every recreational thing they did. Her parents gave her a good allowance, so she had more than enough money. It was what caused the first incident. She wanted to celebrate their year anniversary by going to a nice restaurant. He wanted to do something he could afford.

"But I don't mind paying for you. I never mind," she'd said, putting on her lip gloss. The next thing she knew, her tube of pink gloss hit the flimsy little mirror so hard it cracked it. She'd been slapped and her arm painfully twisted behind her. For a moment she had been frozen in time, seeing his face change and twist into something that had never come out before.

She burst into tears after the shock wore off, and Evan had snapped back to life, crying too because he'd hurt his honey babe. He begged her not to leave him. He was sorry. He was sorry. *Promise me you won't leave me.* He always said that. He made love to her as an expression of his apology. She forgave him, and they ordered in pizza and ate it in her bedroom with the cheap wine he'd brought with him, the light from a wax-worn candle glowing against their faces.

That first time was a rehearsal for how their relationship would play out. But it wasn't when her life had shifted. What she compared it to was when she, as a little girl, had determined to watch the sunset. She wanted to pinpoint exactly when the sky changed to night. No matter how often she tried it, some small distraction kept her from actually seeing it happen. Then she figured out that the sky would grow darker by

27

degrees. Because it did, she didn't notice until it had already happened. That's how her life was. She couldn't pinpoint when and how she had accepted Evan's abuse as normal because it had happened so gradually. That bothered her.

For so long, leaving hadn't been a viable option. If she had wanted to leave Evan, there was no one to turn to. Camille had separated from her family. She had no friends. She told herself that working harder on the relationship was the only solution. To keep peace, she existed daily in the web of a routine that he built for her consisting of work, television, him, and sleep.

She didn't have hobbies. Evan didn't allow it. It took time away from him, he'd said. What should have been her outlet, her job, had gotten lost in the shuffle of her trying to hold herself together as best she could. She'd gotten sidetracked from her career and watched her coworkers, mostly men, grab the promotions and bonuses she'd craved. For the past few years, she hadn't had enough energy to jump-start her career. Evan took so much out of her sometimes that there was nothing left to give. Camille did just enough to get by.

Her low-rated performance meant she had to accept the low-ball raises quietly that had come her way lately. She wasn't about to make any noise over 3 percent raises. She still had her job there only because her boss, Valerie, had mentored her from the start of her career at Braxton Enterprises and kept hoping Camille would lift herself out of the slump.

It hurt to see Val give the good projects to Dean or that arrogant s.o.b. Craig Henry because she knew Camille wasn't up to par anymore. Just these five months alone Camille had missed trips to South Africa, Uruguay, and Japan. But she'd felt powerless and unsure of herself, and it showed in her work. Outwardly she appeared calm and uncaring. Inside she was in constant turmoil, wanting to tell somebody what was happening at home.

She wished she had the nerve to show up in Valerie's office with the black eye or the bruised face, the busted lip, the choke fingerprints around her neck, and say, "This is why I missed the two o'clock meeting. This is why I called in sick." Then Val wouldn't have looked at her with disappointment anymore, but pity. She would have helped Camille find a way to end this ugly roller-coaster ride that she couldn't seem to get off of by herself all those years. Now she would have to take a leave of absence.

Called in sick. Camille thought about that for a moment. She laughed bitterly as she merged onto the turnpike. It struck her funny. *Called in sick.* It was ironic because she wasn't sick at all. It was Evan who was sick. It had been his sickness all along, but she'd ignored it and denied it too long. It was a strange thought to swallow that the man she loved was incapable of controlling himself.

Nora's tape first put the concrete thought in Camille's head that she might deserve a better life. Camille received promo items from her mother's best friend whenever Nora put out a new self-help program or updated a series. There were cassette packs, books, and work journals in a box in the back of her closet. They were hidden from Evan. He thought it was a bunch of bull like everything else he didn't understand or agree with.

One day a single tape came. The title on the outside of the mini bubble package had said, *The Pursuit of Hope.* It was a test copy that Nora's company was trying out on select women, with a response card inside for comment. On the way to work one morning, Camille had listened to the tape. Everything Nora said hit a nerve. "Don't be the wheel," she instructed. "Know that you're a woman and that you have the power to reinvent yourself. Your life."

When the tape finished, Camille sat in the parking garage and cried for an hour. Here she was, an educated woman, as Evan had first called her, with a master's in anthropology, working as a demographer for a good firm. Evan was still a sales associate, immature, and still complaining about working on commission. Seven years later. His insecurities didn't drive him to seek better. He seemed driven only to destroy everything he touched.

Nora's tape had thrust a lot of truths in her face that morning. On the response card, Camille had checked off the box that said she would buy the product and wrote out in the area allotted for comments that the tape made her want to change the way she lived. Camille promised herself then, in her car, that the next time Evan hit her, she would find a way to leave as soon as she could.

Camille had left all of the rain behind halfway up the turn-pike. She cranked her speed up a few notches to seventy-five and set the cruise control. Nothing but clear sky darkness with a forefront of miles of trees lay ahead. She took her glasses off briefly to clean them on her knee and wiped her moist, brown eyes with the back of her hand, wincing as she grazed her puffy cheek. It was two in the morning, and she was almost at Mel's. She had to pull over twice—once to get more Pepsi from a 7-Eleven and again to pee and get directions at a twenty-four-hour Safeway. Once out of the shopping district, Camille traveled a main road in the quiet neck of a modern neighbor-hood.

When the surroundings grew familiar, Camille observed the setting more closely. Suburban Maryland hadn't changed, but at the same token it *was* different. The fundamental dis-tinctions were there: tree-lined streets, cookie-cutter houses, manicured lawns, two cars out front, privacy fencing contain-ing backyards. What was different was the lack of greenery. Even seven short years ago, Camille remembered a lushness that no longer existed. Real estate had taken over. Vast sec-tions of trees had been hewn down and replaced with dou-ble-decker houses. It was like a cancer the way the builders seized wooded areas and piled up houses at every turn. No wonder kids stayed in the house these days to play Nintendo and surf the Net. There was no place to play. Everything was too set up. The small, dense areas where she'd picked wild berries, built a fort, and climbed trees with the Johnson

girls were gone now. Camille felt a sense of loss that surprised her.

She noticed she was sleepy when she reached the familiar
winding road she'd ridden her bike on a thousand times as a
kid. Only then did the enormity of what she was doing hit her.
She was going home. Actually going back to the house she
had determined she would never see again. It was like running from one pain to another one. A waterfall of memories
hit her senses.

"I can't believe I'm here," she murmured, shaking her head.
Her throat was dry. She fumbled in her purse for a stick of
gum with one hand and hung a right onto Causewell—a favorite hangout street for neighborhood kids where one of
those big blue-painted postal mailboxes sat on a corner and
doubled as a good object to lean on. She had hung out there
quietly many times, watching some of the arrogant boys
break-dance on flattened cardboard to Grandmaster Flash and
the Furious Five, trying to repeat moves they'd seen on the
movie *Beat Street*.

Camille made an immediate left onto Reiter Avenue, wishing the tightness in her chest would subside. This was her
street. She had to go slow. The road was narrow and winding,
with cars parked on either side. The neighborhood was
smaller than she remembered. As a child, it seemed that the
neighborhood had been a world in and of itself. When she was
very little, the only confirmation she had that anything else
existed outside this soldiered band of brick homes with four-

columned frontage was when she rode the bus to school or went anywhere with her parents, where looking out the window proved that there were trees, houses, and people in other places.

Camille coasted now, trying to take in everything she passed. The closer she got to the house, the more she wondered if she'd made a mistake in coming. It was too painful. It hurt almost as much as leaving Evan. She swerved to miss hitting a Navigator parked too far from the curb. Then put both hands on the wheel, ignoring the catch in her swollen wrist.

Coming home was different from what it would have been had she come back long ago. The house had been Melanie's for two years now. Her parents weren't there anymore. Her father, Wade, had died after a series of strokes. Catherine took it hard and ended up moving to South Carolina at the invitation of a family friend. Camille hadn't accepted that Wade was really gone. It didn't seem real to her. But now it hit her that when she got to the house, he wouldn't be in his favorite chair anymore—the old brown La-Z-Boy—with a section of the *Washington Post* spread neatly across his knees.

She was ashamed that a promise she'd made to herself brought her back here when the illness and then death of her own father (though Mel had pleaded with her to come) never once compelled her to return.

As far as she knew, Mel had forgiven her for that. Mel hadn't agreed with her reasons for staying away, but she'd respected Camille's decision. Camille prayed Mel would respect this decision too and hoped Mel would understand that she needed somebody.

The sisters had never been that close. They hadn't seen each other since Camille had gone to college. Mel had stayed in Maryland, worked for a few years, then went to Howard University to study architecture. In her second semester, she fell in love with a boy in her English lit class and by the end of the term, dropped out to have his baby and moved in with him in his parents' basement. The relationship didn't last, and before her ninth month, Mel had moved back home to have her baby.

During Mel's pregnancy, she and Camille began exchanging letters. None of Mel's friends from school wanted to hear about swollen ankles, frequent trips to the bathroom, cravings, or how the weight of the baby pressed so much on her lungs that she had to lie on her side in bed if she wanted to breathe. She poured out her depression in pages and pages that Camille read repeatedly. And Camille wrote back, being careful not to show her excitement about New York. She wrote instead about how tough her classes were, how lonely she was because nobody would be her friend, and that she was afraid she would never meet a boy.

They called each other on holidays and birthdays, and Camille sent her nephew, Ben, boxes of toys and clothes. Lately the two had gotten into the habit of sending e-mails once a week. In fact, the more Camille thought about it, the more she realized that there was no question that Mel would welcome her. She was coming back to the one place she knew she could get help. She pressed on the gas.

The next-door neighbor's house where the Johnsons lived came into view as she rounded the corner. Then she saw her old house. Ninety-two twenty-four. All brick, two stories. Mel had kept it up nice. There were new windows, and the shutters had been painted white. The busted lamppost was in the same condition it had been in since '78, when Mel had thrown a wild baseball pitch. Camille smiled when she saw it. The only time she remembered Mel getting punished. Behind the houses, a string of wall barriers had been constructed to block out the noise from the highway.

Camille rolled down her window to breathe in the moist, humid air as she pulled into the well-worn drive and felt relieved. Evan would never find her here. She was safe now. She didn't have one clue what to do next, but she was sure that somehow Mel would help her figure out what her next move should be.

2

*R*EINVENTING RULE TWO: *Know exactly what you want and who you want to be before you begin to make a change. No temple is built without a blueprint.*

———◦———

CAMILLE COULDN'T GET OUT of the car yet. She turned off the engine and sat very still. Her headlights shined on the house. She was home. The prodigal daughter returning. How would Mel take it? Would she feel that she'd intruded on her life? But what other place could she go where Evan wouldn't find her? She couldn't afford to just move somewhere else, and there were no friends to help.

Up close, the house was not all that pretty anymore. The gutters needed work. Mel wasn't exactly a gardener. The flower bed was overrun. The paint on the pillars was chipped and faded. The house reminded Camille of herself, battered and bruised but still standing.

She was overwhelmed by the memories flooding her mind. It made her cry and tremble. A shaky hand gripped the dash. She leaned her head against the steering wheel and closed her eyes tightly. In the center of the yard was where she and Mel set up the sprinklers in the summers so they could put on their swimsuits and cool off when the temperature broke eighty. On the walkway to the house, they'd played hopscotch and jacks. *You cheated!* she would scream. Mel would laugh, and their mother would eventually open the screen just a peep to give Camille a cold look. There was double dutch and kick-ball in the middle of the street. Dodgeball too.

They played hard with the big, husky Johnson girls and the Newmans' boy, Cedric, whose little sister, Monique, tagged along, trying to keep up. Camille had lived outside in the summer, it seemed. *Go somewhere and play,* her mother would tell her. The neighborhood became her haven.

On rainy days she would sit cross-legged on the porch and read Nancy Drew mysteries or Mark Twain's *Huck Finn*. She hadn't thought about that in years. She loved the sound of the rain hitting the roof. Hearing it drain through the gutters. When it was cloudless near the end of summer, she would lean every day against her father's Buick and watch the boys play football in Aaron Hicks's yard across the street, practic-ing for Boys Club tryouts. Mel would sidle up. "That one's mine," she'd say, pointing at the one they called Tall Mike be-cause he had a head lead over the other boys. "I'ma marry him one day," she'd say. "He's not fine," Camille would tell her. Camille had secretly liked him too, but would have died if anybody knew it. Tall Mike didn't know she existed.

What made her homecoming easier was that Catherine was no longer in this house. Camille was numb toward her mother. The woman had never loved her. It was always Mel whom Catherine mothered and took special care of. She was the favorite. Camille never accepted that fact, but she dealt with it. She adjusted to it so that when Catherine would leave her at home to take Mel shopping, Camille wouldn't cry because she couldn't go. When Catherine brought home only enough treats for Mel and herself, Camille made herself act as if she could care less. She got used to being ignored unless she was underfoot. Then it was, *Go somewhere and play,* or *Find something constructive to do.* Catherine had even turned Wade against her, telling him that Camille was getting too old for all of his attention. She made it sound as if girls, once their bodies began to develop, never again needed to be talked to and held by their fathers.

Why couldn't she make herself get out of the damn car? Her face hurt. In fact, her entire body hurt. She was damp and her skin itched from the rough sweater. Her legs were cramped, her lower back knotted and tense. Any length of time spent sitting affected her back these days. She should have gone to see a chiropractor after Evan had thrown her down the stairs that last time he hadn't controlled his temper.

She reached out for the door handle, but stopped. Not yet. Catherine's face was in her head. She thought about the day she left home for good. Ready for college, her brand-new luggage was already loaded in her father's car. She'd reached out to hug her mother.

"Let's not make a big display," her mother had said and had patted her shoulder. "Don't let none of them boys sweet-talk you into anything you can't get out of, and you know what I mean. Be careful on that road, Wade." Catherine dismissed Camille with a wave of her hand and didn't wait to see them drive off.

But Catherine wasn't here anymore.

Camille had to get out of this car. Out of the corner of her eye, she noticed a cat tiptoeing down the block. She followed it with her eyes as it crept. Watching the plump cat, its long white body slinking away in the night, she thought maybe she should quietly slip off too. She was too scared to go inside—that was why this was so hard. What had seemed like the best idea on the road seemed impossible now that she was here. Mel had enough problems. She had a son she was raising alone. Her sister on her doorstep with nothing but the clothes on her back would probably be too much. This was a mistake, she told herself. A shelter would be a better idea than this.

Camille turned the ignition, but paused before putting the car in gear. A light had come on in a top floor window. It was her parents' old bedroom. Camille saw a shadow, then the silhouette of a face in the window. The car headlights must have attracted someone in the house. She hadn't turned them off.

Everything went dark when she did. Few streetlights lit the block, and their house was at a dead end. Too late. More lights were being turned on. The curtains were drawn back from the big picture window at the front of the house. It had to be Mel. Camille sighed, giving up on her plan to find a shelter tonight. She'd been spotted, so she figured she might as well make her appearance at the door.

"Who's there?" Mel, standing behind the door, said it with authority like a soldier, with a threat to it.

"Mel, it's me. Camille." She massaged her aching wrist.

"I've got a gun in one hand and a bat in the other, so whoever you are, you'd better get away from my door before I call the cops!"

"Mel, it's Cam. Open up." Her lip was swollen so her words were slurred.

"Who?" This time it was said more gently, as if she thought she knew who it was, but was trying to place the voice.

"Camille." Her voice came scratchy and forced.

"What in the world . . ."

Locks clicked. A chain slid. Melanie, her older sister by three years, flung open the door with a surprised smile that turned to disbelief when she saw the state that Camille was in. Mel was built thin like Camille, but voluptuous and coffee brown. Her eyes were hazel because she wore colored contacts. She had on Maryland U sweats and a pair of down-trodden slippers. Mel's broad face was framed in a flowing fringe of beaded braids that clicked with every move.

"What the—how in the—Who? Oh, my God," she said. And pulled Camille inside. Camille winced at the pressure of Mel's hand near her wrist.

"I know I must look a mess," she said. It was painful to talk. Her voice shook, and she bowed her head because she was so ashamed.

Mel led her to the family room couch with an arm around her waist.

"What happened to your face?" she asked calmly.

"Evan."

"Evan? You two had a fight?" They sat gingerly. Camille flexed her back and massaged it cautiously.

"I left him. I swear it's the last time he'll ever do this to me again."

"Do this a—you mean he's done this kind of thing to you before?" Mel took Camille's face delicately in her hand and raised her chin. "Camille?" Her eyes were searching Camille's face for an explanation.

"I can't do it anymore. I have to . . . I can't be with Evan any-more."

Her eyes were downcast. Camille pushed Mel's hand away and stared at the lamp on the end table. It was the same one she remembered from years ago, but in a different place. It used to sit beside the chair where her father used to read. A different sadness overtook her.

"What happened?" Mel was asking, and Camille turned back toward her sister.

"We fought. I didn't have anywhere else to go."

Mel blinked.

"I can't believe I'm hearing this, Cam. I can't."

Camille sniffled and said, "I don't mean to intrude." She hated the look in her sister's eyes. She couldn't stand her own weakness.

"Intrude? Cam, we're family. If we don't have anyone else, we have each other. You know that."

Camille sighed. She hadn't known that. That was how other families were, but *they* had never been a real family. At least she hadn't felt part of the family.

"What happened, Cam?"

"Did you get Nora Jordan's new tape?"

"Who?"

"Nora."

"Mama's friend? What's she got to do with your face?"

"Did you get it? Did you listen to it?"

"I haven't gotten anything from her. What are you talking about? Can we speak English here, Cam?"

"I got a tape a couple weeks ago. It was called *The Pursuit of Hope.*" Camille sounded far away.

"It's three o'clock in the morning, Cam. Where are you going with all of this nonsense?"

"I made a promise to myself," Camille said.

"A promise? Look, all I want to know is why Evan did this to you."

"He beat me, Mel." Camille looked at Mel out of the corner

43

of her eye to see how she was taking it. She hoped Mel wouldn't be angry with her.

"Why didn't you tell me? All this time we've been talking and you didn't tell me."

Camille didn't have an answer to that.

"I don't know," she said. "I didn't tell anybody. I was so . . . I never knew what might set him off. He kept saying he would stop, but . . . I promised myself I was going to leave him if he hurt me again. I listened to Nora's tape. I promised myself."

Mel reached for the phone.

"What are you doing?" Camille asked

"Calling information to get the number for the police in Jersey. What's your county?"

"No." Camille grabbed her sister's hand. "Hang it up."

"What? Cam, you have to report this."

"Mel, please."

"You're just gonna let that bastard get away with this? Look at your face."

Mel reached out to touch it, but Camille pulled back.

"You're gonna wake Ben," Camille said.

Mel closed her eyes and took a moment to calm down.

"How can you allow him to get away with this? Again?"

"Mel, you have to understand. I came here because I had to get out. And I have to start over."

"There's nothing wrong with starting over, but look at you. He should be arrested."

44

"No. I came here to . . . Mel, he doesn't know where to find me. I need to figure out what to do. I've gotta—"

"Okay, okay." Mel put up a hand. "You did the right thing. You're here. We'll figure it out together." She put an arm around Camille, and Camille shook her head.

"I wish me and Evan could have made it work. I don't understand why there was always so much anger between us."

"Apparently the man has issues that have nothing to do with you, Cam. You can't help him manage his anger any more than he could help you understand that you don't deserve to be hit. I can't believe you put up with that all this time."

"I know I don't deserve what he did. But if he would have just—"

"If he would have just nothing. No excuses. That's part of the problem right there. You obviously don't realize that this is wrong. Cam, I can't believe I'm sitting here having this discussion with you. All this time I've been jealous of you, thinking you have it all. Big job up in New York. Good-looking man. A master's degree. Your freedom because you aren't stuck with a kid like me. Girl, you have everything going for you. I don't understand you, Cam. How can you sit around and be some man's punching bag?"

Was that all she'd been? She was silent for awhile.

"All I wanted was for Evan to change. I love him, Mel. I don't expect you to understand that, and I don't proclaim it to be right, but there it is. I still think that if he could have just had some positive things happen for him, things would have been different between the two of us."

"Sounds to me like things haven't been different ever since you've known the bastard. I didn't even know what this man was doing, but from what you told me about him before, he sounded rude and controlling. Now here I find out that he got violent with you? Look at yourself. *Look.* You can barely talk with your face like that. Evan doesn't need you to make excuses for him."

"Don't you think I know this?"

"I think you *want* to know this. That's why you're here. Seems to me that part of you wants out of your nightmare, but there's another part of you that's not so convinced. Especially with you sitting here giving me some 'things would have been different' speech. Now what happened between you tonight?"

Camille sighed. "I can't just turn off my love for Evan and throw away seven years like it never happened. I'm not a robot." Camille took off her glasses and groaned, holding the side of her face. Mel put her hand against her forehead and groaned.

"Oh, Cam. You're in pain. And I'm just sitting here making you talk about all this. What kind of sister am I? I'm sorry. Hey. I'll be right back." She went into the kitchen. In a moment she was back with a plastic bag holding cubes of ice.

Camille accepted the ice pack.

"Tell me what happened." Mel rubbed the middle of Camille's back with the flat of her hand to encourage her to talk. Camille took a deep breath.

"Well . . . he called me at work and told me that one of the other guys got the assistant store manager position he was vying for. He had been so sure he'd get it too. He's been there longer than the rest of them, and most of those guys are fresh out of high school. When he called me, he was so blown. I just wanted to do something to show him I was in his corner. I went home early and made a special dinner. I didn't have any good dishes, and I wanted to get fresh bread from the bakery, so I left him a note and ran out to get a few things. Somehow that set him off."

Camille tensed from the weight of the homemade ice pack against her sore cheek.

"What'd he do?" Mel asked.

"Broke the dishes. Hit me." This was too hard to talk about. It was still too fresh. Camille closed her eyes. Her cheeks were wet. The pasty front of her hair sponged up a tear at the bottom of one cheek. Her shoes pushed out against the telephone books under the coffee table.

She said, "I don't feel like getting into anymore details. I can't tonight." The croak in her voice was pitiful. She was so tired.

"Okay. I'm won't rush you. But tell me this. How the hell did you get away?"

"I just got out of there. I left." She didn't want to rehash what had really happened. It seemed surreal. Like something out of movie.

"Least you came here. I'm so glad you came."

"I wanted to be as far away from Evan as possible. I didn't know where else to go. I kept thinking, 'Where can I go that he won't be able to find me?' There was nowhere else but here."

"Hate to say it, but maybe it's a good thing you haven't come back in such a long time. At least we know he can't find you and try to do something crazy."

"Mel, I don't wanna think about that."

"I know this isn't the best time to talk about stuff like that, but I'm just being realistic."

"I have too many other things on my mind. Everything's a mess. My whole life is . . . my job isn't going right anymore. Now I'm going to have to call them to ask for a leave of absence. I don't have any money. No plan. I'm scared, Mel."

Their eyes locked.

"I know." Mel shifted and let Camille rest her head in her lap, soothing her by stroking her damp hair. Mel didn't know what else she should do.

"How can he be two different people?" Camille asked. "How can he be strong for me, and hold me when I'm afraid, and laugh with me, and make dreams with me, make love to me, and tell me that he would die for me, then turn around and hurt me? Make me like this." Camille lifted the compress and placed her fingertips to her cheek.

"I know, sweetie. I know. But you did the right thing. You

got out. And I'm proud of you for that. Cam, please tell me it's over with Evan. Really over." There was hope in Mel's voice.

"It has to be. I don't want to live like that anymore, Mel. I don't want to be afraid anymore. I just wish I didn't still love him, though." She sobbed. Mel waited and rubbed her hair. She knew what it was like to love somebody. To be blind to his deficiencies, putting your life on hold and just holding on, hoping that he would change. It didn't work that way.

"Love can leave your heart the same as it comes," she said. "It just takes time." She was staring at the picture of Ben's father on the mantle, not quite believing her own words. It just sounded appropriate. But still she felt the familiar twinge that came every time she thought about the details of how things had ended with Jeff. Camille shivered. Mel realized she must be miserable in her wet clothes.

"Tell you what," she said. "Let's get you out of these clothes and into a hot bath. I'll make you some tea. You can take the bed in your old room and get some sleep. It'll be good for you to get some rest."

Mel checked the clock on the table. It was after four now. She would call in to work to take a few days off.

"Thanks, sis."

"I'll find you something of mine to wear."

"Mel, please don't tell Mother."

"That's for you to tell if you choose to, Cam. Not me. Come on upstairs." She jogged ahead to start the bath. "Ben's gonna be so glad to finally see you in person," she said.

Camille walked into her old bedroom slowly. Everywhere she turned there were old memories. She hadn't thought she'd ever see this room again. Her posters of Michael Jackson were still up. Her porcelain dolls lined the hutch of the oak desk. The walls were light blue, not white anymore. She was amazed that everything else had remained the same.

"Daddy left it like you had it when you went to college. He told Mama not to change a thing."

"I see."

"You okay?"

"No."

"Give it some time. I brought you some aspirins. Your towel and stuff are in the bathroom."

Camille sat on the bed.

"Thanks, Mel. For everything."

Mel shrugged.

"What are sisters for? There's a bathrobe in there too."

"I mean it, Mel. I know the last time we talked we didn't end on a good note."

"The last time we talked you told me to keep my nose out of your and Mama's business. You were right. I shouldn't have interfered by trying to bring you two back in touch. I'm just glad you came, Cam. We've all missed you. I hate that Daddy didn't get a chance to see you one last time. He asked for you so many times. Even when he couldn't talk, he kept writing your name on that chalkboard."

"Mel, you told me this already. I still don't get why he was

50

asking for me. He never gave me the time of day when I was here. But look, Mel, please don't tell Mother I'm here. I'm not . . . I don't want anyone to know I'm here."

"I told you I won't say anything. Let me go turn off this water before it runs over."

Mel pulled the door closed as she left the room, and Camille sagged. She had to rest. She took the aspirin dry before easing out of her clothes. It felt good to be out of those things finally. The conditioned air drew goose bumps all over her skin.

It was too much effort for Camille to call out to Mel to tell her that she needed to rest before she could take a bath. She had just enough strength left to crawl naked beneath the quilt on her old bed that her grandmother had made her years ago for one Christmas she couldn't quite remember. She fell into sleep, thinking, *What have I got left to lose?*

⨳

THERE WAS MORE TO LOSE. A week passed and the days seemed to meld as she lay tented in the center of her small, square bed like a sick child, unable to function long enough to tackle mundane efforts if Mel didn't insist. Whole thoughts could not form in her head. There was only Evan. Only missing him mattered. And there was nothing she could do but reminisce and cry while Mel sat with her and listened.

By Friday, she found enough strength to call work at Mel's urging. Valerie sounded remote and cold when Camille told her she needed a leave of absence. Valerie asked Camille for a contact number and transferred her to HR, where she was told that she was being let go for poor performance and too many missed days. Herman Manning, the HR director, was very polite, and inhuman. He told her they'd send her a letter and severance. He didn't apologize. She muffled a sob and hung up when he started talking about her health benefits and COBRA.

Mel went back to work the following Monday, leaving Camille alone days. Her depression deepened. She hadn't thought it possible that she could feel worse. But without Mel there to pull her out of bed in the mornings, she spent days in the same borrowed nightgown. She had been with Evan for so long she couldn't remember what she could do without him. She lay motionless in bed and made food her hobby to consume her day.

Nothing she ate made sense or had any particular order to it. She ate whatever caught her eye first. Pepsi and cheese puffs for breakfast. A cup of cashew nuts and raisins. Sometimes cereal for lunch (without milk if she didn't feel like pouring it in). She opened up cans of Ben's Spaghettios or ravioli and spooned up the contents cold. There was too much effort to turning on the microwave and waiting for something to get hot. She ate often, but no matter what she put in her stomach, she couldn't seem to get full. Her stomach was like a bottomless pit. She made herself sick with indigestion at times, but the emptiness remained. She imagined that she was actually feeding her heart.

Dinner was much more controlled. Mel always made large, satisfying portions of something hot and brought it to her on a wooden tray with a glass of juice. Camille ignored the pity she saw in her sister's eyes. All she had strength for was rummaging for quick food and remembering. Some mornings Mel came in dressed in a bright suit, her briefcase under her arm. "You going out today, Cam? Get dressed. Get some sun. Your skin looks sick. You can at least take a walk around the block this morning."

Camille would nod and pretend she'd consider it. But it was as if she were a caterpillar. She stayed cocooned beneath the quilt, her eyes wet most of the time because it hurt so much to remember the past. Her mind took her back to when Evan was sweet and she was wrapped up in everything that he was— the smell of him, his sound, the way he smiled and called her honey babe, his head leaning to one side when he tried to convince her to miss a class.

Evan had been the first person to hold her since she was ten. Her father was a good man. Soft-spoken. A good provider. His big, tall body with his open arms had been her refuge until her body began to change. Catherine sought every opportunity to point it out, and it embarrassed him. He began to distance himself. He took up fishing and deer hunting to keep himself occupied when he wasn't working at the Pepco plant. Camille still remembered the very last time Wade had embraced her.

He had sat in his chair in the family room watching the

evening news with a Löwenbräu on the table next to him. He never said anything. But he would gesture for Camille to come to him. When he was home, she would linger nearby so she wouldn't miss the chance to sit with him. And that last time, he stretched out an arm and motioned with a hand for her to come. That was all it took. In a flash, she jumped up into his warm lap and put her head in her favorite spot against the crisp, white shirt he wore to work, where she could hear his heart thump against her ear.

She liked to curl up to Wade like a cat. Her whole body would form into a ball the way a Muslim prayed. That day he'd smelled like beer and Clorox bleach and the peach cobbler Catherine had made for dessert. He'd stolen a small piece and stuffed it in his mouth before Catherine could catch him, but a chunk of peach fell on him, leaving a stain. Camille had breathed in his smell. She could still remember the way his arms felt around her. It overwhelmed her to be so safe, so that she couldn't open her mouth to tell her father that he was squeezing her too tight. She didn't want it to end. So little affection was saved just for her.

Her mother, Catherine, was closer to Mel. Camille was the one told to go outside while Mel played dress-up at their mother's vanity mirror, spraying on their mother's cologne, putting on her good pearls, and dragging her high heels across the floor.

But Wade's love had been big enough for both of his children. He had hugs and kisses to go around. Looking back,

Camille could see that it galled Catherine, as if she were jealous of Wade's special connection with Camille. Catherine had
looked at Wade that last time as she came out of the kitchen
after finishing dinner and told him that Camille was too big to
sit in his lap anymore. Her body would start changing soon.
You had to be careful how you handled girls. That did it.
Wade never held Camille again. She would hang around near
his chair every night, hoping. It got to the point where Wade
simply spent less time at home, so the chair was an empty
space Camille would sit in by herself sometimes, but there
was no warmth and no safety to be found in it. What on earth
could he possibly have wanted to say to her before he passed
away?

Camille had never had a boyfriend before Evan. She was
shy and kind of plain in high school because she was too
skinny and wore long, bland dresses most of the time. Catherine was strict with her girls. Camille hadn't been allowed to
put on makeup like the other girls, who blotted their lips
bright red and traced their eyes coal black with the little
sharpened pencils they took from their purses. They looked
like little whores, her mother had said. Camille thought they
looked older and knowing. She secretly wanted to look like
them.

The strict rules didn't affect Mel. She had a Coke bottle figure and was extroverted. Her eyes were sexy all on their own.
There was a look in them that eye liner couldn't achieve. Mel
had the boys' track team sewn up (she'd always had eyes for

the stringy, muscled legs of the runners). She wore her skirts as short as she could get away with, and toward the end of the school year when it was hot enough, she knotted her shirt in the front as soon as she got on the bus. Mel had been a natural jokester. But Camille was soft-hearted and quiet. She didn't know how to talk to the other girls.

Camille became a loner. Later, she figured that was why she'd become such a spectator of people. Never included in conversations, she listened. Never invited to be a part of the in crowd, she watched what they did. Some of the girls she picked out and pretended that they were her friends or that she was like them. She spent hours in her room constructing conversations that they would have and plans that they would make. People fascinated her.

After their second date, twelve years after the last time she'd sat curled in her daddy's lap, Evan had taken Camille into his arms. He hadn't kissed her yet, didn't kiss her then. But that one act told Camille she wanted Evan in her life forever. It had taken her off-guard, that hug. They'd shared a milkshake and had eaten vendor hot dogs with chili and cheese on the sidewalk near Columbia.

She couldn't remember now what it was she'd said, but it was something funny. Some candid observation she'd made, like she innocently had a tendency to do. And she stood there smiling, watching Evan shout out laughter. He had virtually ached with it. She giggled here and there just to see it. Him holding his side, bent at the waist, breathing heavily through his mouth. Just when he seemed to be calming down, he was at it again, tears gathering at the corners of his eyes.

When he finally had wrung out the last of his mirth, he smiled at her saying, "You're too much." Before Camille said a word, he had her by the arm and was pulling her to him. Resting his chin gently on the top of her head, he locked his arms around her small frame and caressed her back as if she was something precious that was meant to be kept.

Her eyes had closed. It was like coming home for Camille. It felt so good to have arms around her and a warm body flush against hers. There were no words left. She stood, leaning against Evan, her arms lank at her sides. She could do nothing but breathe because that was automatic, and she knew she was in love because nobody in all those years had ever taken the time to understand that her body needed, screamed for, begged for, a loving touch such as Evan gave. No matter how he hurt her later, he was always sorry. The fight always ended with Evan holding her like a child. Then making love to her with such passion and giving that there was no need for him even to whisper, "I'm sorry, honey babe," in her ear as she gave herself to him.

Camille missed Evan so desperately that she convinced herself that she should go back home. No relationship was perfect. But if a man gives what you need, it's worth it to try to make things work out. And Evan, despite his problems, always gave her what she needed. He was the only person who ever had.

She threw back the covers on the bed, making up her mind. She would take a quick shower. She had seventy dollars left. That would be plenty to gas up the car and get quarters at the shopping center near the beltway. There was plenty of food downstairs to pack a few snacks.

She called Mel at work. "I'm going back." Mel's suitcase was laid out open on her bed, ready for the few clothes that Mel had charged for her at Penney's.

"Over my dead body."

"Mel, I can't do this. I've never left him before. Maybe the separation's made him see he's got to change."

"It's been a week. What about your promise to yourself? What will it take, Cam? How about if he kills you? Will that work for you next time? And trust me, if he's been hitting you all this time, there will definitely be a next time."

"Mel, please. I don't know how . . . how am I supposed to live without Evan?"

"The way you did before you met him."

"I don't remember back that far. But I know I was lonely. I wasn't happy. I wasn't—"

"You're not happy now, Camille. How could you be happy with some man beating up on you?"

"That's easy for you to say. Evan was the only man who ever loved me."

"Evan's love is toxic, Cam. You need to love yourself."

That staggered her. She sat on the bed.

"I don't know how." It sounded pitiful, but it was the truth.

"That's why you came home. To figure it out. Think about it. Daddy died, and that didn't bring you back. But this did. You're here for a reason."

Camille didn't tell her sister that she had been too angry to come back to be with her father before he died. Why should she have come to hold his hand on his deathbed when he had abandoned her long before she ever moved to New York?

"Give yourself a chance to get to know yourself again," Mel was saying. "Figure out what you want. Who you are." Mel sounded so patient.

"What else is here for me but things I don't want to remember? The same stuff I got away from when I went to New York."

"You can make up a thousand excuses, but it doesn't change the fact that you were involved with an abusive man, and you did the right thing by getting out. So stop bringing up what happened in the past. You have to face up to it. It's over with, and I'm here for you now. I'm here. We have a second chance, Cam. You have to stop running sometime."

"Mel, I don't know."

"You have got to stick this out. We're in this together, Cam. You and me. We're gonna make it work together. I promise. You walk out that door and go back to Evan, and you can kiss my support goodbye."

Camille touched her face. "But who's gonna love me now, Mel?" Her voice trailed off.

"Like I said, you are, that's who. If you'd been loving yourself a long time ago, you would never have accepted Evan's bullshit. Now tell me you're not going anywhere before I have to leave work and come home to talk some sense into you."

Camille recognized deep concern in Mel's voice. She hadn't thought that her going back would make that much difference to her.

"I'm not going anywhere."

"Promise me, Cam."

"I won't. I promise."

Mel sighed into the phone. "God, girl, I don't know which way your mood'll swing from one day to the next."

"I said I wasn't leaving."

"Good. Then I'll see you when I get there. I'll be there early. It's my day to meet Ben. I'll see you then?"

"Okay."

"Promise?"

"Okay."

Camille hung up. Pain engulfed her. She laid down the phone, shoved the suitcase off the bed, and wept.

❧❧

MEL WAS HOME BY TWO in time to meet Ben's bus. She came into the house with him, admiring the large manila sheets he had glued macaroni and felt onto in the forms of ships, water, palm trees, and the sun. He was full of questions as usual. Camille heard his voice from her bedroom upstairs. He had the habit, like most other children, of speaking louder than necessary. It was as if they didn't register the sound of their own voices.

"Mom, can I have some juice? Can I go out and ride my bike? Where's Aunt Cam? Is she home today?"

"Yes, baby. But don't you go bothering her. You'll see Aunt Cam at dinner. Now tell me about your day . . ."

Camille listened to their muted voices while she stared up at the ceiling thinking about her earlier conversation with Mel. What was it that she'd said? Figure out what you want. Who you are. How did a woman even start to do that?

The first year at Columbia Camille had a crush on a junior named Alex Brown. Alex was wholly unattractive. Mud brown like the singer Seal. His face was acne central. He had little kernels of eyes like popcorn seeds and kept his hair in cornrows that always seemed to be unraveling. But there was an electricity about him that was captivating. An assuredness in his tense, black eyes that matched his booming Shakespearian voice. He drew women with little effort.

Alex was a painter. Camille followed him around campus for weeks after she'd noticed him coming back to her dorm from one of her classes one day. He would set up his easel on the plaza midafternoons and toss his jean jacket on the ground with great ceremony. Camille would pretend to be writing on her legal pad, but artfully watched Alex stare at the blank canvas for lengthy periods.

She'd follow him with her eyes as he strode back and forth in front of the easel, his hands clasped behind him. He might do this for hours. His brow would furrow. He'd be deep in thought. And then at some point he would grasp his brush in his right hand with a definitive grace and paint with quick, broad strokes as if he was possessed. It amazed her to watch him create. Her heart would race. She would take guesses at what he decided to capture on his blank canvas. But when he finished, she could never tell what his portraits represented. She figured only he knew what the great splashes of vibrance meant.

Her life was like that blank canvas on an easel, waiting for her. Only she could apply that first bold stroke of color and the ones to follow. A thought struck her sharply. She sat up in bed slowly. Freedom was just as scary as imprisonment. There was too much room for choices. Too many opportunities for error. Yet there was something exhilarating about being able to create your own interpretation.

Of course, the problem was where to begin. She'd taken on the persona Evan had created for her. Every particle of her personality, her appearance, had been sucked into the vacuum of Evan's idea of who she should be. The clothes in her closet back in New York were baggy jeans and sweatshirts, over-sized sweaters. Her suits were square and sedate. Dresses shapeless and designed to cover everything. Sensible shoes. She'd been dressing and acting like an old woman all this time.

Camille threw off the quilt and got out of bed. She had to take a look at what she was dealing with in the full-length mirror affixed to the back of the bedroom door. Camille shrugged out of her nightgown, letting it slide down her body. Was she that bad? She was tall for a woman—five feet nine inches. Most men said they liked long legs. Overall, she had an acceptable body. A slim one with small, pointed lemon breasts. Her bony hips held a nice scythe curve. Her arms were too skinny (you could tell by the bones in her elbows and wrists), but she stood up straight the way she was taught to as a child by walking with books balanced on her head. An acceptable body. A decent body. She'd spent a long time covered up like a nun for no good reason. Maybe she would dare to show some of her long legs one of these days. Then again, that might be too much of a change.

She touched her face, almost appreciating its softness. Sans the healing scar, her skin was smooth and clear. A small inky pinpoint of a beauty mark dusting the side of her face embarrassed her because she knew she wasn't beautiful at all. She leaned closer to the mirror. Her eyes weren't exactly exciting, but without her glasses they were at least an honest dark brown, round and just . . . there. They looked out at the world benignly, it seemed, with no emotion and no deeper account of her soul. Her brows were fuller than they probably should have been for a woman. She was naturally hairy. But her features were delicate. A pinched, pert nose with a freckle. Pronounced cheekbones. A sharp, dusky mouth. She wondered if black women ever used collagen too now that more lip was in.

Camille took her hair out of its ponytail and shook her head.

Long, thick sections of curly hair webbed around her face like a black veil. This was her best feature, she knew. But she never knew what to do with it, except let it hang (it didn't hold curls well) or flip it up into a ponytail, which is how she normally wore it. She'd wanted to have it cut into a style. She did her fingers like scissors and pressed a portion of hair between them to see what it would look like shorter. Evan forbade her from cutting it. She was already plain. If she didn't have all that hair, with her body, she'd look like a boy, he'd said. Well she would see about that. Maybe this would be her first definitive stroke of color on the canvas. A drastic haircut. A knock at the door startled her.

"Cam?"

She reached for Mel's ruffled robe on the bed and said, "Just a minute." She belted the sash and opened the door. Mel had changed out of the suit she'd worn to work into some short shorts and a matching tank top.

"Hey. Thought I'd come check in on you." She walked in smiling uneasily.

"Do you think I'm ugly?" Camille asked. She moved over to the mirror above the dresser to look at her ears next, then her neck.

"'Ugly? Course not. You have a nice face. What are you talking about?"

"Think I'm plain?" She put her hair back in its barrette and ran her hand across her forehead.

Mel shrugged. "You could probably use a little spicing up,

but that ain't nothing a little bit of makeup and attention can't cure."

"What kind of attention?" She pictured herself getting a facelift.

They sat on the bed together.

"Oh, I don't know. Wax your eyebrows. Shave your legs. Maybe color your hair. Get your nails done. Definitely put a perm in."

"Perm? Don't they burn your hair out?"

"Girl, no."

"Mother never let us have them."

Mel waved a hand. "That's when we were girls, Cam. I went out and got me one as soon as I got the chance. I couldn't live without the damn thing now, though you couldn't tell with these in." Mel groped her braids.

"Where's all this stuff about your looks coming from?"

"I panicked this morning. It's just that I feel . . . You know, nobody but Evan has ever been interested in me." Mel squeezed Camille's shoulder.

"You're a good woman, Cam. You're sweet. You're smart. Funny. Attractive. You have a lot to offer."

"It must be well hidden. No other men ever notice me, and all I see is twenty-nine-year-old geek."

"That's all you're looking for. I guarantee you that you can take any person on this planet and find there's more to them than that description. You're just shy, Cam. You have to learn not to be afraid of people. That's the only reason I think men might be put off. You're smart as hell. You can run academic circles around a lot of guys, but you don't know how to play the mating game."

"The mating game. Oh, please. Like you could picture me doing something like that. You ever get scared that Jeff'll be the only man who loved you?"

"I'm not gonna lie. I used to. I used to be terrified, thinking, 'Oh, my god. I've got this baby. Nobody's gonna want me with somebody else's child to take care of.'"

"How'd you make yourself stop thinking like that?"

"I saw the situation for what it was. Jeff didn't have a committed bone in his body. He came in and out of my life over and over. Used me at every turn. I had to come to grips with that. I finally said enough is enough. If a man can't be real with me and treat me the way anybody deserves to be treated, I'd rather be alone. A few dates after he and I broke up did a lot to help me see that my life isn't over just because that relationship is."

They were quiet for a moment, listening to Ben play with his Tonka trucks in his bedroom down the hall.

"I lay in this bed at night, Mel," Camille said, putting her palm against the sheets, "and I wish with my whole heart that Evan was here holding me. I miss being held."

"I understand that wish more than you can imagine. I have nights like that all the time. Of course, I've got my little man in there to cuddle up to when it hits me sometimes."

"It's like something inside me is calling out for him."

Mel nudged her.

"Ignore it. Fight it. It's a struggle but it's only been a week. You'll be better off, and you know it."

"Yeah. I hear what you're saying, but I feel so lonely."

"Don't let that make you do anything stupid. That's all I'm saying. Listen, dinner'll be ready in about an hour. How about you come downstairs and eat with us tonight?"

"I guess I could," Camille said.

"Perfect." She clapped her hands together then got up to leave.

"Cam?" Mel turned in the doorway.

"What?"

"It's gonna be all right. Keep remembering that. It's gonna be all right."

❦

QUITE INADVERTENTLY, CAMILLE started taking long walks. She had been waiting for her severance check to come. When the mailman made his drop in the late afternoons, she'd wait for him to leave, put on her sandals, and tramp down to the mailbox at the edge of the lawn in her bathrobe. Then she'd turn around and go back to the house.

Her third day checking the mailbox, she'd noticed an old green Ford truck backed into the driveway of the Bates house. If she remembered correctly, Mr. Bates's son, Ricky, had a truck just like it years ago. They'd graduated the same year. But Ricky had gone into the army after high school. If that was the same truck, it had to be ancient. She decided to investigate. She changed into one of Mel's sundresses and touched up her cheek with foundation.

The truck, she noticed, had rust stains eating away at its body. It was the same one. A bumper sticker that said JIMMY CARTER FOR PRESIDENT next to a cluster of peanuts was still in place. It still had a dent in the fender from the time Ricky was teaching Aaron Hicks to park for his driver's test and Aaron backed into a fire hydrant. Something else caught her eye. A birdbath and pink flamingos in the Nelsons' yard. They were still here too. Camille smiled.

She walked farther up the street, searching each yard for something familiar. Sometimes there was nothing, but every few houses or so, she would remember a broken picket fence and how it got that way. There were the beautiful lemon tree in a front yard, somebody's blue car that looked too old to move (she fumbled with the names of their owners), names on mailboxes that were so faded and grainy she could barely read them.

The next day she took Houser, the next block over. The day after, she hit the main road of Causewell. Then Dayton, which meant crossing over Causewell into another residential development. She had been told never to go to Dayton as a girl because a bully named Cynthia beat her up when she was fifteen for thinking that Camille laughed at her cheap shoes. Camille stood in front of Cynthia's old brick ranch house and laughed out loud.

This freedom stuff was like some kind of expensive drug to a new user. A small dose, and it lasted for days. It was a high unlike any accomplishment she could fathom. She would rummage Mel's closet for things that fit. A taut body shirt. Stretch jeans. Wrap-around skirts that hugged her hips like a glove. She started walking to the end of Causewell and along Route 1 to get to the little shopping plaza, where she could get coffee in the mornings at a bagel shop. She hadn't drunk coffee in years because Evan wouldn't allow her to.

She felt she'd sufficiently scoured the neighborhood after three days. Then she got up early Thursday before the sun got too high. Dressed in a midriff and baggy overalls, she set to work on the outside of the house. The day before at the shopping center, she'd stopped in at Sherwin-Williams for two gallons of paint and the paraphernalia she would need to redo the shutters and posts. Drop cloth, paint stripper, a putty knife, brushes, a trowel. She put on a pair of cotton gloves that she took off again because they were too constricting, and she got to work stripping off layers of paint.

It was arduous but constructive. It took hours to get the posts in decent shape. Then there was dragging an extension ladder beneath the high windows and sitting atop it, praying she wouldn't fall while she brushed layers of cornflower blue onto the shutters.

When she was done, her back was in turmoil. She eased down the ladder like an old woman. Her body hadn't seen so much exercise in years. Reaching the last rung, she groaned, thinking already about tomorrow. There were still the weeds in the flower bed and the ratty lawn carpet to be pulled up. But for all the work, it was good to be doing something. She used the paint-speckled back of her hand to wipe the sweat from her brow.

Camille stood back on the uncut lawn to judge her handi-work. It was amazing what a little paint could do. The face of the house was different already. There was ice tea in the fridge. The best plan was to clean up, take a quick shower, and drink a tall glass of tea while she watched *As the World Turns*. She massaged a kink out of her shoulder and surveyed the mess. Or she could just skip the clean-up altogether and do that later. In fact, she could do whatever she wanted to. She hugged herself and smiled.

Camille's check finally arrived on Saturday. She opened an account at Crestar and spent five hundred dollars on a new wardrobe.

"Look at all this," Mel said, searching the stack piled up on the bed. "Girl, you know you need to give me this. Let me have this, Cam." Mel was holding up a sleeveless mahogany top.

"Mel, please. You have more clothes than you'll ever wear."

"Girl, this is just the right color for these pants I bought last summer. It's got all these different colors in them, and I haven't worn them yet because I can't find a blouse to go with them. This would be just what the doctor ordered."

Camille snatched the shirt. "For me, not you! But . . . I do have a little something for you." She took two hundred dollars out of her purse. "This can't repay you—I don't think I ever can—but think of this as an installment."

"Cam, really. There's no need for this."

"I know you can probably use it."

"You know the house is paid for. And I make more than enough to take care of me and Ben."

"Yeah, well. Let's just say I think I owe you a lot. I mean, I show up at your door literally with nothing. You took me in. Fed me. Let me cry on your shoulder. I'm getting a second chance because of you."

"Thanks, sis. That's the sweetest thing anybody's ever said to me."

Mel opened her arms and the two of them hugged. When the doorbell rang, Mel looked around perplexed. "Who the heck could that be?"

"Maybe it's Jeff." They let go of each other.

"This isn't his weekend."

Camille had been trying on her clothes. She put on Mel's long terry robe and peeked out the window. A yellow cab was backing out of the drive and inching up the street.

"A cab?" she said.

"What in the world would somebody take a cab here for?"

"Mel, go see who it is."

The bell rang again, and Mel went down the stairs to answer the door. A space of time passed. Camille opened her door a crack. Then she heard Mel calling for her. For a half-second, she was sure her heart stopped. Evan. It was Evan. It had to be. She knew he would eventually find her somehow. What should she say? How should she act? More important, what would Mel say?

She didn't have time to dress. She brushed her hair back into a ponytail. Found a barrette and made herself as presentable as possible, and she ran down the steps, her bathrobe swishing.

As she entered the family room, she hoped she was seeing a ghost.

"Mother?"

3

*R*EINVENTING RULE THREE: *Exonerate yourself. You can't progress unless you've pardoned your past.*

WHEN CAMILLE GRADUATED from college, she had written her mother a goodbye letter. She hadn't meant to. She'd intended to write a short thank-you note for her graduation present. But once she finished the letter, she knew the letter had been in her to write years before she ever left home. Evan had given her a box of lavender notepaper with daffodil watermarks on the pages and her name, embossed in gold, centered at the top. He asked her to write to him every day while she was away from New York. She was going to Europe.

That night she sat down at her desk in her dorm room. It was late. Quiet. Camille was in a reflective mood. Her whole life was changing in a matter of weeks. She'd been accepted to work on an intern assignment with the UN that summer that would take her to Europe for the first time. Her adviser had pulled some strings. When she returned to New York, the plan was to secure an apartment and begin fall classes toward her graduate degree.

From her parents, she had received a locket, a check for two thousand dollars, and a card from home. The card explained that no one would be able to make it to her graduation. They were sorry. Somebody needed to take care of little Ben for Melanie (she had just started a new job) and who else could do it better than his own grandma? Your father can't get the time off from work either. Camille had read the card dispassionately, deciding then that since she had been on her own for four and a half years, she might as well go it alone forever.

You never loved me. That was how she started the letter. She wrote her thoughts out in blue ink—the pen Mel had sent with a separate apology. Every frustration she'd ever had growing up hit the unlined pages. The words flowed out of her. There was so much to say that she could barely keep up with her thoughts. She kept reaching for fresh paper.

Maybe if I had been an only child, if I didn't have your relationship with Mel to compare ours to, I wouldn't feel like this. Tears spilled onto the crisp lavender paper and blurred the ink in places. She finished nine full sheets and read them through twice. She didn't change one word. *Everything about you leaves me cold,* she'd ended.

They had not spoken since.

74

She remembered that last line now as she stared open-mouthed at her mother, who stood lopsided in a smart gray Claiborne pantsuit, Ben hugging her waist. When Evan was beating her, not that first blow, or the second or third, but the ones that followed, Camille would get this deep-down hollowness inside. Her body would feel boneless and bloodless. Stark. A moment when no emotion welled up within her. No concrete thoughts. She guessed it was shock.

Seeing her mother face to face after so much time had passed made her feel that way now. She was weak from it. She wasn't ready for this. Her hand went immediately to her face. It was still scarred. An aging scab marred her lower lip. Why did she have to see her mother when she was broken like this? Jobless, homeless, manless, ugly. Her legs were jelly. She sat on the edge of the La-Z-Boy because it was closest to her. The smell of her mother's perfume was heavy in her nostrils, nauseating her. She braced herself.

"I take it you're not glad to see me," Catherine said, easing Ben from her.

"Nana, can I have some candy?" Ben stared up with his hand outstretched, but Mel led him to the doorway saying, "Not now, Ben. Go to your room and play, and Mommy will call you in a little while."

"What are you doing here?" Camille asked coldly. She noticed that Mel was unusually quiet.

"I should ask you the same question." Catherine's face was stone.

Camille turned away. "I don't think I need to explain myself to you," she said.

"I'd like an explanation. What happened to your face, girl?" She was enjoying this. Camille could tell. Catherine had the same look she used to get when she savored a moment. Like the times they played Scrabble and she was challenged. She would whip out the dictionary to prove she'd put down an actual word. She'd tally her points and nod. She looked . . . smug. That was it. Camille couldn't dare let Catherine look down on her with that smug expression, so she stood and leaned against the wall near the french doors for support.

"Did Mel call you? Is that why you're here? Because if it is, you've wasted good time and money coming."

Mel jumped to her feet. "I beg your pardon! I promised you I wouldn't tell Mama you were here."

"Well, how else would she know?"

Camille rolled her eyes and folded her arms. Catherine moved toward her. She seemed to have aged substantially, yet her face was the same. Hard black eyes like marbles of coal. A pink slash of mouth that rarely smiled. Tan skin that freckled easily and a slim neck. Her hair was like the singer Nancy Wilson's—a short, chic helmet. Camille wondered if it was the gray that had taken over the light brown hair her mother had always been so proud of that made her seem so old. She looked to have shrunk. Or maybe it was that Camille had gained height over her mother. She wasn't sure. Catherine

76

touched Camille's cheek, examining its bluish-green hues. Camille tensed.

"Melanie didn't tell me a thing. And why *didn't you* tell me she was here, baby?"

Catherine looked at Mel expectantly.

"Cam didn't want me to say anything."

"She? My name is Camille, Mother." Camille spit it out, making the title *mother* seem disparaging.

"What in he—" Catherine caught herself. She never cursed or used the Lord's name in vain. It wasn't ladylike to do so. This was the first time in years that she'd ever come so close to saying a swear word, and it gave Camille pleasure to see her mother lose her cool.

Catherine's neck stiffened. She clutched her purse strap tightly. "What is your problem, girl?"

Mel rolled her eyes toward the ceiling. "This is so ridiculous. Mama, please don't start in on Cam. She's been through enough."

"The prodigal child. Can't make it down to say a last good-bye to your own father when he lay there for weeks wanting to see you. You didn't try to come to his funeral, but here you are out of the blue now. What kind of trouble have you gotten yourself into?"

Camille threw up her hands. Typical. Catherine's classic behavior pattern hadn't changed. Blame her first, then look elsewhere for explanations.

77

"I'm outta here." Camille stalked out of the room. She made every move up the stairs count.

"Cam," Mel pleaded. "Mama, let me talk to her a minute."

Mel touched Catherine's arm, then followed Camille up the stairs. Camille took Mel's suitcase from under the bed and hoisted it on top of the quilt. The effort hurt her back. She massaged it a second while Mel closed the door.

"That would be a mistake," Mel said, pointing at the suitcase. She leaned against the door as if barring it in an at-ease stance, her arms across her chest.

Camille didn't look up. She haphazardly folded a mint green shirt with Japanese print in red on top of pairs of jeans and swung them into the open case.

"My only mistake was coming here," she answered.

"You don't know what you're saying. Coming home was the smartest thing you've done in years. Where do you think you're going now? Back to Evan?"

"I don't call this home." Camille shut the suitcase and latched it. She took off her robe and retrieved a pair of blue capris and a cotton shirt from the bottom dresser drawer.

"Then where? Where do you think you're going?"

Camille looked at her sister. "How am I supposed to know? This was my last hope."

She flung the suitcase at the wall. It slammed into the edge of the desk and sent a barrage of papers scattering across the floor.

"Camille. Calm down. You're going to scare Ben," Mel said. Her beaded hair tinkled as she bent to gather the papers.

Camille glanced toward the closed door with an apologetic look. "Why is she here, Mel?"

Mel put the papers back on the desk. "Don't leave."

"I can't stand being in the same house with her." Camille walked the floor. She couldn't keep still.

"Where can you go? You don't have enough money. You need time to get your life in order. Stay with me." Mel grabbed Camille's arm gently, but Camille wrenched free.

"I didn't want anybody to see me like this." She ran her fingers through loose tendrils of lank hair that flopped back into her face.

"Stop moving. You're making me nervous. Come on, let's sit down and think about this. Cam, please."

Camille slowed to a stop. She sat on the unmade bed.

"Why don't we just take a minute to look at the whole picture."

"The only picture I see is one of me getting the hell away from her. And how did she know I was here anyway?" Camille asked, sure that Mel was responsible.

"She may have figured it out."

"Figured it out? I knew it. I should have known . . ."

"It's not what you think," Mel said. Camille was quiet, expecting an explanation.

Some kids outside riding their bikes down the big hill were

screaming. Their noise came in through Camille's open window.

"I didn't come out and tell her you were home," Mel said. She put an arm around Camille's shoulder.

Camille withdrew from Mel's arm. "I thought I could trust you."

The past was crowding in on her. She looked toward the brass headboard above the bed. Years ago, when she was hurt, she would trace the ivy pattern with her fingertips for hours. She reached for it now.

"It was supposed to be a surprise," Mel said.

Camille shook her head. "Seeing her," she said, "is no surprise. It's a disaster."

"I'm not talking about Mama. I'm talking about something else."

She looked at Mel, but her finger continued along the headboard.

"What are you talking about?"

"Remember the night you came and you were talking about Nora Jordan?"

"Yeah, of course." She wouldn't forget that night for the rest of her life.

"I got to thinking." She paused. "Wait a minute. The air is on."

Camille stared at her. "That's what you thought about?"

"I told you about opening the window like this. That's money, Cam. Why do people always—" Mel lowered the window, shutting out the noise of the playing children in the street below, "—leave the window open when they know the air is on?"

"It's close in here. Sorry." Camille didn't tell her that she needed the window open every night in order to sleep.

Mel picked up where she'd left off. "So, I'm thinking," she said, putting some of Camille's stray clothes in the hamper. "Cam doesn't have a job. Nora's company is based here. Maybe they have a position Cam could—"

"A job? Hmm. I hadn't thought about that. But what does your mother have to do with that?"

Mel looked in the mirror, fiddling with her eye.

"Turn the lamp up, would you. Feels like something's on my contact. Anyway, before I was rudely interrupted," she said pointedly, "I thought about my little idea. I figured I couldn't just call Nora up and ask her for a favor like we were girls. *Dang it!* These contacts are going to give me a fit. I don't know the woman from Adam. I mean, Eve. Why do we use that saying, anyway?"

"Who cares. I just want to know what happened."

Mel was quiet for a minute, then said, "Cooperate," in the tone she used with Ben when he fought to sleep late instead of getting up for school in the mornings.

"What?"

"Not you, silly. My contact." A tear streamed from her eye. She closed it and said, "There," and sat back on the bed, pressing her bright red toenails into the carpet.

"Uhm, but so anyway, if were going to pull it off, I needed Mama's help since Nora and Mama are old friends. So I called Mama to get her to call Nora and ask about getting you in. Wait. Did I say that right?" She pointed a finger in the air and repeated herself. "Called Mama to get her to call . . . Yeah." She looked at Camille with her one red teary eye as if she'd said enough.

"Still doesn't tell me what I want to know. I'm asking you to tell me why she came all this way if she was just going to talk to Nora about getting me a job when she could do that on the phone? *If* she decided to help me. And that's a major if." The pants she wore were tight. She sat up and unbuttoned the top button.

"Oh that. That part I don't know. I didn't have a chance to find out yet. We'll have to ask her," Mel said.

Camille felt lightheaded. She leaned back across the bed and sighed. This was hopeless. She slid the pillow from beneath her head and hugged it to her chest saying, "Do me a favor. Put this over my face and put me out of my misery. I've had enough."

"You need to stop it. I'm not worried about the thing with Nora right now," Mel said. "What I meant before when I asked you to look at the whole picture was if you realize that having Mama here is a perfect opportunity."

Camille's glasses were on the night table. She put them on to get a good look at Mel's face.

"That's the most ludicrous crap I've ever heard. Big picture.

For what, Mel? For driving me further over the edge? Yeah, this is just what I needed. My life's already totally screwed. Now in walks my worst nightmare in high heels."

"Stop saying that. Mama is not a nightmare, and I wish you wouldn't talk about her like that."

"To you she's not. I have a different story to tell."

"Stop bitching, Camille. All you've been doing is feeling sorry for yourself and taking me along for the ride."

Camille looked at her sister. "How can you say that to me?"

"Am I lying?"

"I don't believe you. You know what I've been through."

"*You* know what you've been through too. So why do you keep playing it out over and over again? You want a prize for being the victim? Too bad they don't pay for it 'cause you could make a lot of money being the professional victim."

"I don't want to hear you. Leave me alone. Don't you have some entertaining to do?"

Camille turned away embarrassed because Mel had struck a nerve. How could she explain to Mel that she wanted things to be different, but she kept finding herself going around in circles?

Mel put a hand on Camille's arm.

"I'm not leaving you alone," she said. "You think you've got the market cornered on being hurt by other people? Everybody knows pain, Cam."

Camille didn't respond, so Mel continued. "What, are you gonna just lay there and ignore me now?"

Camille closed her eyes. Her stomach was doing flip-flops. She noticed that she could smell Catherine's perfume on Mel.

"This is a chance for the three of us to talk," she pleaded.

That broke Camille's silence. She opened her eyes.

"She's not going to talk to me. She's only gonna push my buttons and upset me more than I already am," Camille said. She traced the trellis design of the headboard again and said, "I don't want this, Mel. I'm not trying with her again."

"Haven't the two of you hurt each other enough?"

Camille laughed, thinking of all the wasted years she'd reached out to Catherine, only to find rejection.

"I used to hate you when we were girls. I was so jealous. I couldn't stand your little perfect butt," Camille said.

"Perfect? I think you have that the wrong way around. You were the one getting straight A's and doing what you were supposed to. I was a complete bad ass. Terrible mouth. I was an obnoxious little thing." She seemed proud of it. She was smiling.

"She never saw that," Camille said, turning her head toward the door. "She only had eyes for you. I couldn't stand you for being prettier. For having boyfriends and friends. You didn't let anything stop you. Everybody liked you. For the longest time I wanted to be you."

"What did it get me, Cam, except a man who cheated on me with every girl he saw and a baby at twenty-four? Twenty-four, Cam, and without a husband. I had to quit school and everything. I should be designing buildings instead of planning travel arrangements for people to go to places I may never get to see."

"You can still have your dream, Mel. Jeff didn't take that away from you. You just have to go after it," Camille said.

"I just have to raise my son. Jeff isn't gonna help me but so much. He grudgingly takes Ben every other weekend. How can I go to school, work, and care for Ben? It's just not feasible right now. Maybe when he's older. But that's something I'll figure out later. See, I could play the victim too if I want. So easy, isn't it? But this isn't about me. This is about you and the second chance you're being given. Right now, Mama is downstairs. You haven't seen her in ages."

"That didn't seem to matter years ago, and I don't think it matters now."

"All she had to do was make a phone call, Cam. But here she is. Despite everything that's happened in the past between the two of you, she's here, and I don't care what you say, she came here because you're here. She's obviously reaching out to you, Cam."

"I told you I'm not opening myself up for that, Mel. I washed my hands of that woman a long time ago."

"I hate to say this, and it may sound crazy—"

Camille muttered into her pillow, "What else is new."

"—but I'm glad things went wrong with Evan. Don't look at me like that. I'm serious. It's bothered me a long time that my family's been scattered to the winds. Now here the three of us are, in the house together. I admit I was a spoiled brat when we were growing up. I was rotten to the core. I didn't always treat you the way I should have. But we're grown now, Cam. This is different. We aren't a mother and her two little girls anymore. There're three grown women in this house now. This could be a chance for us to reclaim our family."

"Just hold on. That's all easy for you to say. It hurts, Mel. Despite what you say, I looked at her downstairs just now and I *was* a little girl again. Things would have been so different if only she had been there for me the way she was for you. I know you're the favorite. And that's fine. But I needed her too. I needed her."

Camille shook her head. Mel sighed, thinking how right Camille was about one thing. This did hurt.

"Look, I invited my friend Desnee from work over to have dinner with us tonight. I figured it was time you got out of this room, girl, and Desnee is a riot. You'll get a kick out of her."

"You invited company? Mel, I can't let her see me. My face."

"I already told her about that, and she knows not to ask any questions."

"You told some stranger about me?"

"She used to work at the Hair Cuttery before she came to Trip Planners. And she knows a lot about hair, makeup, and colors and stuff. I told her I wanted her to come see what she would suggest for you. Anyway she thinks you were in a car accident."

"A car accident?"

"I had to tell her something. Des is the type of person that if she sees you she'll ask. Girl, if she asks, your car flipped twice."

"What?"

"I told you I had to tell her something."

"You are nuts."

"That's what they say. So get dressed and be downstairs in an hour."

"I can't. Not with Mother here," Camille sighed.

"Yes, you can. I'm going down to start dinner. Think about what I told you. We can either look at this whole situation as a curse and leave things messed up the way they are, or we can look at it as an opportunity to turn our family into something better than we ever thought it could be. But it's your choice, Cam. Mama already made hers. She's here."

That didn't mean anything, Camille wanted to tell her, but she kept her mouth shut. Mel kissed her cheek and closed the door gently when she left.

❧

Usually Camille could handle only half a glass of wine, but tonight she was on her fifth glass of Merlot. A toasty glow settled in her chest. If she had to sit through dinner with her mother, she intended to do it with her senses dulled. She uncorked the bottle of Mondavi to pour a little more into the goblet she held.

"Haven't you had enough?" Catherine asked in a stern voice.

She was starting already. Camille immediately looked up to see if Mel had heard what Catherine had said from where she stood in the kitchen serving Ben there. Mel was too busy filling Ben's plate with applesauce, a breadstick, and squares of chicken ravioli.

"Why do I gotta eat by myself, Mom?"

"Why do I *have* to eat by myself," Mel corrected. He was at the kitchen table using the crayons that Desnee had brought him on a napkin he'd spread out next to his juice.

"It's just for tonight, sweet pea. I promise. Look. Mommy brought in the TV. I'ma turn it on so you can watch your favorite shows in here."

"I've been taking care of myself long enough to know when I've had enough to drink," Camille responded, and jabbed some pasta with her fork.

The women were sitting at the dining room table eating already because Mel had told them not to wait. The smell of Mel's fusilli with ham, scallions, and smoked sausage dish in their mother's fresh thyme and cherry tomato sauce filled the room. Catherine had made cornbread with blueberries and a simple garden salad.

"Five glasses seems excessive to me."

Before Camille could speak, Catherine turned to say something to Desnee.

Out of the corner of her eye, Camille watched Catherine's

face in the dim light as her mother egged Desnee on to try some of the pasta.

Desnee was saying, "I've made a decision. That's why I'm having the salad. Big girls need love too, and I'm tired of being by myself, Miss Cathy."

"When the right man comes along, baby, he'll want you as you are," Catherine said. "You just haven't met the right one." Camille noted the way Catherine's voice had turned soft.

"It ain't just men, Miss Cathy. I'ma tell you the truth. It's everywhere I go. If I wanna be comfortable, I have to use the handicap stall. It's murder riding the train to work. It's all crowded, and you can look at people and tell they're praying you won't sit next to them. It's embarrassing. Everything is made for slim people."

"Oh, lord. Is she giving the 'I don't want to be fat' speech again? Desnee, you know you're beautiful just the way you are. I forgot to bring in these glazed carrots, y'all."

The room fell silent, and Camille took her chance to broach the subject she'd been hoping to bring up.

"So Mother what brings you to town?" She had definitely had too much to drink. That slid out easily. Normally she would have been less blunt. The only noise to be heard was the faint sound of the television in the kitchen. She was staring at the bottom of her empty glass ready for a fight.

"What brings you, hunh?" She raised her eyes to look at her mother finally.

Catherine pierced her with a heated look. "Camille, now is not the time to talk about it," She said, glancing at their guest.

"I just want to know. It's a simple question."

"Camille, you're tipsy."

"No, I'm not, Mother. I'm drunk. I've had more wine tonight than I've had in months. What does that tell you?"

Her mother looked at Mel as if urging her to do something. All Mel did was take her seat and reach for the pasta as if everything was fine.

Catherine salted her food as she spoke.

"All right. Melanie called me to tell me you needed a new job. She thought I could help. She asked me to give Nora a call to work something out. Nora doesn't have a New York office, so I asked Melanie if you were considering relocating. She said it was something like that. I asked her if you were visiting, and she wouldn't give me a straight answer. I knew something was going on, and I wanted to see what it was. I figured if you were here, you'd bolt if you even had a whiff of an idea that I was coming. So I caught the first thing smoking to Maryland."

"How long are you planning to stay?" Camille asked, helping herself to some carrots. She was on a roll.

Catherine looked uncomfortable. She took small, neat bites of her food. "I haven't decided yet," she answered.

"You brought plenty of luggage."

There was a lengthy silence.

Catherine said, "Since we're being so candid here, may I ask what happened to your face?"

Desnee looked over at Mel. "Didn't you tell me—," she whispered, but the question died. Mel was shaking her head.

Camille swallowed. Her eyes narrowed. Desnee cleared her throat, picked up the bottle of peppercorn ranch dressing from the table, and said, "This is delicious. Doesn't taste lite at all."

"I don't feel like talking about it, Mother. You shouldn't have come."

"I would like to know what happened to you, Camille."

"Look, do me a favor. Don't act like you care now."

"What do you mean by that?"

"That's my first time buying that dressing," Mel said. "I'm glad you like it."

"Do we even need to go there?" Camille's voice had risen slightly.

"Maybe we should. After all these years, it's time to talk about something." Catherine's arms were folded, and she seemed determined.

Camille stood and said, "You have no right to ask me anything about my life."

"I have every right. I raised you."

"You raised Mel. To me you were a presence in the house."

"A presence in the—I tried with you, Camille. You kept your distance from me. You were completely withdrawn. All you did was cling to your father. And even him you forgot about once you left this house."

"You all but pushed me out of this house! You made Daddy hate me. *Of course* I couldn't wait to leave here."

"I never did any such thing. But I guess you couldn't wait to leave because you couldn't wait to hurt me. You sent me that awful letter talking about how you never wanted to see us again to prove it. That killed your father. I couldn't believe you said those things."

Camille threw her napkin on the table.

"You can't believe? I don't believe you, lady. Sitting there all high and mighty—"

Mel broke in. "Wait a minute. Just stop it. My baby is right in the kitchen, and I think both of you are letting things go too far."

"I'm not the one who showed up out of the blue," Camille said.

"It's my house," Catherine retorted.

"Not anymore it isn't."

Catherine sighed. She pushed away from the table.

"Mama, please stop. Cam has been through hell."

"Oh, give me a break. We've all seen a little of that, Melanie. Hell was watching your father mourn for this girl day after day. Hell was watching him be put down by strokes and beg from his hospital bed for me to get her to come. Hell was putting that man in the ground and then lying to people about her being out of the country and saying that was why she didn't attend her own father's funeral. Now she sees a little hell, and I'm supposed to bat my eyes and kiss her foot and cater to her when she couldn't even take a day to be here with your father. Why are you here anyway, Camille, after all these years? Why'd you come?"

"Why'd *you* come?" Camille responded, folding her arms and jutting her chin. Her leaf-brown eyes were defiant. Catherine recalled that look from a long time ago, and turned away because the memory was too painful.

"Here we go with that again," Catherine said. "We aren't going to get anywhere like this." She turned to Mel. "Melanie, would you please tell me what's going on here?"

Mel looked at Camille. Then at Desnee, whom Camille thought was probably trying to figure out how to make a graceful exit.

"Cam was in a car accident, Mama," Mel said. She took a long sip of wine that made it apparent that she was lying.

Camille stared at a framed picture of Mel and Ben. It was a sweet photograph, with the two of them staring into each other's eyes. Camille didn't want her sister to feel she had to speak for her and tell lies on her behalf.

"You've got it all wrong. There's no need to lie about what happened. She wants the truth about me, and that's what she's going to get. That is what you want, isn't it? The truth—right, Mother?"

"It would be a delightful change."

Camille smiled coldly. Then she turned vacant eyes on

Catherine. "Okay. I'll give it to you as ugly as it is," she said calmly. "He beat me, okay? Didn't know that about your black sheep daughter, huh? Evan beat the hell out of me for years. I've been kicked and spit on and called a no-good whore more times than I can count. Every awful thing you can imagine, about anything you can think of, he's done to me. Broke my nose, blacked my eyes, threw me down stairs, choked me, pulled my hair out. He did this to my face too."

She pointed at the healing bruises.

"Slapped me as hard as he could. Like I was a man or something. He was always doing something to me. I had to lie all the time. Calling into work talking about, Oh, I fell. Oh, I ran into the door. Oh, I accidentally hit my head, that's why I have this knot the size of a walnut on my forehead. No more. That's over with now. I couldn't take it anymore, and I left him. And I'll be damned if I'm gonna stand here and lie to somebody like you. Is that what you wanted to hear, Mother?"

Camille lowered her head. Tears streamed down her face, and Catherine stood up and moved away from the table. She looked around the room as if she wasn't sure where she was or how she'd gotten there.

"No," Catherine said finally. "No." She was shaking her head.

Her breaking voice caused Camille to look up suddenly. Catherine was crying. Her lips trembled.

"Mama, please," Mel said. "Come on and sit down and let's talk a—"

"That's not what I wanted to hear at all," Catherine said. She turned and went upstairs to the master bedroom and closed the door.

Mel tossed her fork onto the table.

"Desnee, I'm sorry you had to see that. Sometimes my sister can be a real pain in the you-know-what. You could have handled that differently, Cam."

"She should have stayed away. She has some damn nerve," Camille said.

"She's our mother. She just lost Daddy last year. And she's been through a lot. She didn't deserve that from you. She was concerned about you."

"No, Mel, she wasn't concerned. She's never been concerned. She was just being nosy. When have you ever known her to be concerned about me?" Camille picked up her linen napkin and wiped her face.

"How can you say that?"

"How can you deny that it's true? I busted my butt in school to get perfect grades. I did everything I was told. I wasn't the one sneaking out of the house to go meet boys. That was you."

"Oh, lord. I think we already know this story, Cam."

"Yeah, you and I do know it. But did she ever recognize any of that? No. Did she ever hug me, tell me she was proud of me? No. Not once. It was always Daddy making up for the love she didn't give me, and you know it's true. And then she found a way to mess that up too."

95

"Cam, she loves you. She just doesn't know how to express it."

"No, she loves you," Camille said, pointing at Mel. "She tolerates me."

Mel rolled her eyes.

"You see how she just reacted to what you said. How can you say that she doesn't love you? Didn't you see the look on her face?"

"It's easy for you to say, Mel. Everything you've ever done, she's found some way to praise."

"That's not even a little accurate."

"Well if I'm not altogether accurate, I'm pretty damn close."

"You know what, Cam? I'm sick of this whole conversation. I'm sick of all the anger between the two of you. I'm sick of the bitterness. I don't want to hear anymore about it."

"You never want to hear the truth about our precious mother."

"Well, you know what I think—," Desnee interjected.

"Des, stay out of this, please," Mel said, putting up a hand. And then to Camille, "Why are you focusing on her? You're not a little girl anymore, Cam. You're an adult. You need to get your life in order here." Mel poured herself a second glass of wine.

Camille didn't know what to say. She stood looking incredulous as Mel continued.

"Stop thinking about the past, and start thinking about what you're going to do now. Like if you want to pursue a job with Nora Jordan and what you're going to do about getting your stuff from the house in New York. Evan won't make it easy for you. I feel like I'm a mimic. I could have sworn I said this to you upstairs earlier. When are you gonna get it?"

"I'm going upstairs. I don't need this right now," Camille said.

"That's right. Whenever the conversation gets too hot, you make your exit."

"Give it a rest, Mel. I'm not in the mood." She barreled through the kitchen's swinging door.

"Famous last words," Mel yelled.

"I'd better check on Mama," Mel said to Desnee as Camille walked through the kitchen. Camille went up to her room, slammed the door, and flounced onto the bed. How was she supposed to figure out what she should do with her mother around? She was just beginning to get to know herself. Now she had to deal with this too. There was no way Catherine would help her get a job with Nora after what had just happened. She hadn't ever cared enough to help her before, but after this, she might as well consider herself a stranger to the woman.

Camille always knew she was different. She would spy on Mel and Catherine and write down what she saw in her journal.

"Hmm."

She hadn't thought about that in years. She wondered if it was still there on the bookshelf, tucked in the middle of a mammoth book about the Bolsheviks. She perused the shelf and found the history book still there. To her surprise, when she slid it from the shelf, the journal fell out. It was one of those speckled cow notebooks with perforated pages inside. Camille picked up the book and began to read.

"Today they were cooking a cake," she had written at thirteen. "I hid outside the kitchen door and watched them. They were talking about Prince's new video and boys. I wanted to tell them I liked Jimmy Gray, but he'd asked Keisha to go with him, but she said no because he is not fine and too short. He's not too short for me, but he doesn't know I'm alive. Mel licked the batter from the cake beater, and I wanted some, but I knew that if I asked, Mommy would tell me to go outside and play like she always does."

On March 9 when she was a year older, she'd put, "I got my period for the first time. My stomach was hurting and I didn't know why because I hadn't eaten very much, but when I went to the bathroom there was blood in my panties. I told Mel. Mommy came in and showed me how to use a pad. I already knew how, but I didn't tell her.

"I wanted Mommy to smile at me and give me a hug, but she just gave me some aspirin and tea and told me not to have sex until I'm married. When Mel got her period last year, Mommy hugged her for a long time and took her to Bob's Big Boy for lunch. I asked could I go but she told me it was just for women. I keep crying because I want to go out to lunch too. I don't want to ask Daddy because then I'll have to tell him what happened and he doesn't want to hear about stuff like that. I wouldn't want to tell him about that either. Why does Mommy hate me so much?"

Camille flipped through the journal, remembering some of the events she'd written about and becoming reacquainted with others. It hurt to read it. She had wanted so desperately to be loved then. Not even Mel knew about this. Only Evan. Evan had been the only one in her life who had ever given her the love and encouragement she craved. Had craved her whole life. And she'd had to give him up too.

She hadn't been a faithful journal writer. There were large gaps of time where days, months, a year would go by before she added a new thought. In her last entry, which she'd added the day she'd found out she'd been accepted to Columbia, she'd written, "Finally. I'm outta here. Off to new adventures and new people. I won't miss one thing about this place. I'm headed for New York and I'm never looking back."

She hadn't meant that about not looking back. Secretly she had hoped that one of her parents would find the journal and feel guilty about all the years she'd spent praying for their attention. She had hoped they would throw her a line. But nobody had ever found her journal, it seemed, nor had they ever once given her any emotional support. Only Evan had reached out to offer her love. With him beside her, it was easier for Camille to distance herself from the family. Before she knew it, seven years had gone by. And it hadn't been that hard. The night Wade died, she'd gone with Evan to a Broadway play that he'd agreed to in order to make up for throwing her against a wall. It had been easiest of all not to think about Catherine. There was nothing but pain associated with that woman. It didn't fit that Catherine would show concern now, after so much bitterness between them.

Camille returned the journal to its hiding place and lay across the bed. First Evan, now Catherine. It was too much. She hit the Play button on the small tape player on the floor. She closed her eyes as the tape began and sobbed into her pillow. Nora's voice came running out to meet her.

⸘⸘

"TILT YOUR HEAD. Tilt your head." Camille had never had a perm before. She was sitting in the kitchen on a barstool eating a powdered doughnut while Desnee combed cream relaxer through her hair. The stuff burned. Camille imagined it was eating through her scalp.

"All this hair," Desnee kept murmuring and shook her head. "Lord."

"When are you gonna take it out? It's burning me alive."

"How's it going in here?" Mel asked. She was eating a chalupa.

Camille looked up helplessly. "When's she gonna take it out?"

"Mel, you selfish heifer, you didn't bring me one? I know I'm on a diet, but damn."

"Cam, I told you a hundred times this amount of hair needs

a little more time for the relaxer to work," Desnee said. "Now we don't want to do all this work and then have the perm last a week. Here. Put a little of that soda to my lips would you? I'm parched." Desnee had been parched or dying of thirst, hungry enough to eat a horse or ready to tear up some food as she kept saying, the whole makeover day. Camille was sick of her. But she picked up the Big Gulp sitting on the counter and trained the straw toward Desnee's waiting mouth. She took long, hearty sips.

"There," she said when she was done. Camille put the cup back on the counter.

"Are we almost through with this? My ears are burning."

"That isn't the perm," Mel said, smiling. "That just means somebody's talking bad about you."

"Yeah. I can guess who that is." Camille looked toward the ceiling.

"Mama hasn't said one word to you or about you in two days."

"Sure, and she makes it a big point to ignore me too. She hasn't mentioned a word about the job. She said anything to you? Ow. Towel! Towel!" Some of the perm gunk had fallen across her eyelid. Camille grabbed desperately at the air. Desnee placed a towel in her hand.

"Calm down. It's not in your eye. Be careful how you wipe."

"Can you blame her for not talking about a job after what you did?" Mel asked.

Camille ignored her sister.

"Where did the duchess go anyway?" Camille asked.

Mel grinned, close-mouthed, chewing a bite of her chalupa.

"She said she had a taste for some mangoes. I think she went to Safeway."

"Mmm. Tell me we're almost done, Desnee."

"Mangoes. Mmm. That sounds good. Hold out five more minutes, girl. Just five more."

Camille groaned.

Ben came racing down the stairs and into the kitchen. "Dad's here! Dad's here!"

"Hi, Aunt Cam," he said. She kissed the top of his head. "Hi, Benji."

"My dad's here." He was grinning. His brown eyes sparkled.

"You got your suitcase?" Mel asked him. Camille read the misery on her face and felt bad for her.

"Yeah, I got it, Mom. I put it beside the door."

"What about your kid's meal?" Mel asked Ben.

The bell rang.

"Ya hunh." Mel's face was full of dread.

"You want me to get it, Mel?" Desnee prepared to take off her gloves.

"No. It's all right. I'm good. Don't worry about it. Come on, Ben. Hey, don't be rude. Say see you later to Auntie and Ms. Desnee."

"See you later."

"Bye, man," Desnee said.

Mel and Ben disappeared through the door.

"Two more minutes left, Cam."

Camille didn't hear her. She wanted to get a look at Jeff. She jumped off the stool and peeped through the kitchen door.

"He's fine," she whispered to Desnee.

Desnee nodded. "Not where it counts," she whispered.

Jeff was gorgeous. His picture hadn't done him enough justice. No wonder Mel had had such a difficult time keeping women away from him. Camille wondered if Jeff ever regretted how things had turned out between him and Mel. She wondered if Evan regretted it now that she was gone.

"Cam? The perm?" Desnee whispered.

"Hunh? Oh yeah."

She went to the sink where Desnee was already running warm water and waiting with shampoo. She thought about a silly song: "Wash that man right out of my hair."

⟨❧⟩

"Y'ALL I'M BORED." The three of them, Mel, Camille, and Desnee, watched a videotape Catherine had made of *Who Wants to Be a Millionaire?*" on the family room floor while they finished a pizza with pepperoni washed down with soda.

"What do you want to do?" Mel asked, searching her teeth with a toothpick.

"Dance, girl. I want to shake it 'til I break it."

"Shake it 'til you . . . ?" Camille lifted her head from the crook of her arm and gave Desnee a strange, squinty look. Her newly improved silky black hair hung like a heavy black rope against her shoulder.

"Break it," Desnee said and pushed Camille's shoulder like she was giving her a challenge. But she smiled and heaved herself up, popping her chubby fingers. "Big girls got moves too, honey. Didn't you know that? Here we are, three decent-looking chicks staring in the face of a Saturday night with nothing to do but hang around talking about men and eating ourselves silly. This is a waste of time. I want to dance." She did a Judith Jamison pose.

Camille couldn't remember a Saturday night when she hadn't done exactly what she was doing now. It felt natural.

"Count me out. I'd be out of my element." She finished the remaining crust of her last slice of pizza and sipped Pepsi from one of Ben's Disney cups because none of the other cups were clean. Mel hadn't run the dishwasher.

Desnee paused her antics. "Come on, Cam. It'll be a blast. You need to get out of the house. Been holed up in here like somebody's nun forever, from what Mel tells me. Besides, you've got that fly hair, if I may say so myself. We've got to show you off, girl."

"I'll pass."

Mel massaged her eyes and chimed in. "I don't know, Des. I haven't been out dancing in I don't know how long. I don't think I'm up to it."

"One of the few times Ben is with his daddy and you're tripping."

Desnee sucked her teeth and went into action. "You chickens. Okay. Check this out. I'll be the designated driver, so Mel, you can put on that tight black dress you wore that time when we took Brianne to see the strippers for her bachelorette party. Cam, you can wear . . . something. Maybe something showing some shoulder on you. We get to the club. You get yourself a dirty martini and sit at the bar to scope the dance floor. Right when you're about to turn bored, Mr. Fine with the Colgate smile spots you from across the room. The music is beating in your blood, girl. It's that Brazilian stuff you like, Mel. Or better yet. Some old school, yeah. Atlantic Starr. Shalimar. Roger and Zapp. Those old groups you dig."

"I'm feeling you," Mel was saying, smiling and tapping her foot against a leg of the coffee table. Camille was sitting cross-legged now, caught up in it too. Desnee started rocking from side to side, snapping her fingers to a beat in her head. Her brown eyes were shimmering. Her shoulders rose and fell.

"Mr. Fine Colgate commercial—"

"What's he wearing?" Camille asked.

"Dark blue suit. Tailored. White shirt with french cuffs and some gold links with tiny diamonds shaped like a sphinx."

"Is he tall?" Mel asked.

"Six one. Legs up to his throat like you like them, Mel. Runner's thighs. Linebacker shoulders. He's got Richard Gere's eyes. Milk chocolate Morris Chestnut skin. Muscular, but not Arnold. He's suave, but he's not that pretty-boy type. He's more the handsome intellectual—I threw that in for you, Miss Goody Two Shoes," she told Camille and Camille hid a smile behind her hand.

"He walks toward you. Your legs are crossed, and all kinds of thigh is showing. Every woman in the place has her eyeball on him. But not you. You see him out of the corner of your eye, but you're shooting the breeze with the bartender, Alberto. Telling him about some wicked skiing you did at Wisp last winter. He's freshening your sipping glass and positioning your olive just right. Honey boy keeps coming across the room. Checking you out up and down. You're telling yourself to stay calm. Up close he is even more tasty. He gets to the bar in a slow hurry, and you can smell him as he leans across the bar to make his bold move in your favor. He tells you hello pretty lady. And you say . . ."

Camille looked at Mel. They both couldn't wait to hear what was next.

"What? What do I say?" Mel asked hurriedly.

Desnee looked off in the opposite direction and said, "Heck if I know. According to my recollection, you weren't up to going out tonight, so you missed out on Mr. Fine."

Mel hit her on the arm. "Girl!" she said.

Desnee laughed and laughed, holding her side. Her whole body rocked. The fat around her neck quivered and jumped.

A tear leaked. She wiped the moisture from her eyes as Mel and Camille sat transfixed, arms crossed until Mel broke the hilarity.

"We can be showered and dressed in twenty minutes," she said, fluffing her braids. The beads clicked like pennies dropped into a jar.

Camille looked at her, stunned. "We?" She had no intention of going out to some club. She straightened her glasses across her nose and looked determined to hold her ground. But Mel put an arm around her shoulder and cozied up to her with a pleading look.

"Cam, we can't go without you. You don't have to dance, but at least have a drink with us."

"I don't drink."

Desnee was still smiling, getting out the last giggle, and she said, "Don't drink? Could have fooled me the other night."

Camille regretted that. "That was wine. I don't do hard liquor."

Desnee waved a french manicured hand through the air with blush-pink tips.

"So get yourself some merlot. Chardonnay. Whatever."

Camille felt pressured. She looked at her feet, the toes streaked burgundy with Mel's new polish. With the movement of her head, her shiny, limp hair slid forward like water, and the smell of strawberry spritz hid in her nostrils. She sighed. This was not her, this foreign stuff. Colored nails and new hair. It didn't change her inside. It didn't change the fact that when she opened her mouth to talk to people she didn't know, it was as if her lungs hurt with the effort of pushing up the sounds. It didn't change that her face would flush, her knees would tremble, and she wouldn't have a clue what to do with her hands. How worse would it be in a crowd of schooled men shopping around with their eyes, sifting through attractive women with voluptuous bodies in skimpy dresses? She wasn't one of those women. She would spend the night like she'd spent her days in high school and college, sitting alone and trying desperately to appear at ease and part of the group.

She said uneasily, "I don't know. I've never been to any-thing like that. I don't have those kinds of clothes."

"Excuses. I've got a fantabulous dress you can wear right upstairs. What do you say, Des? Blue?" Mel said.

Desnee nodded. "Blue."

She wanted to burst out that she didn't want even to smell another man, after Evan. It was fun to sit and listen to Desnee's stories, but she needed time to get herself in order.

"I'm not going. I get migraines." Another pitiful excuse that she could tell they weren't buying. "Why is it necessary that I go?"

Desnee took her by the arm to guide her toward the stairs. "I don't want to hear it. Put some makeup on that bruise. I'll be back here in half an hour for you two. Be ready."

The door slammed on Desnee's way out.

"I'm not going, Mel." Camille shook her head, and Mel

shrugged, gliding from the family room with an armful of pizza box and soda glasses.

"You have two choices," she told Camille. "You can go with us. Or you can stay here alone with . . ." Mel looked toward the ceiling making her point clear.

⊷⊶

THE DRESS WAS A VERY DEEP PURPLE, not blue. It wasn't a dress, come to think of it, but a two-piece outfit—a long, fitting stretch skirt with embarrassingly high slits that made her look like a straight stick. A matching sleeved top that had a vee to expose cleavage Camille didn't have, so she resorted to stuffing socks into her padded bra. Olive Oyl. That's what they'd called her in high school. Tonight she'd have to go through humiliation again. Nobody would ask her to dance, she didn't have rhythm anyway, but it was better to be asked than ignored.

She sucked in her cheeks as directed, while Mel put layers of foundation and blush on her face. Desnee was back, supervising in her red finery—a short, backless dress exposing waves of jiggling fat tucked into it. Camille didn't feel so bad when she saw Desnee. A pretty face, perfect personality, but a body that looked out of control. Slyly, Camille patted her sock bra and closed her eyes for the gray shadow Mel would plaster to her lids.

They were on the road in Desnee's Bronco listening to Rick James belch out of the radio speakers. The air-conditioner fogged the windows on high. Desnee turned it off and let her wipers swish the windshield briefly.

"Roll down y'alls windows."

It was still light outside, but dimming. The streetlights would be on soon. The neighborhood was quiet and sleepy except for crickets grinding their legs. Camille watched out the window for elaborate yards with loads of flowers and trees while Mel and Desnee talked about customers at work. Camille self-consciously rearranged her hair with her fingers a dozen times, checking her bangs in the rearview mirror over Desnee's shoulder. Then the scenery changed. They made their way through the streets to the main road with its cherry blossom and pear trees. They wound through the shopping center areas and took the parkway toward downtown.

On the southwest side of D.C. they parked a few blocks from a new club called Limits and exited the truck beneath a streetlight out onto the black road. The smell from the river was bold and stale, reeking of mean fish scents. It made them scrunch their noses and cover their faces with their hands. The club itself was unassuming, but a crowd had formed outside its calm silver exterior, and heavy dance music pulsed in the air all through the street.

They walked toward the music. Camille followed Desnee and Mel onto the uneven sidewalk and carefully stepped over cracks in it where odd weeds grew out. In this block, the smell dissipated, but the music noise grew. There were spotlights in the sky, making patterns against its gray-black haze.

"There's going to be men here galore, y'all. Cam, you gotta loosen up, girl. You're fine." Desnee popped a finger and cracked her gum.

But she wasn't fine. Camille fidgeted with her glasses and tight sleeves, and the block-heeled shoes hurt her feet. A rippling in her stomach made her nauseous. They were slowing now, tacking onto the end of the line crowded at the door where two hefty men dressed all in black with multiple earrings were checking ID's.

Camille dug her license out as she'd seen Mel do. Mel and Desnee were admiring a short, stocky man in gray who had a successful look about him. His face was generously handsome, and he disappeared inside with three other suited men talking investments. Camille watched what other women did and tried to emulate them. The way they smiled a little and worked the crowd with their eyes. The way they posed, carelessly, with hands on hips, leaning with one leg bent, a set of fingers run through the hair. Every now and then, one would whisper to a girlfriend and laugh some. They all showed lots of skin.

Camille's heart beat so fast she was shaking. She felt sick. She tried to readjust her glasses, but somehow dropped them on the ground. A raw-boned man behind her whose face was hiding in a disguise of graying thick bushy mustache and beard helped her pick them up. She smiled thank you.

"You won't find kids in here. Only twenty-five and up," Desnee said. She whipped out her ID for the man at the door, and Mel and Camille followed suit. Then they were inside. And Camille could barely breathe. They squeezed through the crowd like sardines until they reached an open area, where there was a lighted bar that divided a carpeted wall of tables already filled up and a dance floor to the right that was full and seething. This was such a strange place to be. Desnee was right. She noticed no young faces.

It was dark in the club and sweaty and tight. Overhead, colored lights blinked and strobed in yellow, blue, red, green, white to the beat of the music, which was overpowering. As loud as it was, Camille couldn't hear anything else, but saw Desnee turn in the half light, mouth words that Mel nodded to, and then move off in a rhythmic march to join the fray of undulating bodies. Mel grabbed her hand and led her to the bar, where they sat on uncomfortable stools. Camille had to keep an eye on her skirt. It kept falling open to reveal her upper thigh.

"Nobody asked her to dance," she yelled with so much effort that her throat burned. A couple beside her were laughing into the rims of their drinks.

"What?"

"Dance." She walked two fingers of her right hand across her left palm to demonstrate. "Nobody asked Desnee to dance."

Mel caught on and said, "No. Don't have to. Just join in."

Mel ordered them both a drink, and when they came, their bottoms covered in napkins, a tall angular man with square sunshades and an earring took Mel's hand. He wore a mis-matched suit of black pants and gray jacket, but they were quality. He wasn't attractive but he was sexy, and that was enough. He didn't speak. He moved. With silent grace he led Mel toward the dance floor, and Camille felt a pang as she watched them go. Longingly, she stared after them. They dis-appeared, sucked up in the dancing crowd. It made her want to cry. Her eyes stung. She blinked. Desperately, she looked around at the faces near her of people who seemed to be hav-ing a wonderful time. She wished that somebody would ask her to dance too. Not that she would accept, but it would mean everything to be asked. In her high school years of being forced to attend school dances, she'd sat at the back against the wall with other girls who wouldn't be asked to dance. The ugly girls' corner was what they'd called it. It cut her heart. She always ended up crying in the handicap stall of the girls' bathroom in the gym.

Her eyes shifted to the bar. There was the drink in its wide, round crystal glass with two red stirrers and a bobbing cherry. She studied the cherry and plucked it from the liquid to eat it slowly. She took Mel's too. Around her, people were small-talking, dancing in chairs, making dates, checking out the scene. They all looked so comfortable and settled here. She didn't belong. Quiet evenings spent safe at home watching television reruns and specials was all she knew. And Evan. She sucked down half the glass of her bitter drink to get drunk enough to forget this feeling. But it wouldn't go away. She kept on sipping until she was working on Mel's abandoned glass. The music changed, and everybody sounded pleased with George Clinton's "Atomic Dog." The beat thumped in her chest, making her catch her breath. She continued the sip until the second drink was gone and there were only little melting chunks of ice rattling the glass.

After it was gone, she was too afraid to catch the bartender's attention to put in another order. She sat. She rearranged her skirt. The burning in her throat and chest descended to her belly and made her warmer. She could barely hold her head up straight. It spun hard, and the people around her turned to dark fluid. A man and woman at the corner of the bar with their heads together kissed slow and sure, her hand working the back of his head while his arms folded around her body. Camille missed Evan more. Because she was sitting here in the ugly girls' corner with no one to ask her to dance or hold her. She stared at them unashamed and wasn't aware that she was crying until a woman dressed in gold pants and white chiffon touched her arm to ask if she was okay. She was not okay. Camille covered her mouth, crying out with her eyes closed, not caring that the skirt flopped open to expose her entire leg. She felt hands. She opened her tearstruck eyes, and there was Desnee, a perfect sweaty mess, and Mel, guiding her out of the place. Her ears were clogged from the loud music, but a block from the club she heard herself saying it. "Oh, Evan. Oh, Evan. Oh, God."

❦

Nights were hard for Camille. You can make yourself forget anything that hurts when you fill your time with enough people and things. During the day, it's not a major struggle to push certain thoughts to the back of your mind and keep going, keep living. But at night, before sleep overtakes you, in that window of time when your body is still and your mind is moving—worse still, in those hours between midnight and dawn when you're wide awake and there isn't a sound except the slide of your body against the sheets as you toss and turn—you can become vulnerable to your own thoughts.

Camille dreaded it. She held Mel hostage with reminiscent talk until all hours on weekends. Weeknights, she'd stay awake watching *David Letterman* and then *Politically Incorrect*. She did the crossword puzzles from the *Post* because they were so difficult that it distracted her. She began to write in her journal again. When she would reach a point where she was unable to keep her eyes open, a good hour's sleep would follow. But it never failed. Somewhere around two, her brain ignited with the suddenness of a camera flash. An instant memory of Evan would consume her.

The memories were of small things, like the time she was sick with the flu and he'd tried to make her chicken soup from scratch that turned out as salty water with chicken chunks. They'd laughed at that. She thought about their silly contests to see who could make the most baskets in the hamper with Nerf balls they'd bought at F.A.O. Schwartz. These memories made her cry. One moment, she was caught in the fog of deep sleep; the next the emotion of missing Evan was in her lungs and she was sobbing into her pillow, hoping no one could hear. Sometimes it wasn't an insta-memory, but a dream that woke her. She hated the dreams more because they were so vivid that they left her shaking.

One night she dreamed she was climbing the side of a mountain that crumbled with each step she took. She didn't quit. She became more determined to pull herself up toward the pinnacle. As she reached the top, she saw Evan standing there, pounding an omnipotent fist against the rock to break it down. She climbed anyway, with her head down so the boulders couldn't blind her. When she looked up again, she realized it wasn't Evan. She saw herself in Evan's clothes, making the rocks come pounding down on her own head. She awoke suddenly in her dark room.

"When I was sixteen," Catherine whispered, "I dated a boy in high school who slapped my face once."

It was well after midnight, and hot and sticky because Catherine's bursitis meant that Mel couldn't freeze them to death with the air-conditioner. Camille was awake. She regulated her breathing to force herself to calm down after a dream she'd just had where Evan had turned her into a paper doll and ripped her apart. She'd heard Catherine come in her bedroom to sit on the edge of her bed. At first she thought it was Mel. Mel and Catherine sounded alike. Camille rubbed the tears from her face against the pillow. She was about to speak, but then her eyes adjusted and she saw in the specks of moonlight escaping through the window the blurred image of her mother, not Mel, sitting on the bed. The dim light seemed to make Catherine's face appear less sharp. It had been a week since they'd said one word to each other.

"What did you do?" Camille whispered, moving her legs farther from the edge of the bed to make more room for her mother to sit comfortably.

"He slapped me in front of all of his friends and my best girlfriend, Juanita. I had screamed at him for carrying another girl's books. Most humiliating day of my life. I turned and walked all the way home, about four miles, in some worn-down Mary Janes that hurt my feet. I cried all the way. When I got home, I told your grandfather, and he took me to school and threatened the boy with a switchblade he put to his throat."

For the first time she could ever remember, Camille almost felt close to Catherine. She wanted Catherine to hold her like she had ached for her to hold her when she was a little girl.

"Mother, I just want to start over and get myself together."

"Why didn't you tell us, Camille?"

"I didn't tell anybody. I was embarrassed."

"How could you let somebody beat you like that?" It

sounded harsh. The walls were up again and Camille hadn't even seen it coming. She swallowed, cautious again. She couldn't make her mother understand that in between the anger, there was more love, more warmth and affection from Evan than she'd ever had.

"It's over with Evan now," she said, halfway regretting that it was true.

"I know that's what you say, Camille, but how can I know that for sure? You've been in this thing all this time. Didn't tell a soul. You never once called or even sent a card. You just ran off to New York and cut yourself off from your family. Now we find out you were with an abusive man."

"Yeah, I did." Camille didn't want to talk about it. They were quiet for awhile.

"What did you do? Quit your job?" Catherine asked.

"I was let go."

"What? How did that happen?"

"Mother, please. Do you have to know everything?"

"I'm concerned, Camille." Catherine put a hand on Camille's shoulder.

"I don't understand why you would be in the first place, but aside from that, there's nothing you can do."

"Why were you fired?"

"I was slipping. Problems at home interfered with my work."

"I see. Any idea what you're going to do next?"

"Unfortunately, no. Who'll hire me without a reference? All

my things are in New York. The rent there is due in another week, and I know Evan doesn't have the funds."

"Don't worry about the money. We'll take care of that. What I'm concerned about is what you want. Are you 100 percent finished with Evan?"

"I have to be."

"It doesn't sound as if you fully believe that."

"If I say it enough, I'll begin to."

"Maybe if you'd take a close enough look at that bruise on your face, you'd believe it. That man must be like a drug to you. You lose your home, your job, everything you've worked to achieve all because of him. From what Melanie tells me, you're lucky to be alive."

"Mother, why are you even here? This isn't your problem."

"I knew it had to be something desperate that brought you here. We haven't seen or heard from you in years, Camille. I know how you feel about me, but why would you do that to your father? Those last years were very hard. He was so sick. He kept asking for you, and you wouldn't come. He had me put your picture by the bed so he could see it. I had to come here. I made him a promise that I would . . ." Catherine bowed her head.

Camille watched her, thinking that her mother had no clue how she felt. Right now, she only wanted to be held tight. To cry in her mother's arms. But it was too late.

"And what good will it do? We can't go back, Mother. We can't—"

"Why do you call me that?"

Camille sat up. "What are you talking about?"

Catherine switched on the table lamp beside the bed. "Mother. Why do you call me that? You never used to say that. You used to call me Mom. Or Mama." Sometimes it hurt her to see Camille's face, but Catherine forced herself to look at her. She tried to smile a little.

"I outgrew it."

The smile left. "You were always a strange girl, Camille."

"Because you were a strange mother."

"I tried my best with you. You weren't easy to be close to."

"I was a little girl."

"You were a distant little girl."

"Maybe if I had felt some warmth from you, I'd have been more open."

"We aren't going to get anywhere with this. I don't want to get into a debate with you about the past, Camille. You're in trouble now. I want to help you. That should be our objective here."

Camille nearly laughed. Objective. It was just like her mother to make this sound like a business meeting. A day ago they weren't even talking. Now she showed up in the middle of the night to help her strategize her future.

"What are you gonna do? Click your heels together and whip me up a new job? A new life?"

"The question is, What are you gonna do? How long have you been here at the house?"

"A little over two weeks. Why?"

"What have you been doing in all this time?"

Camille looked away. "Trying to get myself together."

"Feeling sorry for yourself is probably closer to the truth."

"What's it to you?"

"How long do you plan on sitting around like a zombie?"

"For as long as it takes."

"You can lose some of that attitude, Camille. It doesn't become you, and you're not in any position to play the smart aleck with me."

"I'm not playing at anything. I just wanna be left alone, and I haven't just sat around either. I'm the one that's been fixing up the house. Oh, but you wouldn't notice that because Mel didn't do it. Why don't you just go now, Mother. It's—" Camille squinted at the clock. "It's after one in the morning."

"I didn't ask for a time check. I can see what time it is. But do you? Are you going back to New York?"

"I told you already, I don't know what I'm going to do."

"It doesn't sound as if there's anything left for you in New York."

"Tell me how I can get a job after what just happened. I don't have a leg to stand on without a reference. Braxton Enterprises is my only source. I haven't worked anywhere else."

"I had lunch with Nora Jordan today," Catherine said.

Camille gave her a wide-eyed look. Catherine continued. "She's interested in you. Especially your background. She tells me her company is in an expansion phase at the moment, and she expects to hire about fifty new people within the next month. She said she could use somebody like you."

Camille didn't want to appear too excited yet. It would be just like Catherine to ask Nora about a data entry job.

"What kind of job?" she asked warily.

"Something dealing directly with her exclusive clients so you can put your degree to good use."

"Her exclusive clients." Camille was blown away. She got out of bed. She was definitely awake now. She walked the floor in a daze.

"I told her you would be there first thing Monday."

"Monday? That's day after tomorrow. It's too soon. I don't think I'm ready."

"Camille, you have no money, no plan, nothing to do but walk up and down the streets all day and cry half the night, and it's too soon to make the first positive step you've made since you left New York?"

"Monday?" How did her mother know she cried half the night? She had tried so hard to be quiet.

Catherine nodded. Camille reached for the pack of Fig Newtons on the dresser.

"I don't have anything to wear."

"I'm sure Melanie will loan you something. I gave Nora my word you'd come, Camille. There's no use in you trying to get out of it."

"I'm not trying to get out of it. I'm just . . . I'm just . . . I don't know what the hell I'm gonna do. Ms. Jordan isn't gonna want somebody like me," Camille said.

"You already have the job."

Camille blinked. "How's that possible?"

"She's a friend of the family. You know that. I asked her for this favor, and she was more than willing to oblige."

"I don't want to get in just because you've got connections."

"Camille, you'll learn in this life that sometimes you use whatever angle you have. We both know that you've got the education and you're capable of doing the job, so don't go looking for reasons to neglect this opportunity."

"Why are you doing this for me?"

"Because it's the right thing. I know I wasn't the greatest mother in the world to you. I know I made a lot of mistakes. I admit that. But I'm not doing this for my child. I'm doing it for a woman who needs help. Nobody deserves to be abused. If this job can help put you back on your feet, then more power to it."

Camille sat beside Catherine on the bed. She put both arms around her and laid a head on her shoulder. Catherine stiffened automatically. But then she looked down into Camille's eyes, reading the yearning in them. For the first time in all their years, Catherine hugged her daughter. It was brief. But Camille was smiling. It was all she'd ever wanted from her.

Catherine cleared her throat. "We'll talk more about it in the morning."

"But—"

"Don't worry, Camille. You'll do fine."

Catherine yawned and rose to leave.

Camille had hoped that this might be the beginning of something between them. Some spark of a beam to start a bridge that might lead them from the past. But she knew from the look on Catherine's face that it would never happen.

"It's late, Camille, and I'm very tired. I'm glad you came back," she said. It made Camille sick to hear her say that. It was like throwing a bone to a needy dog. Catherine turned off the light and left the room.

In the gentle dark, Camille remembered the letter. *Everything about you leaves me cold.* She shivered and buried her body beneath the blankets.

4

REINVENTING RULE FOUR: *Gather your self-help tools. If you know how the game of success should be played, you'll have a better chance at winning.*

CHAOS RULED HERE. Telephone lines rang. Women were crowded into the front office. A young girl with Asian eyes and smooth, dark, bobbed hair served coffee from a pot on a tray she balanced carefully. An older woman in a brilliant pink suit sent a fax, then maneuvered her way to a copy machine and loaded that with papers. Yet another woman asked questions and handed out forms. There was loud, boisterous talking among the women. Some laughter. Some of them read magazines or newspapers, or flipped through books. The reception area was as close and tight as a crawl space.

The Reinventing the Woman headquarters was in a brick townhouse in Alexandria, past King Street but near the Tor-

pedo Factory. The house had three levels. The lawn was perfect. Shutters burgundy. But the door was different. It was
mauve. Open to let air through the screen.

Camille saw the name on the brass plate emblazoned on the
door and felt clean for the first time in weeks. The terrible
bruise on her face was gone. Her bruised wrist had healed.

She climbed the stairs a little anxious, but hoping she
looked the part in a blue DKNY dress of Mel's. Mel had
loaned her the shoes too, some too-snug navy Nine West numbers that made her tense up when she walked.

Two uncomfortable steps into the foyer, and Camille found
herself in the middle of all the chaos.

"May I help you, honey?" she was asked by the woman in
pink over the din.

"Yes. I have an appointment to see Nora Jordan."

The woman smiled encouragingly. "Sure, honey. Your
name?" A list on a clipboard appeared in the woman's hand.

"Camille Foster." She stated her name clearly. She hated
when people called her honey, as if she was a child.

"Oh right. Camille."

"Yes."

The woman stared at her for a long enough time to make
Camille uncomfortable, then said, "I'm Dawn Brooks. Glad
you could make it. Excuse us."

Dawn waved a gaudy, crimson-nailed hand, and the crowd
began to part like the Red Sea. Camille followed her down a
short hallway and into a separate room.

126

"Pardon the ruckus. New Millennium Woman is starting next week. We always get this—"

"New Millennium Woman?" Camille sat on the couch that Dawn had motioned her toward and lay her purse on the floor beside her.

"Yes. That's Nora's newest seminar. It's geared toward the Y2K woman. Anyhow, this week is registration week. It's always like this during registration for a seminar. A mass of women converge on our doorstep. It's a shame we can't accommodate all of them who come, but that'll be over soon. We're moving in another week or so."

"Moving?" Camille had already prepared herself for the traffic-ridden morning drives across the Wilson Bridge.

"Just down the street. Canal Center Plaza. It's a beautiful spot right on the water. How about some coffee?" Dawn straightened her suit jacket.

"No, thank you." Camille said, and crossed her legs to look professional.

"Tea?"

"No, I'm fine. Thank you."

"Then I'll let Nora know you're here," Dawn said, retreating.

The time alone gave Camille a chance to breathe. She surveyed the room, which was small and claustrophobic even though there was a window. The blinds were drawn and the curtains closed. The room was stark with drab white wall paneling except for a blue felt length of famous quotations that hung like a tapestry with a gold epaulet-like fringe at the bottom. There were stacks of boxes in preparation for the move, some with office supplies already inside and others that had yet to be folded into form. The only other items in the room were a water cooler and a small table topped with women's magazines.

Camille sifted through them. She chose an outdated copy of *Vogue* and absently flipped through it to get her mind off meeting with Nora. Sweat from her fingertips stuck to the pages. She dried them against her dress, wishing she were one of the stone-faced models in the pictures, whose insouciance was so pronounced that only their clothes looked alive. These women displayed all of the confidence she lacked, she thought.

"Camille?"

In midturn of a page Camille was interrupted by the woman who had been serving coffee in the lobby. She was smiling pleasantly.

"Yes?"

"Hi, I'm Tracy."

"Hello." Camille put on her friendliest smile too.

There was a pause. The girl seemed to be waiting for something. Camille was puzzled for the girl already knew her name, so she said, "Uhm . . . Is Ms. Jordan . . . ?"

That brought Tracy around. She tucked the auburn wings of her hair behind her ears and said, "Right. Nora's available now. If you go straight down this corridor and around the corner, it's the first door on the right. I would take you, but as you can see—" Tracy gestured toward the hallway as if there wasn't a wall beyond the doorway, but people, "it's a madhouse today. I apologize."

Tracy didn't wait for Camille's response. She left the door open and disappeared down the hall, her heels clicking softly against the hardwood floor. Alone again, Camille stared at the open doorway. This was it, and she was shaking.

On Sunday Catherine hadn't answered many of her questions about Nora. Catherine had provided Camille only bullet points about the woman she was about to meet, describing Nora as commanding, abrasive, and intelligent. She'd been mysterious about how she knew Nora and succinct about Nora's appearance. "She's a black woman," Catherine had said simply, and shrugged as if that particular description said it all about what Camille could expect.

Camille didn't know what to assume or how she should even approach such an icon. She still hadn't decided if she should call her Nora or Ms. Jordan when they greeted. Perhaps Nora. That was what both Tracy and Dawn had called her. They'd said her first name as naturally as they'd spoken their own.

Her stomach growled. The bagel she'd eaten for breakfast seemed to weigh her down. If she took too long to make her legs unbend so that she could stand up, someone might come looking for her. And that would be embarrassing. It would surely get back to Nora and there would be questions as to whether she could handle the job. She pictured that strange

Dawn (she looked like a gossip) telling a perplexed Tracy, "she just sat there looking at the wall like she was crazy. . . ." That was the last thing she needed to happen. This was too important. She had to calm down.

Camille took a deep breath to stabilize her thoughts. *I can do this,* she told herself. *I can do this.* She grabbed her purse and forced herself off the couch. As she walked down the hall, she wondered what exactly she should say and if she should shake hands. She needed an icebreaker. Nothing had come to her earlier in the car. Maybe she could tell Nora how much she liked her work. She would shake hands, call her Nora, and slip in a compliment with the same easy grace that Mel always exhibited.

Camille rounded the corner and gave the door frame of Nora's office a brief knock then timidly walked in. It was smaller than she'd thought it would be for the CEO of a well-known company. Anywhere she looked was dust. It hung in the air like a fragrance might. It was disappointing. But she realized she shouldn't have expected more from this small, antiquated townhouse. And the offices *were* moving soon, as Dawn had pointed out.

Against a short wall were two women sitting in twin gray guest chairs writing on legal pads. They were both smartly dressed in sober suits, and Camille wondered briefly if they were key employees there to check her out and ask questions. She hoped she could hold her own. The two looked formidable.

But it was clearly the dainty woman with mild black hair set in a perfect upsweep and sitting at a computer behind a worn, over-sized desk who was the true presence in the room. She faced away from the door and obviously hadn't heard Camille's light knocking because she continued doing two things at once. Camille could see on her computer screen that she was reading e-mail, and as she paused to use her mouse, she spoke about some project in a sandpaper voice that sounded as if she had a severe cold.

"Ah," one of the women said to alert her. "Nora . . ."

"I'm not finished, Raye," she addressed the woman who wore a buff pants suit. Nora hadn't sounded stern or even angry, but matter-of-fact, the same way she might have asked someone what time it was.

She'd lit up a cigarette when she'd turned briefly to address Raye, and Camille caught a glimpse of the chestnut face that she'd been dying to see illuminated in the light from her computer screen. There were no overhead lights on in her office. The room was dim except for the computer face, sunrays pooling light against the wall in soft circles, and the orange glow from the tip of Nora's smoke.

"Ms. Jordan?" Camille said. The plan to call her Nora had faded as soon as she'd entered the room. You didn't call a woman like this by her first name unless she invited you to. No matter that she and Camille's mother had a history. This was a woman who expected respect and received it without question. Now Camille understood why Catherine had not given her a detailed description. Nora Jordan herself was a bullet point, everything about her as succinct as a pin's head. Had she been a large woman, Camille would not have been able to go through with this meeting. But Nora's small frame made her, from behind, at least *appear* innocuous.

"Ms. Jordan, I'm—"

"Close the door. These are Lena and Raye." Her diction was perfectly crisp. She paused as if she wanted to make sure that Camille remembered. Camille could tell also that this was a woman who rarely repeated herself.

"They are my personal assistants," Nora continued. "You may wonder why I have two, but you will see the reason for that as you become familiar with the company. Raye, go and call Howard and get an update on the build-out. He was supposed to ring me five minutes ago. Find a comfortable spot."

Nora didn't look up from the screen or gesture, so Camille didn't know she'd been addressed until the other one, Lena, offered her Raye's chair once Raye vacated it. Camille determined to pay close attention so that she wouldn't embarrass herself, and she moved to obey Nora's invitation, positioning herself in the straight-backed plastic chair next to Lena, who didn't even look her way to return the rehearsed smile Camille offered. And here she'd gone to the trouble to rub petroleum jelly on her teeth like she'd heard contestants competing in the Miss America pageant did. It had helped get her the job at Braxton Enterprises. Valerie had told her she'd had the best smile of all the applicants. Sometimes it wasn't just an academic record to get you by.

There was absolute quiet except for the noise from Nora's keyboard. This was like being in a library where a person might be deeply afraid (as if breaking a law) of being shushed for even a mere whisper. Camille tired of fooling with a hangnail that she couldn't remove and found the courage to look up from her hands to scan Nora's salmon-complexioned office walls.

A cluster of plaques and certificates took up a whole wall. On another were framed pictures of various scenes of nature offering bold, white-lettered inspirational words like *Teamwork, Success, Spirit.* Beneath each word was a brief quote that identified with its key word.

There were pictures of famous women—Eleanor Roosevelt, Indira Ghandi, Marian Wright Edelman, Susan B. Anthony, Ida B. Wells—and that was as far as Camille got, because in an instant Nora logged out of her computer. She stood abruptly and rounded her desk in what seemed like one fluid movement.

Nora was like a gazelle in a navy, double-breasted pantsuit with white cuffs. There was a refined polish about her, but an earthiness too. Camille noticed she wore no shoes as she padded across the room on her tiny feet.

"You call that a comfortable spot?" she asked Camille. Her eyes were on fire even though she smiled. She pulled on her cigarette once more, then eased into an elegant pose on the black leather sofa on the other side of the room.

Camille rose from the chair, dropping her purse. She picked it up, thankfully without spilling its contents, and moved toward the sofa opposite Nora.

"I didn't think so," Nora said. "New shoes? You can kick them off. Get me a grande french roast from Starbucks." Camille was confused. Why would she take her shoes off to go out for coffee? She was about to do Nora's bidding while she struggled to figure out the whereabouts of the coffee house. She was sure she'd passed it on the way over. She thought that maybe it was on King, but wasn't sure. She didn't know Alexandria. But then Nora said, "Anything for you, Camille?" and Camille almost sagged in the lap of the sofa, she was so relieved. It was Lena to whom she spoke.

"No ma'am. I won't have anything," Camille said. She rearranged her purse so that the strap wouldn't tangle around her feet.

"Camille, my mother is in a nursing home in New Orleans. She is the only one we call ma'am because she's eighty and she's earned it, so a simple no will do in my case. Add some cinnamon to my coffee, darling." Camille understood this time that Lena was the target of that order.

"I'm sorry," Camille said, apologizing for the ma'am. It was a relief to take off those evil shoes.

"Never apologize for being polite, Camille. Be sorry for hungry children and wronged women."

Camille was too afraid to say another word.

"Nora, I need a signature on these invoices." Dawn had appeared in the room just when Lena was sauntering out.

"Give them to Will."

"He's not here. I want to process these today," Dawn said abruptly. Camille was shocked that Dawn would speak to this woman in such a manner. Covertly, she took a closer look at Dawn. Beneath her breezy, childlike demeanor housed in outlandish fluffy pink, bright gold-dyed curls (they couldn't really be all hers), and inappropriately loud nail polish was something peculiar that caused Camille to believe there was more to Dawn than met the eye.

She made a mental note and turned her attention back to Nora to drink her in and make a quick assessment while Nora was too occupied to notice. Tiny as she was, her voice and eyes cut like a razor. At first glance she was severe, but highly attractive in a Carol Moseley-Braun sort of way. Yet there seemed to exist an underlying caring nature in her too. Camille could tell by the way Nora's hair was arranged in front. Tendrils of it framed her absolutely round face. And then there was her mouth. Her lips weren't thin and bitter like Catherine's, but had definition and were colored just the right shade of wine. Her lips were unmistakably sensual. Here was a woman who got what she wanted, but did it with heart.

Nora held out a hand to receive the papers from Dawn.

"So you're Catherine's baby."

She continued talking as she reviewed and shuffled paper, then signed in a swirling scrawl.

"I'm the youngest."

"Oh, the youngest, not the baby. Well, well. I see. Such a pretty girl. You look just like your mother, you know that?" Nora smiled.

Camille didn't know what to say. Nora was looking at her strangely. She leaned over and fingered Camille's hair. "I saw you once when you were just a little thing, propped up in your mother's arms. You were squalling and wanting attention."

Some things didn't change, Camille thought, but she said nothing.

Nora smiled softly and said, "A long time ago, your mother did me a favor, and I'll never forget her for it. Did she mention anything about it?"

Dawn spoke up. "You forgot to initial here." Nora obliged.

"No. My mother didn't mention anything about a favor. How did you know my parents?"

Nora gave a sharp, short laugh that Camille thought was unbecoming of such a dainty, attractive woman.

"The three of us went to high school together. Poor Wade. I can't believe he's gone. He was such a darling of a man. Your father was the star of the football team."

Camille smiled another contestant's smile, but like clockwork, there was that image in her head of Wade asking for her. According to Mel, at the end, he would look at her picture on the nightstand in the hospital and blink at it furiously to communicate that he wanted Camille to come home. The thought made Camille sad.

"Your mother and I," Nora was saying, "were on the pep squad together, if you can believe that."

Camille couldn't believe that even if she were shown photographs. She didn't think her mother had an enthusiastic bone in her body. Nora went on to talk more about Catherine, but it made Camille uneasy. She had to change the subject. She didn't want to talk about her mother any longer than necessary, especially since she'd insisted on staying on at the house and refused to offer a reason why. Camille secretly believed Catherine stayed to make her miserable as payback for the last seven years.

"I'm just so honored to be here," Camille said. "I have all of your books and tapes."

"And what do you think of my work?"

"I think it's fantastic. The way you get people to look at their life and the things they go through differently. You really break it down. You changed my life."

Camille hoped she wouldn't be asked any pointed questions about Nora's work since she hadn't touched any of Nora's material other than the *Pursuit of Hope* tape.

"Remember that nobody can change your life but you, darling," Nora said.

Camille was relieved. For some reason she didn't mind that Nora called her darling.

"Well, yes. I agree. Your work helped me start seeing myself differently. It made me want things to change. Or . . . I mean, want to change things."

"Thank you, Camille. I love hearing women tell me that. It means I'm doing my job. So tell me your story."

Nora took a puff and put her feet up on the table in front of her as if she were preparing to hear a bedtime tale.

Camille blinked. "I don't understand."

The smoke was beginning to sting her eyes. She was thankful when Nora dashed out her cigarette. The intercom buzzed.

"Nora, it's Diane from the Center." Tracy's voice came through clearly.

"Excuse me a moment, Camille. Put her through," Nora told her and then picked up the phone on the first half-ring.

"Lady Di." Nora balanced the phone against her shoulder. Lena came in with her coffee, and Nora took a sip.

"Of course. Yes, that's on Wednesday," Nora was saying. She had made herself comfortable on the end of her beveled-edged desk. "I think I'm going to speak to them about body image. You know, I had a young girl—cute little thing—walk up to me with her mother in Sutton Place and ask for one of my cards the other day. Her mother said she was showing signs of becoming obsessed with being thin. Said she had plastered a bunch of pictures on her walls of models from some of these popular magazines."

There was a pause. Then, "I know it, Di. I know. Well, I took the woman's number, so I think I'll have one of my assistants

138

give her a call and have the woman bring her baby down to the center Wednesday. Okay, darling. Keep your head to the sky." Nora put the phone in its cradle.

"Take the coffee back, Lena. It's been sitting."

"But, Nora . . ."

"Thank you, no. Tell that girl behind the counter that's always smiling that she knows better than to send me old caffeine. Now back to your story." Nora sat again. She'd brought with her a peach that she softened by squeezing it in her palm. She bit a chunk out of it and looked at Camille, waiting.

Camille looked down at her hands, ashamed. You couldn't blurt out that your boyfriend had abused you for several years and that you escaped and lost your job in the process.

"I don't have a story," Camille said without looking up. She was afraid of what Nora might be able to read in just her eyes or in her demeanor.

"Not so."

"But I don't, Ms. Jordan."

"Call me Nora. How old are you, Camille?" Her lipstick smeared the peach when she took another bite.

"Twenty-nine." Camille eyed her cautiously.

"Then you have a story. Every woman has one. Most have two. An a and a b."

"A and b?"

Nora nodded. Her eyes were cold, almost lifeless. But there was something electric in her still.

"Remember this well. The first story a woman has up her

139

sleeve is the abridged version, but tucked deep is the bare truth. The abridged is dished out to whomever—friends, foes, family, anybody. Almost like the things you put on your resumé that you've dressed up so you can appear to be somebody who has it all together. But the b version . . . Darling, that's the one that cuts to the heart. The bare truth is the story that most women take to their graves. That's the one I like to hear."

"I'm not . . . What do you mean by bare truth?" Camille asked.

"I'll give you some examples. The bare truth is when a woman tells me she stole money from her mama's purse. Bare truth is when she's slept with a man just to get her rent paid. It's when she begged some man not to leave her and had no shame about being on her knees screaming his name as he walks out the door. It's naked and pure. No fiction. No massaging. So tell me, Camille. What's your—Oh, hi." Nora was smiling, and Camille turned in the direction of the doorway.

Two men came in with Raye. They were both tall and attractive, but the one with the shorts and a tank top stood out. His muscular body glistened. The front of his tank sported a vee of sweat as if he had been jogging or lifting weights. The other man was older and polished. His eyes were a light cinnamon brown. Everything he wore looked expensive and carefully assembled on his medium, deep chocolate frame.

"My two favorite men besides Denzel Washington."

The taller of the two, in the suit, said, "How's my angel?" and kissed Nora's cheek.

"Cam," she said, "this is my handsome fiancé and partner, William Mathis. And this is Greg Emory, the most amazing director of marketing I could ever have been blessed with. Gentlemen, this is our new programs manager, Camille Foster. To start, I'm assigning her to work on Complete Woman."

Now she wouldn't have to ask what her title was. Camille traded formal hellos.

"So, you got Complete Woman," Greg said, his hands in his pockets. He smiled warmly.

Camille shrugged and adjusted her glasses. "I guess so." This man made her terribly nervous.

"Lucky you. It's a neat program. I'm doing a lot of work on it, so I guess we'll be doing some collaboration."

"Great. I look forward to it." How would she concentrate working with such a handsome man?

"How's Kis, Greg?" Nora asked. She lit up a fresh cigarette. The intercom buzzed.

"Nora, it's—"

"Take a message, Trace. I'm holding two gorgeous men hostage in here. How's Kis?"

"Kis is just fine. He misses you, though. He was kind of antsy in the car when I went to drop him off at my house."

"Nora, put that cancer stick out," Will said.

Nora ignored him and turned to Camille. Lena walked in and set the new coffee on the desk.

"Hi, Will. Greg," she said.

"Raye, did you get that update on the space from Howard?"

"He sent you a detailed e-mail."

"Perfect. He never does what he originally says he'll do, but he always winds up giving you just what you need. Isn't that just like a man?" She laughed at her own joke by herself, and it seemed natural.

Nora picked up a photograph from her desk. "That's my black lab, Kismet. Come on over here, Camille. Don't be a stranger. Greg's going to take care of him while we're in New York tomorrow."

Camille walked over and took the small gold frame that Nora held out to her.

"He's beautiful. You're going to New York tomorrow?"

"Correction. We," Nora said. Camille almost dropped the frame.

"We?"

"Of course, we. You have to keep up with Wonder Woman. Anybody who works for me learns that things happen quickly around here."

"What's in New York?" Camille asked apprehensively.

"Tall buildings, concrete, evil people," Nora said, chuckling. She spewed smoke and continued to eat her fruit.

Camille set the frame back on the desk. Evan was in New York too. That was the only evil person she was afraid she'd see. But of course, Nora didn't know about that.

"*We're* going," she said, "because I'm scheduled to address a group of women execs at Goldman Sachs. It's a brilliant new plan of Greg's that we're launching for Complete Woman so we can reach out and touch women who have cracked through the glass ceiling. It's a high-pressure, competitive game they're in. It would behoove them to make sure they have their personal and emotional outlook in check. I'll explain it on the plane."

Camille was relieved. Evan wouldn't be in that part of town.

"When do we leave?" she asked.

Nora checked her watch. "Eight tonight."

Camille couldn't believe what she was hearing. It was already four. Nora was oblivious to her distress.

"Will is traveling with us. Is everyone ready? First, let me get a napkin."

"Ready to roll as soon as I change my shirt," Greg said.

"Good. We'll have supper and a drink at Chadwick's. Then Greg's going to drop us all off at National Airport."

"*We* as in me too? Nora, I don't have any clothes."

Nora waved a hand. "Details, darling. Just details. Haven't you heard about not sweating the small stuff? When we reach the hotel tonight, we'll have them launder what you're wearing. I'm sure Lena packed me an extra set of something you can wear to bed tonight. You'll be fine, darling, you won't melt. Go change your shirt. We'll be waiting for you in the car."

Camille understood this time that Nora was speaking to

Greg, but still her head spun. Nora was a slow whirlwind the way she spoke and moved. Somehow she had managed to slip into three-inch blue patent leather pumps without Camille's noticing. Camille stood back watching her, amazed.

Leaving the coffee untouched, Nora took her purse from a side desk drawer, then extended the handle on a piece of black luggage and wheeled it out of the office. Camille followed her out of a back door and into a slick black Benz with personalized plates: Nora J. Camille was impressed.

Nora turned to her and said, once they were comfortable, "Question, Camille."

"Yes?"

"What made you come to me? What made you want to take a job here?"

Camille thought a moment about how to respond, then decided to settle on the bare truth. Without flinching, she stared Nora square in her penetrating eyes.

"To save my life," she said.

Nora smiled, then touched her arm and told her, "Well, darling, you've come to the right place."

⳾

THE GRACIOUS NEW BUILDING for the Reinventing the Woman headquarters overlooked the sweeping sienna waters of the Potomac. A large brick building, it was six stories and part of a group of five. It was at the bottom of a dead-end street in a semiresidential neck of Alexandria where half-million-dollar brick waterfront townhouses were stacked in a row four stories high. Nora had just bought one, she'd told Camille. She kept it, she'd said, for late meetings and special guests. Camille was welcome to stay there anytime.

The new building was part of a beautiful setting. A pseudo park with a patch of green lawn that had volleyball nets, benches, and weeping willows was off to the right. Between the building and the water was a maze of paths and brick arches where people lunched and watched recreational ships and chalky sailboats drift by. In the distance, you could see planes taking off from National Airport. There were statues and a majestic waterfall if you started down the walkway from the farthest left building where Reinventing had the top two floors, and continued along the meandering path. Camille thought it was the perfect setting.

She drove in to the new office with the top down on her car. It was a clear September Tuesday following the Labor Day weekend. She was still stuffed from eating too much of Mel's sweet, smoky barbecue. The sky was vibrant and cloudless, so bright that she wore sunshades though the air was crisp. She crossed the bridge, and the smell from the vast Potomac was hard and rank. The first exit off the bridge was hers. Thankfully, traffic subsided once she entered the residential area a mile off the exit. She studied her surroundings. The neat townhouses like the old Reinventing office, some with courtyards and flower gardens. The businesses were petite, painted brick—a cleaner's, an upholstery shop, a deli with ultra-large windows in the front that said: F-r-e-s-h S-a-n-d-w-i-c-h-e-s. She drove, passing King not far from the water, until she reached a section of office buildings in Reinventing's block. She turned down the street of the train tracks and parked in the underground garage.

It was early, so the office was sparse of people when Camille arrived. But Dawn was there, directing the architect to have one of the painters redo a wall in the reception area. She waved as Camille walked by, and kept talking. Camille smiled and nodded, but not too enthusiastically. She didn't like Dawn with her transparent phoniness. Camille stepped over a box and walked down the hall toward her new office.

Her nameplate gleamed on the door. PROGRAMS MANAGER. This small triumph overwhelmed her as she touched the engraved lettering. So much had happened in a month that her head was spinning. She and Nora had traveled to five separate cities. She'd spent most of her time playing personal assistant to Nora while they traveled and then helping coordinate the move and hiring new staff. This week she would finally get a chance to get acquainted with her job.

She turned the light switch, and the recessed bulbs overhead lit the room. Her new mahogany furniture gleamed. This was a miracle. She had a midsized office with a window that looked out onto the muddy black river. At Braxton Enterprises, everyone, even the senior people, had cubes.

Camille grinned. She slung her shoulder bag onto her desk and took off her shades. After closing her office door, she

146

darted to sit in her high-backed, black leather chair and leaned with her feet on the desk. So much was changing so quickly that sometimes she had trouble processing it. A month ago, there'd been no job, no money, no hope. Evan's absence was still hard to accept. She struggled constantly with her need for him. But the best thing about this job was that it didn't leave much time for her to think about him. Keeping up with Nora was a constant effort. Camille was grateful. The only time she missed Evan was late at night, but nobody else knew that but her. And she figured that in time, the need would subside, just like Mel had said it would.

A knock on the door startled her.

Camille took her feet off the desk. "Come in."

"Hi, neighbor. You busy?" Greg stood in the doorway with two containers of coffee from Starbucks. His office was next to hers.

Camille shook her head. "No. Just basking. Come on in."

This was the first time she'd seen him in business attire. He cleaned up well. His full, masculine physique was enhanced by his well-cut black suit. His shirt and silk tie matched his lucid wheat eyes. He was fine. Over the past couple of weeks, he'd grown a short, trim beard to go with his neat mustache. The look made him seem even more suave and sexy, as if he had something wicked on his mind. Camille felt like a wallflower under his gaze. She wished she'd dressed in more than black cotton slacks with a matching undershirt and a button-down electric blue top.

147

"How do you like your new digs?" he asked.

She ran her hand across her desk and said, "Love it. Especially the furniture and the view." They shared a smile.

"I know that. This is worlds better than the old place. No creaky stairs. No cracked walls."

"No dust," she added and he laughed. It pleased her to make him laugh.

He set one of the containers he held in front of her.

"Brought you an office warming gift," he said.

"Thanks." Her ears were growing warm. She couldn't look into those crystalline eyes. She pulled off the coffee container lid and inhaled.

"May I?" Greg motioned in the general direction of an empty guest chair and moved toward it when Camille smiled at him and said, "Sure."

"Well. You like the job so far?" He reclined comfortably in a jade side chair facing her desk. He made her uncomfortable, but she fought it.

"To be honest, I don't know what the job is. I mean, I've been here a month, and all I know is my title."

Greg laughed lightly as if he understood. "Well. I know how you feel. This place has a tendency to suck you in and pull you in several different directions at once," he said. "That's why I'm here."

She gave him a perplexed stare.

"What do you mean?" She sipped. The coffee burned her tongue. She set it aside to let it cool.

"Oh my gosh," Camille said sheepishly and licked a bit of cream from her lip.

"What?"

She pointed at her cup and said, "So good. That could be addictive."

He leaned forward, frowning.

"You've never had 'Bucks before?"

He made it sound like a crime. She shook her head no.

"Man, Camille. You've gotta get out more. Speaking of . . . What are you doing for dinner tonight? You have plans?"

Everything stopped. The sound of the plane outside her window that had just taken off from National Airport a few miles away, a phone ringing in another office, the blunt odor of fresh paint assaulting her nostrils from the last set of touchups the painters were making. All that filtered into her mind was one thing: Was he asking her on a date? The thought was almost too delicious to entertain. She sat there for half a second with a detached smile until Greg said her name.

"Um." Her hand swept out nervously, accidentally knocking her telephone off the hook. It went careening across the desk and struck Greg's hand.

"Oh," she said. "Oh."

She grabbed the receiver quickly to replace it in its cradle. Her hand slipped, and she hit a button. A dial tone blared from the speaker. She pressed the release.

"Sorry. I'm normally this clumsy. I mean . . ." She took her time. "I'm not normally this clumsy." She blushed. She hated that he made her so nervous. Greg didn't act as if he was aware of it. He was smiling good-naturedly, straightening a cufflink. Then he sipped his coffee casually and smiled again. She hadn't noticed the dimple when he smiled before. The hair on the back of her neck tingled.

"It's okay. No harm done," he said.

She made an embarrassed face. "I'm so sorry."

"Don't be." He waved off her apology. "So what about dinner?"

"Oh. Um. I don't know . . ." She fiddled with a paperweight, trying to figure out how to tell him that she couldn't go out on a date. The break with Evan was too new. Too fresh. Besides, she wondered what a man like Greg would want with her.

"Strictly business, Camille." Greg raised both hands as if swearing. "Honest. Nora asked me to fill you in on Complete Woman. I know you have a full plate today, and I'm much too busy to take time out of my schedule to do it. Doesn't seem right to be stuck in this office half the evening, so I thought maybe we could mix business with a good meal." His voice was smooth oil. Especially the way he drew out her name. Caaa-Meel. It was soothing the way he said it. If only he would say it again. But his game face was on. He was all business.

She shrugged. "Yeah. Sure. Dinner'll be fine. After work?" She tried for nonchalant but she thought her voice sounded airless. Like a deflated balloon.

She did force herself to smile, hoping she didn't look disappointed that he wasn't asking her on a date. An ego boost from a good-looking man like Greg was just what she needed. It didn't surprise her that she wasn't going to get it. Years of disappointment made this one another marker for the books.

"Let's say eight. I've got a few errands to run after I get out of here this evening."

"Okay. Eight." She nodded, smoothing her hair back from her face. She straightened her glasses.

"It's a plan," he told her.

She grasped for conversation to keep him there. "Ah . . . but where?"

He thought a moment. "Tell you what. Why don't you e-mail me directions to your house and I'll come pick you up after I'm done. We'll decide from there."

"Will do." She gave him a thumbs up.

Greg stood, nodding toward her coffee and said, "Don't let that get cold."

She shook her head as if she would never let that happen. "Course not."

"See you later," he said.

She waved. He closed her door when he left.

"Will do?" she whispered, thinking how silly she must have looked putting up her thumb like that. She laid her head on her desk and wished she could be more like Mel.

CAMILLE SPENT THE DAY GATHERING STATS for a report she was doing on the *Pursuit of Hope* responses and writing a speech for Nora to give at an awards ceremony the following night at a downtown hotel. Most of the staff was still unpacking, so she wasn't disturbed except at noon when Tracy let her know that their catered lunch had arrived. Around three, she decided to knock off. Mel would be home because it was one of her days to get Ben. And Camille had an idea.

"Mel?" She called out to her sister as she entered the house. Camille followed the sound of music and found Mel in the den with a book.

Spread My Wings was blasting from a portable boom box. The beat pulsed in Camille's ears.

" . . . To a place that I've loooonged foor . . ." Mel was singing in a Lucy Ricardo screech.

"Can you turn that down!" Camille yelled, but Mel didn't hear her.

"What?" she said.

Camille demonstrated a turning motion with her hand.

"Oh." Mel modulated the sound and then said, "Sorry."

Camille stopped herself from using Nora's saying.

"Why is it that when these groups get together and get a little success, they split up thinking they can do the solo thing and then you never hear from them again. I mean really. I used to love me some Tony Toni Tone. And what about Troop?

Remember them? Weren't they bad? I mean, this song used to be my jam. And . . . New Edition. Bobby left and the whole thing went awry. Now he's married to Whitney, and the last good music he made was like way over ten years ago. Why don't these groups just stay together—"

Camille didn't have the patience to listen to another one of Mel's tangents. If it wasn't music, it was why, when you're waiting for a parking space in a crowded lot, does the person leaving the spot take forever to pull out, or some other nonsense thought.

"Where's Mother?"

"Out back doing some yard work."

Where's Ben?"

"He's playing at Marlon's."

"Marlon?"

"Hicks. His dad is taking them for ice cream and to the park. You remember Aaron, don't you?"

"Of course I do." She'd had a tremendous crush on him as a girl. "Mmm," she said, remembering Aaron's confident stride through the neighborhood, "he was so arrogant. I thought you told me he lived in Florida, though. They visiting?"

"Nope. Back. He's not the same person. His wife died last summer. Ovarian cancer."

"Aw. I'm sorry to hear that."

"He needed help with his son, so he came back here to stay with his mom."

"Mmm. At least he has his family. Listen, I have to—"

"He's an attorney. Still cute too," Mel said. Camille could see the wheels turning. Camille waved a hand in front of her face.

"Earth to Mel. Listen, I really need your help."

"What's up?" Mel laid her book face down.

"What was that stuff you were telling me that day about arching my eyebrows, coloring my hair . . . you know."

"Hunh?"

"Okay. Would you turn me into . . ." she'd started to say Naomi Campbell, but that would have gotten a laugh from Mel. She was way out of Campbell's league. She tried a different tack.

"Can you make me pretty in four hours?" Camille glanced at her watch.

"Girl, what are you talking about now? First you want a perm. Now—" Camille sat on the couch.

"See, there's this guy. Greg. Remember I told you about him?"

"The marketing guy?"

"Director of marketing."

"Whoop de doo. Whatever. What about him? You have a date with him? Is he fine?" Mel pinched her arm and Camille grinned and looked away. She was too embarrassed to admit the things she'd thought about all day.

"Oh, my God!" Mel said. "You like him! Is he fine?"

"Before you get all carried away, it's not a date. It's a business dinner."

"A business dinner that you want to mix with pleasure?" Mel winked and did a shimmy.

"Mel. I . . . I just want him to notice me, that's all. He doesn't ever . . . really look at me. He's all flirty with the other women in the office. Even Nora, and she is not the type to flirt with."

"You sure it's not because he doesn't know you well enough yet?"

"I don't know. I just know I want him to notice that I'm a woman. Men don't ever see me, and I'm the only one Greg doesn't compliment."

"Well, I guess we could sexy you up a bit."

"Sexy me up? Mel, just do the best you can. What do we need to do to color my hair and do my eyebrows and stuff?"

"No, no. We can't color your hair. First of all, that would take too much time, and aside from that, if you went in brunette this morning, coming out of the house with red hair tonight would scream, *I'm desperate.* And what if the color didn't take right?"

Mel stood over her a minute making her feel self-conscious. Camille wanted to give up and go upstairs. She could still call Greg at the office to cancel.

"You're right," Camille said. "Who am I to think anything can be done in this short amount of time."

"That's not what I'm saying at all, girl. First, we'll do this." Mel plucked the hairpins out of Camille's bun, laid them on the table, and fluffed out Camille's hair.

"You have all this hair. Des gave you this stunning perm

that's got it laying down like silk, and you still refuse to show it off. Well, Mr.—what's his name?"

"Greg," Camille offered.

"Mr. Greg is going to be in for a treat. But first I'll need my supplies." Mel ran up the stairs like a child, she was so excited.

For the next few hours, Camille thought she could have been at a spa. Mel washed her hair and gave her a wet set that she promised would hold the curls better than simply using hot curlers. Her face was cleaned, rubbed, plucked, powdered, and painted. Mel manicured her uneven nails and polished them a bright red that was not as bold as Dawn's, but close. By the time Mel finished her beauty treatment, it was after seven. Ben had been dropped off back at the house and sent straight in to take a bath, he was so filthy from playing in the dirt. Mel was trying to convince Camille that the brief little dress she wore with matching low-heeled spaghetti strap sandals looked perfect.

"I don't know if I can pull this off," Camille said uneasily.

She stood looking in the full-length mirror in the living room. For the tenth time, she tugged at the bottom of the skirt, trying to pull it down. It went no further than mid-thigh.

"Looks to me like you could be on somebody's street corner," Catherine offered. "Less is more I always say."

"Mama, behave. Cam, you look beautiful. Benji, doesn't Aunt Cam look gorgeous?" He was adorable in Toy Story pajamas and a matching robe.

"Yeah, Mom. Like a million dollars."

Camille and Mel laughed.

"Boy," Catherine said, "where'd you learn that?"

"TV."

"Lord." Mel smiled. Then, "You're wearing it." She pointed at Camille.

"I'm showing everything." Camille had to admit that she did look better than she ever expected to. Especially her hair. It was alive with curls.

"Ain't nothing wrong with showing the man some skin."

"You didn't even dress me like this when you and Desnee dragged me out to that dang stupid club."

Mel sucked her teeth.

"In my day there was a lot wrong with showing skin. We called girls like that fresh."

They both looked at Catherine.

"Mama, would you please just peel the potatoes? Ben and I would like to eat in the near future."

"My name isn't McDonald's, Melanie. I'm not running a fast food restaurant."

Mel rolled her eyes and ignored her. She turned back to Camille. "Do you know how many women would kill to have your body? Me for one."

"Well, you can have it if I can take your hips."

"Girl, I'll give you every pound."

Camille turned to get a side view of herself. She shook her head. "I'm going upstairs and change. This is not comfortable."

"All this fuss over a man," Catherine muttered.

The doorbell rang. Camille looked at Mel with wide eyes.

Mel laughed. "Too late," she said and pushed Camille toward the front door.

"Hey." Greg was wearing his suit from the morning. His smile was the sun.

"Hi." There was little air in Camille's lungs. Her face felt like a weight when she smiled back. She should have used the petroleum jelly. She was afraid that maybe she'd overdone it with the new look.

"You look very . . . very nice." His eyes rode her from head to toe.

"Thank you."

If she let go of the door handle, she might fall on her face. The strap on her left shoe was eating into her corn. At some point she was going to have to stop wearing Mel's narrow shoes. She struggled for what to say next, but then Mel saved the day.

With a friendly smile, Mel sort of walked toward Greg and at the same time casually nudged Camille and the door aside to widen the entrance and said, "Won't you come in? I'm Cam's sister, Melanie. This is my son, Ben. And in the kitchen there is our mother, Catherine Foster. Pleasure to meet you." Mel stuck out a hand that Greg shook firmly before he walked in as Mel stepped out of his way.

"How do you do," he said to Mel. "Ma'am." He waved and nodded at Catherine.

"Excuse my rude behavior Mr . . ."

"Emory. But please call me Greg, Mrs. Foster."

Catherine knew how to pour on the charm when she felt like it. "Thank you, Greg. It's a pleasure to meet you, but my elder daughter here has me working my poor fingers to the bone peeling potatoes for supper."

"And I'm sure it'll be a delicious meal, too, Mrs. Foster."

Greg glanced at Camille, smiling. She still held the doorknob. Her heart beat in her ears.

"You ready to go, lady?"

She nodded. A sickening jolt burst in her abdomen. Mel handed her the black beaded purse she would carry tonight and the short wrap from the small round foyer table, giving her a quick, pleased look. It didn't register. Camille was in the midst of serious worry. For instance, she wondered how she was going to get through this night alone with this attractive man. But her worst and most immediate issue was how she was going to get to Greg's car because she couldn't make herself move. She was frozen against the door.

Greg solved the problem. He offered his arm to escort her to the car. Thankfully, she let go of the doorknob, shifted her purse and wrap to that hand, and took his arm. She needed something to hold onto. She reminded herself that this was just a business dinner, and Evan would never know.

"You like Copeland's?" It was a muggy evening. Greg put the top down on his gray Infinity.

As they delved onto the parkway, he sped up, and Camille

struggled to keep her hair in place saying, "I've never been. What kind of food do they serve?"

She remembered Evan's question when they'd met. *You like chicken wings?* For years she'd thought it was sweet and endearing. Now it seemed pitiful.

"Well, it's Cajun. Very good food. Nice ambiance." Greg fiddled with the radio stations.

"It sounds lovely. Where is it?" If he didn't realize soon that the heavy breeze was giving her a fight to the finish, she was going to look like Frankenstein's bride when they reached their destination. She settled for trying to look like she was freezing.

"Annapolis." He looked over. "You cold?" Camille was hugging herself. Her poor curls were flying every which way.

"Some," she said.

"You should have told me." She was already scared to death about being alone with him. Now he wanted her to complain too? She didn't want to be a nuisance.

"It's not so bad," she said, shifting hair out of her eye.

"No, if you're cold, you're cold." He wound up all the windows. It made a big difference. She relaxed a little.

"Copeland's okay with you? 'Cause there are other places around there if you don't like New Orleans fare."

"No, it sounds great. I'm sure it's nice."

"Yeah, well, it's one of my favorites. I think you'll like it a lot."

They reached the deco restaurant within a half-hour and

were seated on the upper level in a quiet corner where they could barely hear the soft new school jazz piped in through the walls. She was glad that Greg had thought to make a reservation. Judging from the line, they would have had to wait for some time to get in. The place was knee-deep in people. Camille wished she could observe them freely, without making Greg think she was abnormal. She couldn't help herself. She was fascinated by how elegant the decor was, yet half the people who'd come wore shorts or jeans and brought small children with them. She looked over the railing from her seat on the second tier. A man loafed near the front, unconcerned while the woman with him petted up a fussy baby. She watched them awhile, struck by the familiar pang that she and Evan would never have a family now. She turned away to focus on her menu.

"Find something you like?"

"Quite a few things. I'm narrowing it down."

"Cam—can I call you Cam?"

"Sure." Camille cleared her throat. Her voice sounded old and breathless.

"I have a confession to make." He stared into his water glass and ran his fingers along the edge of its stem.

"A confession?"

He nodded. Camille sat calmly, but inside she was on the edge of her seat. He was like a little boy when he wasn't looking at her with those eyes, turning her into jelly. His cell phone rang suddenly.

"Excuse me," he said.

She took the opportunity to scan the room again. A lot of women in the restaurant were older, and many of the young ones, she noticed, looked like housewives whose husbands did well. Most were light-haired, square-bodied women who were living the lives they'd been taught to acquire with a husband/provider and a couple of kids. They probably lived in those quickly built cookie-cutter houses that were two and three hundred thousand dollars a pop.

Their men looked casual and unstressed—from the loafer leaning against the wall downstairs in an Ab and Fitch T-shirt, whose baby was still acting out, to the older men with their button-down cotton shirts over potbellies and their khaki pants.

What Camille found most frightening about Maryland was the lack of originality. At least in New York, everyone seemed to have a stamp of individuality as unique as their fingerprint. Here you knew that most people fit into two categories: politics or technology. There were very few men who peddled their music on the street corner or women working in deadbeat diners who thought they were destined for the stage. She missed living close to New York. She missed her old way of life.

"Hey, you with me?" Greg waved a hand in front of her face.

"Hunh? Oh. Yes." She accidentally knocked over the bread basket.

"I've got it," he said.

"What's your confession?" She swept bread crumbs from the table with her hand.

"Oh. Yeah. Well . . . I do have to brief you on the Complete Woman project, but . . . I wanted to get to know you better too. I don't really relate to anybody in the office. Half of 'em just came on board, and the rest are jealous of my close relationship with Will. They're kind of spiteful. You don't strike me as that kind of person."

"You think the other women in the office are jealous?" She took a bite of one of the warm rolls the waiter had placed on the table.

"Unfortunately," he said.

This was news. The way he carried on with them, Camille was sure they were a closely knit group.

"I'm surprised. Lena and Raye seem a little cliquish, but Tracy seems nice. I'm not sure about Dawn. And then with this slew of new people, I guess we won't form opinions of them until later."

"I'm talking about you, Camille. I want to get to know you."

"Oh. Well."

"You think we can?" he asked.

She didn't understand at first. Then she smiled and said, "You mean get to know each other better?"

"Yeah. How about it?"

The food arrived. She'd ordered a pasta with duck that was so warm it steamed her glasses. Nobody had ever wanted to take the time to get to know her. Not even her own family. Not even Evan, really, because he hadn't gotten to know the real her. He had turned her into someone else. Here was this man who could easily have any woman he wanted, sitting across the table asking for her friendship. The offer was too tempting to pass up. Camille placed her glasses on the table, then took a sip of chardonnay the waiter had just refreshed.

"That would be nice," she said, shaking her head. "That would be nice."

5

*R*EINVENTING RULE FIVE: *When performing self-surgery, remember that life incisions must be made in the place the pain began.*

"STRIKING," NORA SAID, looking up from her desk.

"Hunh?" Camille walked into the large corner office with its heavy double doors. It was like an apartment, fully furnished with sofas, oriental rugs, wall hangings, and a full wall credenza with a built-in wet bar. Off to the left was a balcony with a hot tub. Nora had said a good soak in hot water kept her nerves intact. A private bathroom decked out with marble was hidden in what appeared to be an alcove. This was the first time Camille had been on this floor. She could barely contain herself.

"Nora, this is so beautiful."

"Look at this," said Nora, looking her over. "Loose hair. Makeup. New suit. Makes me think you've got your eye on somebody."

Camille laughed and said, "Look at this artwork. I've always admired good art." She thought briefly of Alec and her blank canvas with its shaky start. She was embarrassed by the attention from Nora, so she gave the paintings a closer look than she normally would have. She personally didn't think she looked striking at all. Her hair had lost all of its curl. It hung hippie flat. But at least it was smooth. The only makeup she wore was a gentle fuschia lipstick that she didn't think was the right color for her skin. She wasn't sure what color she'd worn the night before, and Mel had gone to work too early to be consulted.

"So you like it? I do too. Howard did a bang-up job." Nora smiled. "It's a hell of a lot better than the office on Union." Nora searched her desk for something.

"It's breathtaking." Through the window Camille could see more of the river than she could from her own office, and then a stretch of buildings beyond. The sun touched the dark water with streaming light, making it shimmer.

"Greg sent me an e-mail last night telling me he was going to give you background on Complete Woman. Was he able to fill you in?"

Nora looked at her watch. "Where is that man?" she murmured to herself. He was supposed to have shown up for their meeting at nine. It was after nine-thirty and no Greg.

"Yes, we met." It was more than that. Camille hadn't had such enthralling conversation since she and Evan had first met. But it was better. Greg was a real man. He had experienced things. He seemed to understand so much about life and the world that Camille had hung onto his every word like a student with a crush. At times she had found herself unable to concentrate on their conversation. The shape of his mouth was full and bowed. Almost every time he began a sentence he said, "Well," giving emphasis to his W's. Camille thought it made him look as if he wanted to be kissed.

"Last night he told me about CW's inception and the kinds of clients it attracts," she said.

"Last night. Hmmm," Nora said thoughtfully. "And?"

Nora was scanning the morning paper above her glasses. Camille knew she was weighing the words in her responses to letters she'd answered in her "Dear Nora" column that appeared in the *Washington Weekly* newspaper.

"It was good information. But what I didn't quite get was a true understanding of what my role will be, so I—"

Nora lifted a finger.

She intercomed Raye and said, "Raye, call Dr. Landry's office. Tell him I'm not going to be able to make the eleven o'clock. Tell him I'll be in touch. Have you seen Greg this morning?"

Raye responded that she hadn't.

Nora pushed back from the desk and rose from the chair. Kismet lay in an ebony furry heap on the carpet beside the desk, nursing his sensitive stomach. Nora knelt to rub his black coat.

"Poor baby," she said softly. He lifted his head and stared with sad eyes to receive a caress to his head.

"That medicine I have you on is making you lethargic. Yes, darling."

Then Nora looked up as if remembering that Camille was in the room. She put on her game face and said in her husky, commanding tone, "As I started to say . . ." Both Camille and Kis tensed at the volume. "Reinventing receives thousands of letters and calls from prospective candidates. Currently we have no definitive criteria for allowing women into the program." Nora soothed the dog again.

Camille mentally shook her head. She couldn't figure it out. The woman had two separate personalities. A soft, casual one who went barefoot in the office and petted her spoiled dog like a baby, and the no-nonsense, abrasive businesswoman who spouted advice like a fountain. Camille liked the casual Nora better. She took the lid off her pen and wrote: c-r-i-t-e-r-i-a.

"Loosely," Nora continued, "Complete Woman is understood as a program for women execs who want to attain full quality of life. The only weeding-out process is financial. It costs about five thousand a year to be a member."

Camille was floored.

"Five thousand? Greg, you didn't tell me that."

Greg had breezed in straightening his tie, a paper tray in one hand, and kissed Nora's powdery cheek. Camille remembered the way his mouth had felt brushing her hand when he'd taken her home last night. Or the look on his face, for that matter. Evan used to get that same look when he took her in his arms. The strong attraction she felt made her nauseous. She looked over at Kis. Too bad she couldn't lie down on the floor with him, nursing her upset stomach.

"Well, it's a minor point," Greg said. "Sorry I'm late, ladies. Had to run an errand on the way in. But, Cam, I didn't mention it because the fee is a drop in the bucket for the women we deal with. Coffee?" He set the coffee tray on Nora's credenza.

"Ooh. Caffeine. Greg, I don't care what anybody else says about you, you're a gem to me," Nora joked. She pressed her hands together. The rhinestones on her flamboyant blue suit sparkled with every move she made.

"I try," he said.

Camille inhaled his dimpled smile and watched him lift out the containers to hand them one each. She put her pad down next to her on the sofa to take her container from him.

"Your favorite," he told her. "Sumatra." Their fingers touched.

"You remembered. Thanks." Barely noticeable, Nora's brow rose. Camille cleared her throat and focused on the coffee. If Nora could tell that she was warming up to Greg, she was going to die.

Nora sat on the couch with her coffee.

"Camille was just telling me that she's unsure about the

specifics of her role. I had just begun to explain to her that our clientele are all over the place."

She turned to Camille. "We need somebody to take a look at who our current clients are. We have about thirty, I believe. That doesn't include any of the women with the Fortune 500s who bring us in for the life-building lectures, of course. It's so refreshing when companies understand that personal health affects professional health. They're always talking about team building this and that, when what some of them don't get is that each individual block must be strong if they want a fortified foundation. Tangent. 'Scuse me. Anyway, we'll continue to view company life-building as a separate and distinct category, minus any new actualization techniques that come out of that area. What we need, however, is to put together some demographics on the individual women. Pinpoint exactly what the needs are, so we can better address them."

Camille thought a moment. "I have a question," she said. "What specific types of issues do—"

The intercom beeped. "Nora?"

"Yes, Trace."

"Sorry to disturb you, I know you're in a meeting, but Maureen Tripp is on the phone."

"Thanks, Trace. You did the right thing. Which line?"

"Line two."

"Tell her to give me two minutes, and I'll be on ASAP."

Nora straightened her suit as if she was preparing to talk to the woman in person. "I need a cigarette for this one," she said.

Greg immediately closed the door. He opened a credenza drawer and took out a cigarette pack and a can of aerosol.

"Will in?" asked Nora.

"He's gonna get you if he catches you smoking up here."

Nora lit up and took a long puff. "I couldn't care less. Who does he think he is, anyway, my fiancé or something?" She giggled wickedly.

Forget catching her, Camille thought. The smell was the tell-tale sign. She couldn't stand the way the stuff burned her eyes and got in her clothes.

"This call couldn't have come at a more perfect time," Nora said.

She started giving Camille background. "Maureen is with Merrill Lynch in New York. At the top of the food chain. She's one of my newest Complete Woman players—I call all CW members my players because I'm the coach. Maureen's married, three kids, has a live-in mother-in-law. She came to me about three months ago when I was speaking at Cornell. I'm acquainted with one of the professors there who's a friend of hers. He recommended her for the program, and now I know why. The woman's an emotional basket case. Well, you'll see." She stubbed out her cigarette and said, "Watch me make magic."

Camille held her breath, poised as she watched Nora hit the Speaker button.

"Maureen?" Nora said and was answered with a wail not unlike a frustrated child's. Greg and Camille exchanged a perplexed look. The woman sounded as if somebody was killing her.

Nora rolled her eyes and took a seat in one of her side chairs. She was totally unmoved. "Calm down, Maureen. Calm down. Now breathe." She put her feet on the desk, and it made Camille smile. Nothing seemed to ever ruffle Nora's feathers. She would have freaked out if she had to be the one trying to get this crazy woman to pull herself together.

"Okay," Maureen gasped out. She went into what sounded like obscene panting.

"Okay. That's good. Now. Did you close the deal with that AT&T exec you were telling me about last week?"

She blew and sniffled. "Of course, I did," she said indignantly.

Nora stifled a laugh. Apparently shop talk was the cure for whatever was ailing her.

"How's Art?" Nora asked. She absently picked up a small pad and began making notes.

"Fine. He finally made partner after kissing major ass. I swear it's about time."

Nora looked at Greg.

"And the kids?" she asked.

"Bobby broke his arm playing soccer two days ago. Such a rough-houser. I rush him to the hospital like a madwoman, and he doesn't shed one tear. He's already charging around the house like nothing happened. Kelly got a bee sting on her ankle and was in bed for three days. The little thing didn't let me sleep a wink the whole time."

"Well, she's only four, Maureen."

"That and Art spoils her to pieces. I don't understand how these kids can be so different. Like night and day."

"And how's mommy-in-law dearest?" Nora sipped her coffee. Camille's mouth watered. She followed suit.

"That bitch," Maureen whispered with venom. "You know what she did, Nora?" There were tears in her voice again, and Camille almost groaned.

"What happened?"

"Nora, the woman is out to get me. I can't talk loud because she's downstairs. Hearing aid, my ass. The bitch isn't deaf when she's watching *One Life to Live* or anything else she wants to hear about."

"Maureen." Nora was like a mother admonishing her child.

"But honestly, Nora, she seems to know just when somebody's talking about her. I swear, that woman goes out of her way to make me look like a fool, and Art doesn't do a thing. He sits there and lets her hurt me."

"Are you planning on telling me what happened?"

Camille wished she would get to the point too. She had drained the last of her coffee and an earlier cup she'd had was making her squirm.

"Okay. Here's the deal. Now, you know I can throw a good party with the best of them, right?"

"I've never been to one of your parties, Maureen."

Maureen was in another zone now. "It was a dinner party," she said. "An informal. An impromptu celebration at the house for Arthur's big promotion because, I swear, it was down to the wire. For a while we weren't certain that he would get it, but then, God bless my Art, he did everything short of mow Old Man Carter's lawn."

"Okay." Nora drew it out, leading her along.

"So . . . he called me at two to say they'd taken him to lunch and offered him the partnership. Okay?"

"Yes."

"Well, Nora, that meant I had about four, five hours tops to throw together some sort of mini-celebration. So what do I do? I hop on the horn to our best friends, Laurie and Hugh—you know I told you about them—and then I manage to get two of his racquetball buddies from the firm to commit and bring their spouses. I was on a grand roll. So what were we talking? About eight people, ten max."

"Sounds like," Nora said. Kismet finally woke up from the dead and sauntered around the desk to where Nora was on the other side. He pressed his chin against her thigh and whined low for attention. She gave him a rubdown that seemed to satisfy him.

"So I immediately call Gourmet Gathering," Maureen was saying, "this adorable little gourmet shop that doesn't mind doing last-minute parties as long as it's for ten people or fewer and it's kept simple. So this is what I do. I order a sampling of hors d'oeuvres, a cake that says *Congrats, Art*—they already have the cakes made up, chocolate truffle, if you please. On top of that I get chicken breast with coconut curry sauce, a simple rice dish, a couple of salad bowls, and a vegetable grill mix."

"Uh-hunh," Nora said, pausing from petting Kismet to jot something down.

"Then I called Donna, the kids' after-care nanny—Nora, I couldn't live without her—and got her to put a half-dozen bottles of wine in the freezer to chill. Well, little old me, I pull the whole thing off, and let me tell you, everybody seemed happy. Everybody. But what does *she* do? The hairy old hag! In front of all of our friends, she asks me couldn't I have done any better than to serve some measly old chicken, as if her son is hard up for money? That measly old chicken cost me twenty bucks a serving, I'll have you know. It was free range, for God's sake. And Nora, I could have died on the spot."

"What did you do? Did you say anything to her?"

"It's Art's mother. So I'm standing there thinking, *Now she's gone too far. Now he's gonna tell her off good and proper and throw her in a nursing home like any other red-blooded man who sticks up for his wife.* I mean, there we were, all our friends looking on, and of course she talks loud enough to be heard even if a subway was to burst through the living room. So I looked at Art, my protector, my rock of Gibraltar, and my eyes are big as saucers, Nora, because all I'm wanting is for the floor to suck me up or a friendly aneurysm to flare up in her brain, and what does Art do? I'll tell you what he did. He laughs. My very own husband stood smack dab in front of my face and laughs and says, 'Now, Mom.' *Now, Mom?* They laughed at me, Nora. I swear, she makes me feel like I can't do anything right."

The tears were back in full force, but Nora didn't bat an eye, and Camille knew at that moment that she wanted to be just like Nora. Out of the corner of her eye, Camille sneaked a peek at Greg to see if he was enjoying the show too. His face was too closed to tell. She refocused on Nora, who was calmly tapping her pen against the desk.

"Maureen," she said suddenly. "Aside from this incident . . . how are you?"

"How am I? I'm on the brink of despair, and you ask me that? What's that got to do with anything?"

"Answer my question."

"I don't understand." She sniffed, seeming to calm again a little.

Nora sighed and jotted another quick note on her pad.

"Okay. Forget that. How about this . . ." she said. "Go and get something to write with and a sheet of paper."

"Something to . . . ?"

"Write with and a sheet of paper, Maureen."

Camille tugged Greg's sleeve and mouthed, "What is she doing?"

His answer was a shrug.

"Nora, is this another one of your exercises? I'm so not in the mood for this." She had switched from the tearful voice back to the frustrated victim.

"Just do it. Trust me." Nora could have been sighing, her voice was so tender.

Maureen huffed out, "All right. Hold on a minute."

They heard fumbling and murmuring. For a few seconds, it sounded like a police search was going on. Crashing, slammed drawers, falling objects. It made Camille uneasy. She gripped the edge of the sofa. A flash came back to her. *When I get my hands on you, girl* . . . What would Evan be doing right this moment?

Camille looked at the wall clock behind Nora's desk. Eleven-fifteen. He was at work. Probably unpacking new merchandise or straightening suits on hangers, repositioning mannequins. He was particular about the displays. The way things looked. She thought, *What if he saw me now, sitting here, my breath smelling of coffee, in bold lipstick with my hair down in public and a tight skirt above the knees?* How often did he think about her? Had he given up looking for her? Had he stopped calling Val, crying himself hoarse on the phone and begging for her number?

She must be sick, she thought, to miss somebody, to still love somebody who had caused so much pain. The man must be in her blood.

"I'm back."

Camille was sucked back into the reality of sitting on the sofa next to Greg, breathing in the faint staleness of cigarette smoke and watching Nora "make magic."

"Perfect." Nora was as patient as ever. "Now here's what I want you to do. I want you to take two minutes to draw me a picture of your world."

"My what? My world?"

"Yes. Your world."

"Nora, all the money I pay you? What kind of hare-brained—"

"I want you to put in it everything that makes up Maureen's world. Two minutes."

"I don't see how this is going to help."

"We'll get to that in a moment."

Maureen threw out an exasperated sigh. "All right. But I still don't see how this can help."

"That's why they call me the expert. I'm timing you, Maureen."

Nora guided Kismet away from her and stood up with the newspaper in hand to show Greg. She wrote out on the pad of paper, read it. Then she walked over to her filing cabinet and rifled through the top drawer until she found what she needed.

"Nora?"

She stepped back over to the desk. "I'm here," she said, skimming the contents of a file. "Finished?" She looked at the clock. Two minutes weren't up.

"I'm done, Nora. But I don't see why . . ."

"Tell me what's there."

"Uhm. My world." Maureen said mockingly. "Let's see. There's my job, my house, my husband and the kids, our best friends, his mother, my parents . . . and . . . that's it."

"Just as I thought," Nora said.

"What's just as you thought?"

"Aside from your job, is there anything in your life that is yours alone, Maureen?"

"I don't know what you mean," Maureen said, a little guarded.

"Listen, Maureen. Listen to yourself. Look at your picture. I mean, really look at it. There's a bit of everyone else in it but you. Where are you, Maureen?"

"I don't . . ."

"Where are your interests and your friends and your hobbies? What do you do for yourself that is separate and apart from your family? You know, there's one thing I've noticed that's been present in every conversation that we've had: each time we've spoken, I've gone down a list. I've asked you how's Art, how are the kids, how is the mother-in-law, and each time, you've given me an update, but when I ask about you, I can never get an answer."

"But that's because—"

"You've made your family your entire world, and it's to the point where they define you, Maureen. It's like your family and friends fuel your opinion of yourself. Therefore, in order to feel validated, you look to Art. In order to feel validated, you look to your mother-in-law, who herself is not a complete woman." Nora winked and Camille was sure she was the greatest woman who ever lived.

"Your family and the close friends you and Art share have your power, Maureen, because you gave it to them. You know what you have to do? You have to create a world for yourself and do things, experience things that allow for personal validation. And then . . . ," she said loudly. Kismet looked up with concern. "And then . . . ," this time more quietly, "when someone makes a cruel remark out of ignorance, you'll be strong enough to speak up for yourself and whole enough so that someone else's jealousy won't bring about an emotional outburst that leads you to make frenzied phone calls."

Camille put her hand over her mouth and stared at Greg, who was equally impressed. She had seen Nora in action on stage and gotten a glimpse, in her lectures and from her tapes, of what Nora could do, but this was different. She'd actually witnessed Nora soundly pick this woman's problem apart with skill and expertise in a matter of a half-hour. Who needed years of therapy if you had enough money to afford a life coach?

There was static in the line on the other end. Other than that, pure silence. Camille imagined that the light bulb was going off in Maureen's head in living color.

"Oh God, Nora," she said finally. "Is it really that simple?

But it must be. Why else would it make such good sense? All this time I've been making sure that I give everyone else in my life what they need, and I haven't given myself a thing. Not in years." Her words came out in a tremble.

"Exactly. As women, we tend to do that," Nora said. Camille couldn't wait to hear more.

"We were taught to nurture others, and that's what we do. When we're girls, those of us who are lucky to have good parents and a two-parent household, which you and I had, we get that emotional nourishment from our parents. Our worlds are created for us. I don't know about you, but I was a Girl Scout and I was a pep girl and played violin in band. I participated in school plays. And everything I did, one or both of my parents were there to cheer me on and tell me I was wonderful. If it wasn't a parent, then most often it was a teacher or a classmate. In the school plays, the entire audience clapped, and I remember feeling powerful and accepted. But when we grow up, our worlds center around home and family. I don't have children, but my husband-to-be takes up a great deal of my time. And along the way, some of us tend to lose sight of everything else. And all to participate in the most thankless job in the world. Mom is expected to cook and clean. Mom is expected to car-pool. Wifey is expected to entertain, to make love with him, to take his shirts to the dry cleaner. You don't get any thanks for what you give anymore because it's expected. You don't get any validation that you are good. That what you do is appreciated and valued. That's why the pot-shots cut so deep.

"So what you have to do is get a group of friends all your own. Join a club. Volunteer somewhere so that you can give back to your community. Find a hobby that you can excel in. Ensure that your job is one you enjoy and can gain recognition from. Validate Maureen for a change. So that when jealousy or meanness attacks you, you'll be able to see it for what it is and not take it to heart."

"Oh, Nora. I had no idea. Oh, God. Look at me." A barrage of sniffles came next. "I can't believe I overreacted this way."

Nora smiled. "You'll be all right, Maureen. Often our reactions to insignificant behaviors of others is in most cases indicative of a deeper issue within ourselves."

"Oh, gosh. Thanks, Nora. I owe you so big."

"Yes, you do. But quick before you go. I'm assigning you a mission this week, and I want you to send me a detailed e-mail report."

"What's my mission?" She said it like a child forced to do homework.

"Your mission, should you choose to accept it . . ."

The two women laughed.

Camille and Greg smiled at each other.

" . . . is to do one new thing for Maureen alone that you can add to your world."

"I accept," Maureen said. The last thing they heard was her laughter.

⊰❦⊱

CAMILLE RUSHED THROUGH THE FRONT DOOR full of excitement.

"Mel, you will not believe the day I had. And what happened to the lamppost?" Camille yelled out. The television was on in the family room beyond the french doors, and there were noises toward the back of the house. Camille entered the family room and set her briefcase on the sofa, ignoring Catherine, who sat on the love seat listening to *Judge Judy* and perusing the *P.G. Journal.*

"Hello, Camille," she said without looking up. She peered over her glasses at the front page. The fact that she was still at the house was the most annoying mystery. She seemed to have settled like the old La-Z-Boy and some of the other outdated pieces that Mel refused to get rid of. Whenever Camille asked her when she was going home, she would tell her that when it was time, she would go. It was like old times. They hadn't once had a civil conversation since the night Catherine had sat on Camille's bed to tell her about the job with Nora.

"Hi," Camille said. It was a let-down to have to come home and put up with her. "Mel?"

"What?" Mel called from the kitchen. Camille could hear her starting the dishwasher. She unbuttoned the jacket of her burgundy suit and reached for the knob that opened the french doors leading to the kitchen.

"What . . ."

Laughter hit her as she entered the kitchen. " . . . happened to the lamppost?"

A tall, good-looking man with a bushy mustache that curved upward with his friendly smile was bent over the counter next to Mel wearing her Kiss the Cook apron, deveining jumbo shrimp on the cutting board.

"Hey. You know Aaron," Mel told her casually.

It was more like she'd known *of* Aaron. The way Mel said it, you'd have thought she and Aaron had been close friends as children. He was five years older and had never glanced her way years ago. He'd aged so well too. He looked as if he worked out because his upper body beneath the jean shirt he wore rolled up at the sleeves was all puffed up like a hot-air balloon, but below the waist he was compact and lean. His hair was neatly cut, and just like his father, his hairline had receded slightly, but it didn't detract from his chiseled features.

"How you doing?" He dipped his head toward her.

Camille didn't remember to respond to his greeting. Instead she looked at Mel and said, "What happened to the lamppost?"

She'd removed her earrings on the way to the kitchen because they were clip-ons, and if she kept them on too long, her ears smarted. She dropped one.

"Lemme get that," Mel said. She was wearing the tightest jeans Camille had ever seen, and Camille wondered how she would ever retrieve the earring. Amazingly she did it, although she was slow about it. It didn't escape Camille that Aaron watched Mel's every move. Then she realized that Mel had choreographed the whole scene. This was way too much.

"I took it up," Aaron said.

"Pardon?"

"The lamppost." He slit the body of another shrimp.

"We bought a new one," Mel said, washing her hands with liquid soap.

"A new . . . ?"

"Yeah. That other one was older than dirt. It was too rusty to repaint. Aaron said we might as well get another. He's going to put it up tomorrow. Remember when I broke that thing? I don't know why we never got it fixed or got rid of it. Sentimental, I guess. Isn't it a trip how people keep old stuff that doesn't do them any good anymore? You look in somebody's attic, and they've got all kinds of worthless junk—old furniture they'll never use again, their children's toys that don't work anymore, clothes that'll never come back in style. And all because of their memories. Mama made me promise I would never get rid of Daddy's old chair, even though it's all beat up and the lever's broken off so it won't recline anymore."

"I see," Camille said blandly. She had loved that old lamppost.

"It's in the garage if you want to take a peek."

Her heart pepped up. "Our old one?" she asked hopefully.

"No, the new one, silly. It's gorgeous. That old mess went to

185

the dump. Aaron's teaching me to make étoufée. You want some?"

Camille tried not to grimace. "No, thanks. I had a late lunch. Where's Ben?"

"With Aaron's mom. He's staying over with Marlon tonight so I can get a break."

The picture became clear to Camille. The spark between the two of them was virtually tangible. They seemed so comfortable together.

"You sure you don't want any? You know, Aaron's mother is from New Orleans. She taught him everything she knows about Cajun cooking. Right?" Mel looked up at Aaron as if he could fly.

Aaron confirmed with a nod and said, "Yeah, she did." He didn't look up from his surgical task.

"I'm sure," Camille offered. "But I'm sort of busy. I brought some work home that I'm going to see to in a minute. You guys enjoy."

Camille backed out of the kitchen. On Fridays, she and Evan would cook together on the grill all summer. They'd listen to George Benson as loud as the portable CD player could go out on the porch while Evan prepared the grill because his was the only music that Evan said he could cook to. He would put his lean, T-shirted body into the task on "Never Give Up on a Good Thing," turning his famous vegetable shish kebabs to the beat of the music.

They'd marinate their steaks in a touch of Jack Daniels with

A-1 and Worcestershire while they talked. They always could talk. No matter what. She'd have been able to tell him all about her day and how lucky she was to be working with someone as great as Nora Jordan. He would have listened. Camille picked up her briefcase and started to exit the family room.

"I'd like to talk to you, Camille." Catherine licked a finger before turning a page, then folded back the paper. It was one of Mel's pet peeves. She'd say, if someone else decided to look at that same newspaper later, there would be finger-lick germs all over the pages. Camille never reminded her that several unwashed hands had already touched the paper before it arrived at the house in the marked slot next to the mailbox.

"Mother, what is it now?"

"I take it the job is going fairly well."

"It's a living," Camille said. The last thing she wanted was for Catherine to get into her business and try to meddle.

"I think it's time we had a real discussion and stop avoiding each other." Catherine looked up, but Camille stared at the television. Judge Judy was hammering down on a defendant about some money he'd borrowed.

"I don't have time, Mother," Camille answered. She looked toward the kitchen longingly. Loneliness had the most interesting habit of creeping up on a person. One minute you could be just fine, giddy about how well your day had turned out. Then the next thing, there it was, a sudden pop in your head, a sudden hollow feeling in the crevices of your bones. It made a person wish and want. It would have been fitting had Billie Holiday sang, "Good morning, loneliness," as a sequel to the one about heartache because it similarly invited itself inside a body to render it helpless.

"When will you have some time?"

"I'll let you know."

Camille walked upstairs and sat on her bed. She needed somebody to talk to. Without thinking, she picked up the phone and dialed the house in New York. Evan answered on the first ring as if he had been waiting for her call.

"Hello?"

There was so much she had to tell him, but she couldn't speak. Her whole body went numb.

"Hello?" Evan's voice was ghostly.

Camille shivered thinking of how the rain had beat down on her head, blinding her. When she'd made it safely inside her car and finally fumbled her glasses out of the glove compartment as she backed down the street, she'd seen Evan one last time running desperately out of the house to stop her.

"Honey babe? Is that—?"

She hung up. Mel shrieked with laughter in the kitchen, and Camille felt an urge to run from it, to drown it out. She pushed Play on the tape player, and there was Nora in midsentence admonishing weakness. It helped her breathe more easily. Keeping the phone in her lap, Camille rifled through her night table drawer and found the yellow sticky she'd written Greg's telephone number on.

"Hello."

"Greg?"

"Camille." She almost burst because he knew her voice. He sounded pleased that she'd called, but there was music in the background and she assumed that he was tied up.

"I guess you're busy."

"No. Not at all. I'm listening to Miles and cooling down from my workout. I'm about to finish preparing dinner."

"Oh." She didn't know what to say and tried desperately to think of something. He could be one of those people who hated getting phone calls from friends who had nothing to talk about.

"What's wrong?"

"Nothing. I am . . ."

"What are you doing right now?"

She stared at the ceiling. If only she could come up with something interesting like tutoring an underprivileged child or gazing at brochures to plan an impromptu trip to St. Barth's. Instead she took a deep breath and said, "Nothing. At the moment," hoping it implied that she had been doing important things before calling him.

"Well, they say it's better not to eat alone. I just made a lasagna, and I could use some help tackling it."

"Some help?" Yes was on the tip of her tongue, but she was afraid to say it.

"If you're willing to come out to Silver Spring, I could use the company."

"I . . . Okay."

"Great. Got a pen, so I can give you directions?"

"I'll get one. Hold on." She didn't mean to lay the phone down so hard on the night table that it banged. She had to work on calming down. Her eagerness was much too conspicuous.

She pressed her hands together wondering what she was doing. She was agreeing to go to Greg's house to be alone with him. Compared to staying at home to eat étoufée with Mel simpering all over the place and Catherine's dour comments, this was definitely a welcome opportunity. Nora was relating an inspirational story about Althea Gibson.

An hour later Camille sat comfortably in a papasan chair in Greg's tastefully decorated loft with its twelve-foot ceilings and well-glossed hardwood floors. She had been greeted with a glass of pinot grigio that she nursed while she observed his furnishings and intermittently watched him prepare the dining table for dinner. His home was elegant. He'd either had someone decorate, or he had a real eye for style. Either way the setup was impressive. He owned a lot of deco pieces, and she noted that he was into cubism. Gris, Picasso, and Braque liths sprawled over two textured walls painted in an easy shade of blue. His place fit his personality, she thought.

"I'm glad you came," he said, arranging a clear vase of irises in the center of the simple fruitwood table. It jarred her. She'd been looking at the *Guernica* print, remembering a PBS special she had seen.

"Oh. Me too."

He was watching her. It made her nervous. As usual she spilled something. Before coming, she'd changed out of her power suit and into bell-bottom jean Paris Blues that miraculously fleshed out and rounded what she thought of as her modest hips. Her shirt was a shell pink cotton see-through with elbow sleeves that she'd been modest enough to wear a ribbed gray tank top under. The shirt was what she was wiping spinach dip from when Greg suddenly said, "Well. So tell me."

"What?" She pressed her shredded paper napkin into a ball to wipe the bottom of her shirt some more. The dip would leave a slight, unnoticeable stain, but would still make her feel self-conscious for the rest of the evening.

"What's wrong, Camille? Let's talk."

"I'm fine." If she explained to him that her life lacked direction and foundation, he would want to know more. She couldn't open up to him like that. The details were too harsh.

"You're fine." He didn't believe a word she said. He walked slowly over to where she sat and she couldn't take her eyes off him. He was as gorgeous as Evan in black nylon sweat pants with double white stripes up the sides and a black Everlast T-shirt that was kind enough to allow her to take pleasure in the definition of his pecs.

"We haven't known one another very long, Camille," he said, "but I think you're a wonderful, attractive woman."

She was flustered and taken aback and had to coerce her

tongue into helping her say, "Thank you." It came out thickly, the way someone just learning the language might say it, favoring the t-h.

"I'm sure my instincts about you are on point." Greg crouched in front of her chair to look up at her.

She laughed nervously. A warm thrill spread through her.

"What do your instincts say?" She couldn't believe she'd blurted that out. Just like the day she'd first met Evan and flirted with him in front of his friends. She couldn't look at Greg. Her breath became tangible and liquid as he rose from his knees and laid one hand on the arm of her chair.

"Well. They say . . . They say . . . this."

His kiss was a feathery kind of thing. A sort of tickle against the mouth. Or maybe it was wisps of hair from his mustache teasing her lip. But whatever that feeling, it was good. Like climbing into a warm bath at the end of a long day. The need within her unfolded in a sigh. She was sure there were a thousand reasons why this kiss shouldn't happen, but thoughts began to slip away from her like dying fall leaves and melted into her heartbeat, his humid breath.

She struggled for control. Camille opened her mouth to ask him to stop, but nothing came because Greg took it as a sign of encouragement and his gentle tongue found its way there. Shards of light were filling her up inside the way an evening train might illuminate dark tunnel corners. It was a terrifying thing. She felt caught in midair. She was a helium balloon accidentally let go by a forgetful child to float against the sky, and she needed something solid to hold onto. She needed him to hold onto for strength and centering and anchoring.

Just one of her arms went up to go around his neck because her other hand was in her lap and he was holding it in place. Her elbow grazed the wine goblet, knocking it over, and the glass hit the floor with a vengeance, startling them.

"Oh, Greg. I'm sorry. Let me—" She scrambled from the chair, feeling like a fool. The second man ever to kiss her, and she'd ruined it. Tears sprang up hot and quick.

"No, I'll get it," Greg said, calmly. "It's all right."

He patted her thigh to reassure her. Then he was up on his feet heading for the kitchen. Seconds later he was back with a hand sweep and a dry dishcloth.

"I'm so sorry, Greg." She worked her hands together.

"Don't worry about it."

The oven alarm began. They both looked toward the kitchen.

"Dinner's ready," he said, shrugging.

"You want me to get that?"

"No, you're my guest. I'll bring it out in a few minutes."

"Okay." Trying not to cry, she paced a path from the chair to the window where there was a view of a park. Sane reasoning was returning to her by degrees, and she knew that this couldn't happen between them. This was what she'd convinced herself she'd wanted from Greg, so why now did it seem so misplaced? There was only one reason for that. There was still Evan.

193

"Greg, maybe I should go."

"No, you can't. Don't go. Look, if my kissing made you un-comfortable, I'm sorry you feel that way, but I wanted to, Camille."

She felt bad. He seemed disappointed that she might have regretted it.

"I didn't mind. It was nice." She'd given a more passionate critique of a movie. A handsome man had kissed her, and though her body had responded, that was all. It wasn't like with Evan, where the expression of passion was a peripheral display of a deeper level of emotion.

"Then why would you want to leave? The evening's just begun."

She just wasn't ready nor could she bring herself to explain it to Greg, but she chose to stay despite her apprehension. It was better than sitting in front of the television or watching Mel and Aaron fall for each other.

"You're right," she said and sat at the dining table in one of the four mismatched chairs. She toyed with the irises. They were sweetly fragrant.

"I'll get the lasagna. It's my special recipe. You're gonna love it." Greg had cleaned up the mess and dashed to the kitchen to turn off the alarm.

She wished she'd loved their kiss. It had been good. But she guessed a good kisser did not make for a perfect kiss. She'd fooled herself into believing that a kiss from Greg might re-move the numbness that had stayed with her ever since she'd left New York. But someone had once said that only time healed all wounds. They never mentioned anything about what a kiss could do. Maybe time and distance would help her see beyond Evan some day. It would be a miracle from heaven if that happened.

As if in answer to that thought, Greg was back with dinner, his oven-mitted hands boosting up the steaming pan. The way the sunlight swirled around his face, it was almost easy to believe he was a guardian angel waiting to guide her.

⤙⤚

THE WEATHER WAS BEGINNING to grow cooler in the mornings now. Car windshields became opaque with overnight dew. It was that in-between stage when bleak-sky mornings were brisk enough for a sweater and a thin jacket. But miraculously by midday the sun would be heavy and high, and going outside, people were surprised that it was warm again, even though the same weather sequence happened like clockwork each day. The trees were changing. Blood reds, fiery golds, and burnished orange lit the curling leaves with vivid color for a season.

Camille's relationship with Nora was changing too. Though Nora never truly got close to anyone, she was slowly taking Camille under her wing. Camille sensed it was because of Nora's bond with Catherine.

"I was twenty-two," Camille was saying, looking up at the meshed-branch trees lining the sidewalk, thinking how funny

195

it was that this was the first time in years she'd appreciated the onset of fall. For the first time, there was someone other than Evan to talk to. It felt foreign.

She and Nora walked arm in arm. Nora's free hand was wrapped around Kismet's leash. They were both bundled up more than was necessary. Nora's arthritis was acting up. She walked Kismet herself to exercise the stiffness out.

" . . . and I couldn't for the life of me see that Evan was toxic."

"Darling, nobody sees anything that young. When I was twenty-two, I was busy falling in and out of love with all the wrong men. I didn't have a clue."

Camille laughed. "I can't imagine you were ever that way."

"Believe it. Real wisdom costs. The only way you can get it is to experience some hurt and setbacks along the way."

"It was more than falling in and out of love for me. I just wanted so desperately for somebody to care about me."

"Oh, darling. It breaks my heart to hear you say that. That's what drives most people, especially women, to accept less than they deserve."

They turned the corner onto King to look in the Old Town shop windows.

"All I saw was this cute guy. He was easy to talk to. He was so affectionate. It didn't matter to me that he was broke and childish. He was somebody. When he looked at me, it mattered that somebody was looking, you know. Nobody else had ever paid any attention to me."

"As pretty as you are?"

Camille blushed. "I'm not." She turned away and saw her reflection in the window of a resale furniture store and had to admit that she was at least attractive. Switching from glasses to contacts made a big difference.

"Darling, you don't realize what you've got. Such a pretty face. Greg can't take his eyes off you."

"Nora." She hadn't thought she could get any more embarrassed, but now . . .

The aspirin must have kicked in because Nora bumped her hip and said, "I'm serious. He's got you in his sights. Always asking questions about you. He's a very handsome man. He's definitely interested. And I think you are too, but I advise you to be careful."

Camille turned and said, "Why?" as if she had already planned to seduce him.

"You have to take time to heal. Be Greg's friend. Deal with yourself and your feelings for Evan before you jump into something with another man. A man like Greg doesn't come along often. It would be best if you went into it with your head on your shoulders straight. That way it'll be a thing of beauty, sweetie. It'll last."

"It's like . . . It's like, Nora, I don't know. I know where I want to get to. And I know what the template answers are for leading a healthy life, but here I am—a great job, my sister and I are closer than I ever thought we'd be, I have people in my life who want to call me their friend." She threw Nora an affectionate look. "But still something's missing. I still lay awake at night wishing Evan was here to hold me. I sometimes pick up the phone to call. I've gone as far as writing him e-mail, and then talking myself out of sending it, thank God."

"That's just it, darling. You've got a misperception going on. Unfortunately, there *aren't* any template answers to life. If there were, my job would be done because my definition of satisfaction—and I say satisfaction because I don't believe happiness is attainable in the sense that we use it in, meaning a perpetual state of true contentment with everything in your life—but my satisfaction is different from yours is different from Greg's is different from everybody else you'll ever see. And you talk about something missing. Well, that something missing is you, dear heart. You have to go back, Camille, all the way back to where the void started. You have to examine your past."

"I don't know if I can." She'd spent years pushing away her childhood.

"Would you tell me just a little about it? Maybe I can help. They tell me I'm a self-actualization expert or something akin to those words. I don't know." They smiled.

Camille didn't want to talk about it anymore. It was too pretty a day to think about Evan or Catherine. Or her father lying in some sterile hospital room, calling her name with his dying breaths.

"I . . . I've been looking for a rug just like that one for my bedroom." Camille pointed at a simple oatmeal chenille throw displayed in the window of an odds and ends shop.

"May we stop in a minute? I wanna go in and get a closer look. See if it's what I really want."

"What you really want . . ." Nora said, her wise, keen eyes searching Camille's face. "Sure, darling, that's what it's all about."

⁂

AFTER THEIR FIRST WALK, whenever Nora was in town now, she and Camille began making a habit of taking a long walk with or without Kismet. They would stroll the five blocks to Starbucks for their coffee, then drift back toward the building and wind down the paths, enjoying the sound the water made against the jagged rocks. Camille treasured their time. She soaked up Nora's knowledge about life like a sponge. It helped that Nora offset Catherine's presence at the house. When Camille came to work, she knew somebody was there to understand how she felt. Nora actually listened to her.

"What was it like for you as a child?" Nora asked on one of their treks. They dodged a roller blader and took a path they hadn't explored before, up a set of stairs that led them past the top of the waterfall.

"Strange."

"Strange?"

"Yeah, it was different. My mother was . . . different toward me." They reached the top of the stairs and started down the walk.

"In what way? Oooh." Nora slowed. She placed a hand against her hip as if to hold it in place.

"You okay?" Camille asked. Nora handed Camille her coffee cup and limped forward, still holding her side.

"I will be. Darling, I think we need to have a seat for a few minutes. Those stairs were something else. This body isn't what it once was."

They strode over to a bench so Nora could rest awhile. Nora leaned her head back. She was glamorous in the Jackie O. sunshades she wore.

"You all right?"

"Right as rain now. So Catherine was different with you, you say?"

The only thing Camille disliked about Nora was the way she probed into people's personal lives. She would have much preferred to talk about what was really bothering her right now. But she didn't know how to say it.

She sighed and said, "She's always been close with Mel. Not with me. I . . . Maybe it's me. For some reason, people have never been able to get close to me."

"How is that possible as sweet as you are? You don't put me off. Seem a little shy sometimes, but everybody here has nothing but good things to say about you."

"Thanks. That means a lot coming from you."

"I'm telling you like I see it."

Camille didn't respond. She stared out across the water, absently sipping her coffee. Nora sensed that Camille had retreated. A sudden chill wind came from off the sluggish river. Camille sank deeper into her coat, and Nora lit a cigarette.

"I always say," Nora told her, "that to understand the middle, you've got to start at the beginning."

"The beginning?" Camille asked. She watched a cruise ship slide quietly by.

"Of this." Nora waved a hand back toward the buildings. "Of my vision."

"I don't understand."

Nora unbuttoned the top button of her flowing trench. Her gray-patterned scarf was arranged thickly around her throat.

"I had a sister too," she said.

"Had?" Camille sipped her drink and looked at Nora with some surprise. It was rare that Nora ever talked about her own life. What little Camille knew about her was drawn from what she saw each day and what Greg mentioned.

"You really are a sweet girl. Woman, I should say. My sister was like you. Her name was Julia."

"What happened? Where is she?"

"I lost her twenty-seven years ago. She passed away. I wish you could have met her." She took off her Jackie O's and let the sun caress her face.

"I'm sorry," Camille said.

"Be sorry for—"

"I know, hungry children and wronged women." They shared a laugh.

Nora took Camille's hand and squeezed it, saying, "You're a quick study, darling." Then her face became reflective. She propped her feet on the railing in front of her.

"I was twenty-three and had dropped out of college because I thought I was in love," she drew the word out, making a mockery of it.

"You didn't finish college?" It was hard for Camille to believe. Nora had such great wisdom

"Darling, I was living with a man, Steve Tolbert. Steve sold cars at a Ford dealer."

"You, with a car salesman? I can't picture that."

Nora pursed her lips and said, "If you'd seen Steve . . . The man was long, strong, and lean. Couldn't piece two sentences together to save his life, but all he had to do was look at me, and I fell all over him like rain. You know, the way you do with Greg."

"Nora, I don't." Camille hid her face behind her hand and blushed.

"Lies you tell. As handsome as he is?"

"I hadn't noticed. I guess he's all right."

"That's like saying I guess the pope is Catholic."

"Nora, please. Back to Steve."

"All right. Fine. But one of these days I'm gonna get you to open up. Anyway," she went on, "all I wanted to do was be up under this man, cook for him, clean his little rinky-dink apartment, beg my parents for money to buy him nice clothes to wear to work, and then lay on my back for him at night."

Camille blushed. "Nora." She still hadn't gotten used to Nora's plain language.

"Well, the truth is the light. I'm just letting it burn. Sex is nothing to be ashamed of."

"I'm not ashamed of it."

"Then express yourself, girl. That's what's wrong with too many people in this country today. Sex is made to be a taboo topic. But bodies are beautiful. Lovemaking is the most gorgeous expression of giving I know when you're in love. We should savor that and be proud of it."

"So you were living in a rinky-dink apartment with Steve."

In their short time together Camille had already learned to steer Nora in their conversations if she wanted to hear a finished thought. Nora's mind seemed to work on several different thoughts at once.

"It was bliss back then. And I say that because I was ignorant." Nora grinned.

"While I was throwing time down the drain, my sister, Julia, was doing things. She studied fashion in college. She planned to go to Paris and design clothes. Model too. Julia was gorgeous. She was a very pretty girl."

"What happened?"

Nora's eyes were vacant. "Heroin. It wasted her. She came back home looking like an old ghost, and it broke me in two."

"Heroin?"

"It woke me up. Mind you, this was the early seventies. So blacks, especially black women, weren't encouraged to make their mark. Not to mention that women in general were still trying to kick doors down. I mean we still have some hill to climb, but at that time, it was virtually a pipe-dream to think about owning your own business if you were a woman and you were black. But Julia put a fire under me. I wanted to do something to help women." Nora adjusted her flowing hair-piece, a waterfall of waving auburn hair on the back of her head to match her newly dyed hair.

"I don't get it. Why'd her addiction make you want to help women and not addicts?"

"Before she ran off for the last time, she admitted she'd started using because she didn't feel good enough about her-self. She felt she lacked something. Thought she wasn't good enough. Her misperception of herself was what put the nail in her coffin. My family almost didn't survive it."

"I know you hate to hear it, but I am sorry."

Nora stubbed her cigarette and lit another, chuckling. Camille wanted to gag. In between puffs, Nora took small bites out of a peach she had in a napkin in her pocket.

"I'll accept it this one time. But don't get used to it."

"So it was Julia's death that made you want to start Rein-venting."

"I struggled a long time trying to get backing. I went into the schools and talked to girls. I went to girls' homes. I talked to women in shelters, halfway houses, prisons. In the meantime, I married and divorced two men. Went through a financial crisis. All kinds of emotional hell."

"Nora, why are you telling me this? You're such a private person."

"Because I trust you with it. And I remember what you told me the day we met."

"What I told you?" Camille racked her brain trying to remember.

"I want to help you save your life, Camille. I see so much of myself in you. The hurt in your eyes. Someday I hope you'll tell me your story. And I want you to know that I'm here when you're ready. You know, Camille, you can turn your life into anything you desire it to be. It can be saved, darling."

"You keep asking me for something that's not there, Nora. The only story I have is an abusive boyfriend that I left in New York and an unfeeling family I left here a long time ago. That's all."

Nora tossed the remainder of her fruit in the trash. "I won't push, Camille." She patted Camille's leg and said, "Come on, let's go inside. I have some work that's calling my name."

Later that afternoon Camille went down the hall to the staff lounge for a soda and returned to her office to find a man standing behind her desk. He was a towering figure in a gray pinstriped suit that matched his thick white hair. An elegant salt and pepper goatee crowned his chin. He faced the window. He'd moved the phone cradle to the window sill and was pressing buttons while he balanced the receiver between his ear and shoulder.

Camille placed her Sunkist heavily on the edge of her desk so that it clinked. He turned his bold black eyes on her.

"May I help you?" she asked rudely. She was tired and irritable, not having slept well the night before.

Deep grooves lined his cheeks when he smiled, but his friendly face didn't move her.

"Oh, I'm sorry. Is this your office?" he asked. He pocketed a hand in his trousers.

"Yes, it is. I'm Camille Foster." She pointed toward her nameplate on the door.

"I'll be just a moment. I'm checking my messages." He whispered it, then fell silent, furrowing his brow while he listened intently.

Camille wasn't sure what to do, so she sat in one of her guest chairs. He had some nerve tying up her telephone. It was bad enough that the property managers had been bringing in these prospective tenants for the past week to show off their office space, but now these people were going way overboard using her phone.

"We have guest phones in the reception area."

"Here you are," Dawn said. Lena was with her. "Camille, have you been properly introduced?"

"Introduced?"

"To Mr. Mathis. Will's father. Harold Mathis, this is our program manager, Camille Foster."

Camille was surprised. Will looked nothing like the old gentleman with his fluid, granular brown face and bulbous nose. He looked like the kind of man who craved stress, although he appeared debonair and calm. Whereas Will was the type who seemed not to have a care in the world, every line in this man's face told a different story.

"Young lady." Harold Mathis nodded, still holding the receiver to his ear. As he dipped his head, its bald center shone like polished marble beneath the overhead track lights.

"Nice to meet you." Camille shook his strong, veiny hand.

"It's my pleasure."

"Mr. Mathis, excuse me, but Will asked me to let you know that he and Nora are waiting for you in the lobby."

He replaced the receiver. "Then I guess I'd better go. Thank you, Dawn. And thank you for allowing me to use your telephone, young lady."

Allowing him. It was more that he had barged into her office without asking. She'd had no choice.

"Not a problem," Camille lied.

She just wanted them all to leave so she could be alone long enough to lay her head on the desk. But then Lena stayed put. Her attitude toward Dawn didn't go unnoticed. Camille saw the look she gave Dawn's bright orange suit like it was the most distasteful ensemble she'd ever seen.

"So how do you like us so far?" Lena asked Camille. And without being invited to, she made herself at home in the chair that Camille had just risen from. Lena grabbed a stress ball from Camille's desk that she'd gotten at a vendor exhibit during a function where Nora had spoken.

"It's good here," Camille said.

She picked up her soda, opened it, and poured its contents into a tall glass mug, then sat behind her desk. Lena repeatedly molded and squeezed the ball.

"Just good?" Her light southern accent was somewhat flat.

"I like it a lot."

"Greg tells me you came here from New York. You grow up there?"

"No." Camille wondered where this line of questioning was going and why she'd decided to be extra friendly all of a sudden. If only she could have a few minutes to herself.

"Where'd you grow up? Here? 'Cause you know, Camille, I've been trying to place your face since you got here. There's something so familiar about you." She pointed at Camille as if accusing her.

"Really."

"I don't know what it could be, but I know I know you from somewhere. First time I saw you it was one of those déjà-vu moments."

"Hmm. I doubt we've ever met unless you've been to New York. I haven't lived in this area for years." Camille sipped her soda through a bendable straw.

"Cam, got a minute?"

It looked like no alone time would soon be coming. Greg

was there in the doorway carrying an armload of something that he lugged into Camille's office when she told him to come in. Her heart stood at attention as he walked over to her meeting table. She couldn't help drinking in the sight of his well-cut body in maroon suspenders and matching tie over a cream shirt that was tucked into charcoal slacks.

"What's that?" Lena asked. Camille was embarrassed by her thoughts. She hoped Lena hadn't noticed.

"Well. These are the new CW kits. Jerome just delivered these, and I came straight here. Nora was on her way to lunch and didn't have time to get a peek at 'em."

"Oh, let's see," Camille said. The caffeine must have been working because she was feeling a little less annoyed. Greg fumbled the box before he could set it on the table and blushed. He was nervous, she thought. Why hadn't she noticed it before?

"Oh. Sorry. Wait a minute." He hefted the box onto the table.

"Sure, Mr. Butterfingers," Lena said. She grinned.

"Well. Check this out."

Greg slit the box open with a key from the ring holding at least a dozen other keys that he brought out of his pocket. Then he was pulling out a set of material to hold up for display. Camille smiled when she saw it. The designer had done a terrific job. The artwork was splashy and obviously female, yet understated and professional—a workbook in crisp, conservative blues, a sturdy two-pocket folder with scalloped edges, a notepad with a sky background and workplace affirmations in wispy gold letters.

"Oh my," Camille said. "I'm impressed."

It all fit into a three-inch notebook with a cobalt and gray Complete Woman insert. Inside the front cover was a welcome page from Nora herself, with a head and shoulders shot of her at the top left of the few paragraphs introducing the package. This picture was very different. For once Nora wasn't wearing one of her signature wigs or hairpieces. Her own sheer hair hung softly around her face, and she was smiling, not looking serious and haughty like she usually did.

"Doesn't Nora look good?"

"Yeah, she does."

Lena stood up. Camille and Greg looked up.

"Well. What do you think, Lena? Like it? Something wrong?" Greg said.

Lena moved toward the door, looking at her watch. "I," she pointed toward the hall, "just remembered I have to relieve Tracy for lunch. I've got to run." She turned and left.

Greg and Camille shared a perplexed look.

"What was wrong with her?" Camille asked.

"Who knows. She acts funny sometimes. Just a weird woman, I imagine."

"When are we shipping these out?"

"In a week. So you like the results?" Greg asked.

"I think it's perfect. CW clients will love them."

Greg took the moment that Camille admired the notebook again to watch her.

"This picture of Nora is so great," Camille said.

"I know. That reminds me. You and I both still need to get Randall to take our pictures for the Reinventing intranet site. He asked me about it in the hall this morning."

"Why'd he ask you about me?"

"He stopped by your door, but you weren't here. He asked me to tell you."

"Oh. I guess I can do that in the morning. Why do we need an intranet site anyway?"

"We're expanding so much. Getting so many new people in so quickly. Will thought it would be a useful tool to help new staff and old learn names, faces, and more details about the company."

"Makes sense, I guess. I hate taking pictures though."

Greg wished more had come of their kiss. Ever since it had happened, his whole game plan to get closer to Camille had gotten confused. It was frustrating. There didn't seem to be a vibe from her anymore.

"Well. How about we celebrate," he said.

"Celebrate?"

"The new CW kits. Let's go to Chadwick's for dinner tonight. If you're free."

"That would be nice. Maybe Nora'd like to join us. I'm sure she'll love these."

He wanted to say that Nora wasn't invited, but that would

have been inappropriate. If Camille wanted to play things cool, he was willing to allow whatever happened or didn't happen between them to take its course.

❧

CAMILLE DREAMED SHE STOOD in the middle of the highway behind the house trying to stop traffic. A brass whistle was clamped between her teeth. She blew it hard. Her cheeks puffed out with air, but the whistle wouldn't work and cars came at her from all sides, barely missing her. She kept trying to get out of the road, but there were too many cars to dodge. Just before she was hit by a bus, she saw a flash of light, and there was Catherine at the wheel with a devilish look in her eyes. Evan was standing beside her pointing.

Camille awoke suddenly with a headache and nausea that sent her straight to the bathroom to crouch on her knees and vomit. The retching racked her body in quick, violent waves that left her gasping for air. Once it was done, she was left trembling and didn't want to move.

"C, you all right?"

Mel walked in belting her yellow silk robe over shorts and a black lace bra.

"Unh. Could you wet me a cloth?" Camille croaked out. She leaned her head against the floral papered wall to catch her breath. A section of hair was pasted to her cheek.

"Not pregnant are you?" Mel found that funny.

"If immaculate conception is still in practice, then sure."

212

"Getting the flu, you think?" Mel reached under the sink for aerosol first and sprayed a liberal amount of Lysol that made them both cough.

"Ooh. God. You're trying to kill me with that stuff. I don't think I'm catching anything. I feel better now. Might have been the gumbo."

Aaron had cooked again the night before. He'd taken to bringing over large crockpots full of Cajun foods to impress Mel after she'd raved so much over the étoufée. Secretly Camille thought it was a put-on. She'd tasted the étoufée herself and had thought it was too salty. It was probable that Mel would make a fuss about Aaron's burned toast if he brought her some, just because he had made it.

"If it was the gumbo, then we'd all be sick," Mel said defensively. "I had two helpings, and I'm healthy as a horse this morning. Here."

Camille smiled weakly, accepting the steaming cloth.

"What do you know? You're too infatuated to get sick."

"I'm not infatu-anything."

"Uh-hunh. Handsome man, single, convenient, interested." Camille paused to gargle with Listerine.

"Hmm. That's a familiar song. Sounds more like you and what's his name. Mr. marketing director."

Camille rinsed her face with cold water, then said, "For the last time, the name's Greg. And no, it doesn't."

She hadn't told Mel about the failed kiss. It was too embarrassing to talk about. She and Greg hadn't even discussed it, but had pretended their kiss hadn't happened. It was safer that way. She liked Greg a lot, but she was nowhere near ready to be intimately involved with anyone.

"Oh yeah? What about, 'Make me pretty, Mel, I want him to notice me.' What about that?" Mel had the same smug look that Catherine was famous for.

"That was one time." Camille held up a finger to give weight to her statement.

"Well, Cam, the man *is* cute."

Mel glanced toward the window. The grayish light of morning oozed through the slats of the shutters.

Mel said, "I better get ready for work in a little while."

She tucked the shower curtain inside the tub and turned on the water to scrub out the tub. A cloud of steam erupted.

"If I'm infatuated with Aaron, sis, you're infatuated with Greg."

"Cut it out, Mel. You seem to forget that only a month ago I was with Evan," Camille snapped. She couldn't help being angry. Mel and Catherine acted as if she could just pick up and forget Evan existed. That in itself was a tremendous fear of hers. Every day she seemed to move further away from him, and it upset her. If she didn't have his picture in her wallet, she wouldn't at this point have remembered how he looked.

Sometimes she felt as if the real her was on the outside of her body, watching this new woman say and do things that Evan's Camille would not have thought about. She would never be able to make Mel understand that all she wanted was her old life and the man she really did love without the beatings.

"This is the part I don't get, Camille." Mel's hand was on her hip.

A stale taste was still on Camille's tongue, so she had layered her toothbrush with Colgate and started brushing.

"What are you talking about?" It came out as wha-a-u-tah-eh-ba. Mel gave her a funny look.

Camille rinsed and exhaled.

"I said, what are you talking about?"

"I'm talking about you, Cam. Why do you still love that fool?"

"I've never said one derogatory thing about Jeff."

"Jeff never hit me."

That hurt. Camille took a step backward. "Maybe not, but he wasn't faithful. Evan was never unfaithful."

Mel was bent at the waist scrubbing out the already spotless tub with Tilex and a vengeful brush. She was a fanatic about germs.

"Right. You know that for sure. Look, I'm not trading mud with you, Cam."

"Trading mud? I'm not trading mud. That's not what I'm doing at all. I'm only trying to . . . I wish you wouldn't minimize what I'm going through. I can't just turn it off, Mel. I mean, I like Greg, but I was with Evan for seven years. Seven. He's been with me through everything. I thought we would get married and have a family one day."

Mel stopped scrubbing. "That could have happened if he wasn't nuts. It seems like you should be remembering that shit. But you keep going in and out of this fantasy world. One minute you're totally excited about the future. You've got your job, a new look, a cute guy liking you. You've got Nora, me. Here, you've got so much going for you. So many people behind you. Then sometimes you wrap yourself up in that plastic bubble of yours, that Evan bubble, and it's like you're living on Fantasy Island. All I think about is seeing your face the night you came. You were scared, you were exhausted, you were bruised up. And I think, why in the world would this girl put up with something like that for all those years? Open your eyes, Camille."

Camille's stomach churned. Mel stared at her, challenging her. The scrub brush dribbled water on the delicate lavender bathmat.

"Thanks, Mel. Thanks a lot. But what you're asking for is impossible. I would have to be a robot to be able to forget about Evan the way you want me to. Do you think I'm an idiot? I may be about some things, but I do know that it takes more than a month and a half to recover. I know I go back and forth sometimes about my feelings, but there's a constant battle between my love and devotion for Evan and my well-being. Most days, I don't know if I'm coming or going. I don't . . ."

Camille was quiet. She leaned on the edge of the cabinet.

"What is going on in here?" Catherine asked.

Mel and Camille's eyes met.

"Do we have any ginger ale?" Camille asked. It was Saturday, and she decided she would stay home today instead of going shopping in Georgetown with Nora, just in case she really was catching the flu. The gumbo had been bad, but not so bad that it would make her ill.

"Some in the fridge. Good morning, Mama," Mel said. "Aaron's picking Ben up to take him and Marlon to soccer practice at ten. Can you help him get dressed and fed?"

"I surely will. Now what's going on?"

"Cam and I were just talking."

"Well, you're going to run up your water bill, you let the water run wild like that, Melanie."

"Oh. Right."

"Why were the two of you yelling?"

Both of them ignored the question.

"What is Benji gonna be for Halloween?"

Mel played along. "Girl, would you believe he and Marlon wanted to be Teletubbies? All I need is my son portraying a purple character carrying a purse. No way. I talked him into doing Woody, and Marlon's going to be Buzz Lightyear instead."

"Who?"

"You're so out of touch. *Toy Story.*"

"Oh. I know *Toy Story.* I just didn't know the names of the characters. Sor-ry. I don't keep up with kid stuff."

Camille left the bathroom. Halfway down the stairs she

stopped, realizing suddenly that she hadn't had a period in two months. Stress was one thing, but nausea was a red flag. She figured she'd better find out if there was something to worry about. After drinking a tall glass of ginger ale, she was going to head straight for the CVS down the road to pick up a pregnancy test kit.

She laughed at her own paranoia. It couldn't be true. She'd been on the pill forever, held strictly to its regimen, and hadn't had one mix-up or moment of forgetfulness occur. It surely wouldn't happen at this point when she'd made a break from Evan. Nobody would play this kind of sick joke on her.

She reached beneath the waistband of her pajama pants and explored her abdomen to check for some foreign arm or swell that hadn't been there before. What parts of a baby developed first? How did one tell? It was hard to think what a normal stomach felt like. Reasonably in shape, her stomach was rather flat, but pancake soft and gushy. A baby would be too cruel a turn of fate. Absently, she searched for a heartbeat or at least something strange. There was nothing. Ginger ale forgotten, she went back to her bedroom to change her contacts and dig out some clothes to get to the store quickly. She wasn't going to be able to rest until she knew one way or the other which way the wind blew.

6

REINVENTING RULE SIX: *Don't fall back into old patterns.*

"KNOCK, KNOCK. You wanted me to . . ."

The hair on the back of Camille's neck tingled.

" . . . take a look at my report on the CW findings. Yep."

Greg came into her office. The scent from his cologne preceded him, and Camille inhaled it. She loved that smell. What had he said it was? Nautica?

He avoided the tendrils of cotton hanging above the door with its dots of fake black spiders.

"Some setup you have in here." He looked at the fake pumpkins in a corner on the floor. Orange and black paste-up pictures of a witch with a cat and a wicked jack-o'-lantern were stuck to the window behind her desk.

"I love decorations. When I was in New York, I would do

my whole house every year. Christmas, Thanksgiving, Easter, Halloween. Christmas was my favorite."

Camille noticed dark circles under Greg's eyes, as if he hadn't slept much the night before. She wondered if he was stressed about something. She thrust a bound blue folder into Greg's hands, then turned back toward her computer and said, "Thanks."

He responded with "My pleasure," in a way that made her stomach quiver.

She was glad that she wasn't looking at him. She hated that he still made her nervous even though they had agreed to remain platonic. They'd been friends for over a month now, and she couldn't quite pull herself together inside. It was a mystery. It was like playing a childish, inverse game of pulling petals from a flower . . . "I like him. I like him not." She wondered when she would ever understand her own brand of reasoning.

"Aren't you going to say anything else?" he asked.

She had gone to the Haircuttery for a blunt-cut bob Desnee had finally talked her into. It wasn't short-short, but close around her neck and she loved the way it felt when she swiveled around in her chair. Like a caress.

"Say what?" she asked.

"Don't I look different to you today?" He laid the report on the desk.

"New tie? I like it. Where'd you get it?"

He cleared his throat and said, "Bachrach. But—"

"The colors are nice. I like the gold highlights," she said.

Her mouth twitched. He looked so put out, she struggled not to smile. It was a scam that she'd agreed to play a part in because his office was at the start of the hallway, and nobody could figure out how else to get the cake down the hall without him seeing it before they were all assembled and ready.

Greg's back was to the faces crowding in Camille's doorway, and he couldn't see the group of people behind him, with Dawn out front holding a white-iced sheet cake in her hands like a square, dense cloud.

"Ha-ppy Birrthdaay tooo youuuu." They sang low, watery, and off-key. Not quite in unison. But the smile on Greg's face was full of thanks as Tracy aimed her disposable Kodak and snapped photos. The crowd—Nora, Lena, Dawn, Raye, William, and at least eight new people Camille didn't know— spilled into her office in languid step to their singing. He cut his eyes fondly at Camille.

"You guys . . . ," he gushed.

"How o-old are you? How o-old . . ."

Greg refused to tell, and to his chagrin Tracy yelled out thirty-three. Camille already knew. She'd asked Nora yesterday when they'd hatched the plan to have the party in her office.

"He looks forty-five to me," Raye joked and touched Greg's arm intimately, smiling a little too much. She had her eye on him, Camille could tell. She wanted to snatch every drop of curly weave out of her red-dyed head. As Mel would have said, the hussy looked like somebody's clown.

Greg didn't notice. He was too much in his element as the center of attention.

He gave an airy breath and said, "Yeah, well, that's what working here'll do for you." As if on cue, a round of good-natured laughter exploded.

Dawn was setting the cake carefully on the round table in a corner. Camille withdrew a card from her desk. From the bottom drawer where files were supposed to be kept, she took out a wrapped box with the Palm VII they'd chipped in on (mostly Nora and William) because Greg was always complaining about his inability to record verbal commitments on the spot. She handed it to Dawn.

"Happy birthday," Nora said above the din of talk. "We got you good, didn't we?" A cupful of laughter spilled out.

"You certainly did." His arm came up and rested around Nora's shoulder.

"I'm glad y'all came in when you did. He was ready to give me the business for not remembering his birthday," Camille said softly, speaking more so to Nora than the crowd.

"Payback, Camille. Remember that," Greg said.

William was lighting the candles. "I heard him in here carrying on. 'Don't I look different to you today,'" he mimicked in an offkey voice that sounded nothing like Greg's silky tone.

"Ha ha. Very funny. Just wait until March gets here. I'll make sure your birthday is forgotten," Greg said.

"By all means, man. I wanna forget. I don't wanna be forty-seven anyway." William licked icing from his fingers.

"Well. That's good," Greg said, always quick with a comeback, " 'cause if my memory serves me correctly, brother, and it usually does, you've been forty-seven about three or four times now."

Everybody got a kick out of that one.

Camille could barely gain her composure to answer the telephone.

"Camille Foster speaking . . ."

"Honey babe . . ."

She couldn't breathe. The walls closed in. Something had planted itself in the pit of her throat and was stretching its cotton body all through her esophagus. Once she'd had the TV on in her dorm room in college while she dozed off and on after a heavy exam. She was listening to *Entertainment Tonight.* RuPaul came on the screen. She'd wanted to see what dress he'd worn to an Essence function. In her haste to get her glasses off the night table, she'd broken them in two. She'd spent all the next day bleary-eyed, trying to make it through classes until she could get to the optometrist's office. The whole experience had been disorienting. She felt that same feeling right now, because looking across her desk, all the faces looked fuzzy. Everyone else in the room appeared abstract and incomplete.

A wave of nausea overtook her. She couldn't face them. Not when they looked like this. She rolled her chair out from behind her desk and swiveled toward the window. Maybe everything looked normal outside. She looked down. A little girl, a toddler, was showing off her new walking skills for her mother on the path outside. Her square little body hurdled. Her raven finger-length of ponytail jiggled with each step. She looked as if she was tap dancing forward on a tightrope.

"The peanut butter went bad, honey babe. It got all oily on the top, and it ain't smell fresh—you know how it do when you throw it out, so I went and got another one. Jif. I know how much you like Jif. You know I don't like peanut butter. I wouldn't eat it if you paid me to. That was you that called me, wasn't it?"

"I don't eat that anymore."

"Cam, you're missing the party. Don't you want some cake?" Lena was holding up a slice on a plate. Camille turned around briefly, then turned back toward the window. Her eyes burned.

"Who's that?" Evan asked cautiously.

"A birthday party." Camille was barely coherent. She kept her eyes on the little girl, wondering if there were such a thing as having too many emotions at once. Being overwhelmed by emotions is what she guessed it was, because inside she was laughing, crying, angry, happy, wistful. Inside she was needing something. Evan, perhaps. But wasn't it wrong to need him still? Lena asked her again if she wanted cake, and she shook her head no for Lena's benefit. The slice of cake was given to one of the new tech guys.

The biggest emotion of all was relief. This wasn't a dream that she would awake from sweating. It was happening, and so far, there was no need for a straitjacket. Thank God for that. But then this other thing that was going on inside her. It was so good to hear Evan's voice again, she closed her eyes for a minute trying her best to process what she felt.

"Oh. Well. I . . . I bought you some. I got it."

This was the part of him that made her so vulnerable. He was a little boy, eager to please and desperate to be loved. Did she still . . . ? She was afraid to ask herself that question. She couldn't ask herself that right now. There were people in her office, and a proper breakdown was necessary for that kind of introspection.

"How did you find me?" Camille asked.

The air strained against her vocal chords. Her whisper into the phone was scratchy and full of tears that couldn't be shed. She cupped the top portion of the mouthpiece as if to keep the conversation secret.

"How did you—" She repeated herself, thinking that maybe he hadn't heard her the first time, but he interjected with, " . . . I walk in the closet and smell your clothes, babe. Like flowers. So sweet. Everything's just the way you left it. All those soft dresses on the hangers. The one I bought you for your birthday, baby. You remember? The gray one. You told me you loved the pleats so much. You never got a chance to wear it."

She hated that dress. It looked like something straight off

the osteoporosis back of an AARP member. Camille looked down at the tight blue wool slacks and low-cut lavender cashmere top she wore. Her appearance had changed so much. She didn't even look like the same woman. Haircut. Arched brows. Contacts. Clothes that fit the personality of a woman still in her twenties.

"Your sweaters," Evan was saying. "You should be wearing your sweaters right about now. It's getting cold out. You know how easy you get cold. Soon as a breeze think about blowing, you all shivering." He gave a far-off laugh like it was his fondest memory.

"Uhm."

"I found your bathrobe in the closet too. It was all bunched up on the floor. You probably wanted to wash it 'cause it got some kind of stain on it, chocolate or something. But I couldn't wash it. It smelled like you, honey babe. I put it on the hook behind the bathroom door, 'cause I know when you get out the shower, you like to put it on so you won't be cold."

Why did he make her feel these things? It was too much to handle.

"Evan." She caressed the phone as if she were stroking his soft jet of curls.

Somebody stuck a CD into her disk drive, and Camille looked up for just a second. The next thing she knew, Gladys Knight's church-shouting lungs were filling up the speakers with tight harmonic Pip backup following close behind on "If I Were Your Woman."

"You look beautiful on TV. Your hair's different. I can't believe you cut it, but it's nice."

How quickly things changed. Not long ago he would have knocked her down for touching her hair. She was breathing so hard that her contained breath made her hand moist. How could he possibly know what she looked like now and where she was? Then it hit her. The NOW function at the Convention Center in D.C. where Nora had spoken. A news piece was done on that. She'd been there right in front of the camera next to Nora and Gloria Steinem, trying not to look too terrified.

"I need you. I need to be with you," Evan said. "I can't keep myself together without you, honey babe. You know that."

She wondered if he looked the same or if he'd lost weight because he couldn't cook. He was probably existing on fast food these days. Wasting away without her.

"Evan, I—"

"Tell me how to get to you, and I'll come. I'll be there. I can take a couple days from work."

"This isn't the right time to talk."

"I need you, Camille."

Her heart sagged. How long had it been since anybody needed her? Not before Evan and not now. The work she did at Reinventing was rewarding, but not unique. It wasn't rocket science. Anybody putting their mind to doing the job could make it work. At home, there was Catherine, whose love would never include her, and then there was the ache of watching Mel and Aaron fall in love. Even Greg was just a trip for her ego. She only wanted his friendship, and he probably had enough friends not to need her in any special way. Evan had always been the one who needed her.

She closed her eyes and plunged in.

"Things can't be the way they were." An olive branch thrown in his lap.

She sat silent, listening while Evan told her he'd done a lot of soul searching. He said that the time without her had given him an eternity to understand what his problems were. He had conquered them and was ready to make changes. They could get married if she would have him. Just tell him where she was staying so that he could come. God, she'd missed him.

Camille opened her mouth to speak, but Greg touched her cheek with gentle fingertips. His warm hand on her face sucked her back into the room. She could smell him. Wisps of that cologne emanated from him. The conversations the others were having were tangible again. Raye was making fun of Dawn's print skirt, calling it a bargain basement throwback from the seventies. William was talking shop with the new guy (what was his name? something like Ron or Rob. No, Rod. Rod Keegan. He was heading up the newly established HR department). The music was less papery. Gladys was singing about the midnight train to Georgia saying, "I ga ta go! I ga ta go!" and Camille could feel the coarse texture of Gladys's determination.

"Come have some cake," Greg said. Camille smiled okay.

Beyond Greg, Nora was standing close, leaning against the wall in her bare feet as usual, checking them out. She could tell by the light in Nora's eyes that she knew something was up.

"I'll call you later." Camille hung up before Evan could say a word. She forwarded her calls to voice mail.

"Is it good?" she asked Greg. He picked up his paper plate with its large slice of cake. Sometimes people can tell when you are dying inside. Camille looked down at her manicured nails, hoping her eyes didn't betray the storm churning inside her. Only Nora seemed to notice it so far.

"It's delicious." Greg forked another puff of icing into his mouth.

"Great, I'll have some."

"May I have a word?" That was Nora from across the way. She was much too observant for her own good.

The two of them left Camille's office unacknowledged and closed the door on the noise. They stood in the hallway near the printers.

"Either learn self-defense, or leave him the hell alone."

"Who? Greg?"

"Don't Greg me. You know I mean Evan."

"What are you talking about?" Camille folded her arms. How did Nora always seem to know what was going on? The woman had a sixth sense.

"You can fool some of the people some of the time . . ."

"Nora, please. I don't need one of your lectures right now."

"Don't play simple with me, Camille. This isn't about a lecture. It's about your life, the one you're finally starting to piece together. I'm not going to stand by and watch Evan ruin it."

"He just wanted to talk. Just because we talk doesn't mean—"

"Lie to yourself, but don't play me for a fool. Tell me the truth."

"Nora, I'm not playing you for anything. It was a conversation. That was all."

Nora gestured for Camille to follow her. She looked both ways down the hall and just about tiptoed to her office with Camille following.

"What are we doing?"

Nora entered her office and told Camille to come in.

"What is—?"

Nora lit up a cigarette.

"Child, come on. Hurry up. Close the door." Nora brushed the fringe of bangs of her brown wig out of her eyes with one long manicured nail.

"Mmm," she said. "Just what this old girl needed. I'll have to listen to one of William's lectures, of course. He can always tell when I smoke in my office, no matter what I do. He pitched the biggest fit last time. Talking about the lease and the law and what if the property manager got wind of it, no pun."

Nora grinned wickedly at Camille, then pushed a tunnel of

smoke from the side of her mouth. She pulled a small spray can from her drawer to spritz the air.

"As I was saying . . ."

"I still love him, I think."

Nora stared. "You think?"

"He's a good man, Nora. He just has some issues he needs to work through." Camille put a hand over her nose. It was nearly impossible not to want to vomit.

"Let's be real here, Camille. Over the past few weeks, you and I have gotten pretty close. I think of you as a friend, and to be honest, you have some issues you need to work through yourself. You can't babysit a grown man and his issues."

Camille lifted her chin. "Why are you always preaching to me? I'm much better than I was."

"Bravo. You've done what no one else has ever accomplished. In two months' time, you have learned all you need to know about yourself. That should be our next campaign. Get a few clothes, a new do, contacts, and voilá! Instant perfection."

Camille grimaced. There was no way to get Nora to understand what she was going through. With her, everything was so black and white. She looked out the window into a froth of fog surrounding passing boats.

"I know I have a long way to go, Nora. You've been so wonderful to me. I couldn't have gotten to this point without you. I know you're concerned, but let me tell you what it's really like for me. Every night I go to bed all by myself. Alone. I wake up in the morning, and it's still just me. But look at you. You have a great business. Power. Money. Fame. You have William, Nora. You're about to become somebody's wife. How can you propose to know how it feels to be totally alone? Your life's perfect. And I don't see anybody but Evan knocking my door down to be with me."

"What about Greg? I know I advised you to take that slow, but don't shut him out completely, darling."

"Greg is . . . Greg's not Evan. I don't want to talk about this anymore."

She turned and left the office and made her way to the elevator. Thankfully no one passed her as she exited the building into the brisk sunny day. Hugging herself, she shivered from the cool wind and wandered down the walkway past the statue of a defeated Roman warrior. She turned a corner and found herself smack dab in the path of the little girl just learning to walk, her arms stretched out from her sides to balance her staccato bounce while her mother inched just behind her, ready to catch her if she fell.

7

R EINVENTING RULE SEVEN: *Face hard tasks first.*

———

CAMILLE WAS IN A DARK, restless sleep when the phone rang at three in the morning. The sound jerked her awake. She groaned and sighed, groggily trying to figure out what was happening. First, she had to remember where she was. For a moment, she looked around the dark room. When she re-membered that she was in her old double bed, she realized that the phone was ringing its slow, persistent chime. She slid a quick glance at the clock and reached to pick up the phone before the call could go to voice mail.

At the end of the call, Camille got out from beneath her warm down quilt into the cool air in her bedroom (her win-dow was always cracked) to throw on jeans, canvas shoes, and a sweatshirt beneath a new long gray wool coat. She left a quick note on Mel's nightstand and took the stairs two at a time. Outside, the chilled air grabbed hold of her skin. She shivered, buttoning her coat to the throat. Tiny pinpoints of rain fell from the blue-black sky in a quiet mist.

Camille looked to her left and right to give the street a quick once-over before she shut the front door. Her pepper spray was ready. It was a low-crime neighborhood, but you could never be too careful. She dug her keys from the bottom of her purse quickly, and held the key she would use to open the door out like a weapon.

The minute squeak from her car alarm echoed in the stillness, and she gave her surroundings one last look before she got in and locked the doors, starting the car and the wipers. Nothing was on the radio. She flipped through the stations twice, then rummaged for a tape in the storage space hidden in the armrest. The *Bodyguard* soundtrack was the first tape she pulled out, so she put it into the cassette player and sped off.

When she reached her destination, she stood outside the building and pressed two numbers on the keypad to the left of the secured door. She was buzzed in and took two flights of stairs and knocked on a burgundy door. The door budged. Camille realized it was already open so she walked in haltingly and closed it behind her.

"Hello?"

The lights were on but dimmed. Camille turned them up and crept to the end of the foyer. Each room flowed into the next. The tiled foyer spilled into a spacious living room that melted into a dining room. Off the dining area was a tacked-on kitchen separated from the dining room by a breakfast bar with three hunter green velvet-covered stools.

The apartment was airy with nine-foot stucco ceilings and flawless creamy buttermilk walls. Everything from the carpet to the furniture was neutral. No pictures were hung. No photographs were up. No accents graced the tables. The only splash of color was in the heavy dark lemon-colored swag and curtains hung artistically at the picture window. The furniture was expensive and simple. Clean-lined butter-colored sofas and chairs, a white-washed entertainment center that spanned a wall and was empty save a thirty-two-inch television, and in the dining area, a full mahogany dining set complete with buffet and china cabinet. But there was something else. A smell. A burning. At first, Camille thought it was the fireplace, but it was something else. She realized what it was.

"Hello?"

Kismet came lumbering up solemnly to sniff her and licked her hand.

"Hey, Kis." She scratched his head. "Where's Nora?"

She went over near the sofa and turned her head at a noise that resembled the clearing of a throat. Camille blinked, surprised. Nora sat on the floor in a corner beside one of the chairs in beige pajamas and a matching robe with a snifter between her knees. A bottle of wine was on the floor at her feet beside a cordless telephone. She blended into the room like a chameleon, except that she was smoking as usual. The ashtray on a small, low table was full of dashed-out cigarettes. Camille didn't know what to make of this scene. She had never seen Nora in anything but conservative, no-nonsense designer suits and three-inch heels, armed with full makeup and elaborate hair.

"Nora?" Camille said.

"What you said to me earlier got next to me."

"Nora, what are you talking about? Why'd you ask me to come here? What is this place? Whose is it?" Camille knew Nora lived in Oakton, not Springfield.

"My life's anything but perfect, Camille." Her words were liquid. "Want a drink?"

Camille declined with a hand and asked what was going on. She walked toward Nora to sit near her on the plush tawny carpet. The smoke was almost overwhelming.

"For the past week, this is where I've come about three times now. Nobody else knows that but you. Nobody else knows."

Kismet stretched out on the floor beside Nora.

"Why? Why would you come here?" Camille asked her. Nora's laughter was bitter. It sounded awful.

"Be sorry for me, Camille."

Camille dropped her keys into her coat pocket.

"What are you talking about?"

"Hungry children and wronged women. I got this place because I can't sleep in my own house when he's screwing her," Nora said and drained her glass.

Camille had to swallow several times, wetting her dry throat for words that didn't want to come. This wasn't real. This was some fictional place. This wasn't Nora sitting here with tears in her eyes talking like this. It was an apparition. It had to be.

"What . . . what's going on?" Camille tried to sound calm.

"I've known almost a week and a half now."

"Known what?" A real sense of dread welled up inside Camille. She had the feeling that she didn't really want to hear this.

"He thinks I don't know," Nora continued. "'It's late, baby. Time got away from me. I'm not coming tonight.'" Nora attempted to affect William's slick, easy baritone. "He always comes to stay the night with me, Camille. Unless he's . . ." Nora nodded matter-of-factly.

"Will," was all Camille could say. Her limbs felt heavy. Her arms flopped down at her sides, and she stared at Nora hard.

"He leaves his car and takes a cab to her house," she said. "I figured that out a few nights ago. A cab, like he's being sneaky. So I won't by chance see his car. He doesn't think I know he's popping rocks off in that whore. How could he think I wouldn't know? When you've been with somebody long enough, you just . . . Right up the street from my house. Right under my nose."

"With who? Who are you talking about? Is it somebody you know?"

"I had him followed for a couple weeks. Had a PI take pictures and everything. Tracked his comings and goings. He gave me all the evidence when I returned from St. Louis. Her bedroom has a balcony. I went to her house one night last week. I sneaked over there because I couldn't believe those pictures. I kept saying, *Not her.*" Nora closed her eyes tightly, as if to shut out what she'd seen.

"Who?"

"I had to witness it myself, you see. To believe it. You know she lives three blocks from my house? They were there that night. It was too dark in there for me to see. I put my ear to the window because it was open, but I didn't need to. They were so loud. I couldn't make out what they were saying, but I heard them. One minute they were laughing. Everything was so funny. So damned amusing. Then they were . . . It sounded like . . ." She covered her ears, narrowing her eyes. "It sounded like somebody was dying. Some filthy dying animal. Or maybe it was me, Camille. Maybe it was me dying while I stood there and listened to two people I love make a fool of me." Nora poured out another glass. She struggled to gain control of herself.

"Two people you love? God, Nora. Who is William—"

"I bought Dawn that damn house. Five bedrooms, a solarium, a gourmet kitchen just like mine, an enclosed hot tub out back that she's probably been entertaining my fiancé in. She was my friend. Like a sister to me when I lost Julia. Camille, she was there from the very beginning. At Reinventing's inception, she was right with me every step of the way. But dammit, I was there for her too. I took her in when her husband left her years ago. She didn't have anybody else. But I was there for her. I was always there."

"Dawn? Our Dawn?" An image came to mind of Dawn the first time Camille had seen her in hot pink, her frizzy, dyed curls framing her fox-like honey brown face. Blood-red nails that clicked like castanets. Everything about her was larger than life. Her more than ample curvy figure, her makeup, even the jewelry she wore was always large and assuming, like she screamed inside to be noticed by acting out through her appearance. She didn't have an ounce of the sophistication that Nora displayed naturally. Camille had wondered why Dawn and Nora were friends at all. That a cultured, Vernon Jordan type like Will could fall for such a low-standard set of charms was beyond belief.

"No," Camille said. "Nora, I can't believe that. Anybody else but her. How could she attract a man like Will?"

"Who knows how these things happen, Camille? I'm a busy woman. I travel all the time. Maybe he thinks he needs more attention than I give him. They stopped for awhile after I came back from St. Lou. I think they figured I was catching on. Maybe I seemed suspicious of Will after I spied on their little love fest. Little do they know, I've done more than catch on. Then here it comes again tonight. I get a call around ten, and he tells me he can't make it. He's tied up. I guess what they say is true. What goes around comes around." Nora gestured with a hand and some of the liquor sloshed in her lap and onto the floor.

"Nora, I can't—"

"I know he's there with her. He didn't answer his phone at home, and his cell went straight to voice mail. Do you still think my life's so perfect, Camille? Do you still think it's gravy? Because I will tell, you darling, it may be a cliché, but you can't judge a book by its cover."

Camille couldn't think straight. She had to get up. She wanted to scream until she lost her voice. She wanted to run out of the room. This wasn't Nora Jordan sitting here falling apart drowning her anguish in a full glass of liquor to obscure something too ugly to accept.

Camille walked back and forth saying, "I can't hear this. I'm not hearing this."

Nora spoke up again, and Kismet moaned low.

"You admire me, don't you, Camille?" she said. "You can't even handle seeing me this way." Nora followed Camille's movements for a moment, then topped off the liquor in her glass. She took another drink.

"Are you kidding? Ever since I met you, I've wanted to be just like you," Camille said, running a hand through her hair distractedly. She was exhausted. She sat on one of the couches where she could still see Nora, who was staring into the fire. Camille unbuttoned her coat finally and tossed it across the arm of the sofa.

"No, you don't, Camille. Don't ever say that. Don't ever say you want to *be* just like anyone. You have to learn something. Love the act, not the actor."

Nora's smile was mysterious.

"What are you talking about?" She hadn't meant to sound impatient, but she was fed up with this whole scene. She was sick to death of Nora's having a saying for every occasion. Pretty words of wisdom hadn't gotten her anything but a man who was cheating on her with her best friend. She didn't want to acknowledge these flaws. Camille couldn't explain why, but she felt Nora had betrayed her. Having Nora present in her life had meant that a whole and happy life did exist. Now that too was a farce.

"It's okay to admire the things I've done," Nora was saying, "but you don't know me from anybody else you've ever just met. I'm just a woman, Camille. When it's all said and done, I'm just like you. So many look at the people who've accomplished great things, and they put the burden of perfection on their shoulders. Who knows if Mother Teresa went to bed at night wishing she had a man to hold her in his arms and give her support and comfort to carry on her work? And look at Bill Clinton. Tall, poised, handsome. A Rhodes scholar. President of the United States. The man has more power than most men ever realize during their careers, a brilliant, attractive wife who appears to be loyal, and a nice daughter. But guess what? He was still so insecure and in need of love and attention that he had to prove his personal worth by tricking some gullible little fat girl into getting on her knees to cater to that insecurity inside him. Now that's a bare truth if I've ever seen one."

"Why are you saying these things?"

"I want you to face something, darling. When the camera is off and the lights are low, Camille, you don't know what demons people have to fight. You don't need to want to be like me. I'm just a woman. And you're already that. All you have to do is make sure you're the kind of woman that you can respect. That's it." She threw her three-carat diamond engagement ring across the room. It bounced off the CD player and landed silently on an intricately patterned oriental rug. Kismet raised his head briefly.

"If it's that simple, Nora, then why are you sitting on the floor feeling sorry for yourself? Why are you calling me at three in the morning to come see you like this?"

"I hoped you'd understand. It's an uncomplicated reason. My best friend is screwing my fiancé, and I don't have anybody else to talk to about it. I feel helpless. Everything I thought was true is a lie," Nora said. "And I guess I wanted you to see that nothing is perfect in this life no matter what side the dice land on. I take care of my business, sure. I believe in the work I'm doing. Thousands of women have been helped because of my work. That makes me proud. And I know that Julia would have been proud too. But when it's all said and done, Camille . . . when the office is closed and the telephone isn't ringing and the cameras aren't rolling, here I am sitting in the dark, guzzling pricey liver poison in the middle of the night because my man and my best friend are cheating liars. So when I tell you that you should stay as far away from your ex-boyfriend as humanly possible, darling, I know what I'm talking about. That's the—"

Camille couldn't stand to hear another word. "I think I should probably get an abortion. I don't know," she blurted out.

She lay back on the cool soft pillows on the sofa to look up at the ceiling.

It was Nora's turn to be shocked. "What?"

"I don't know how far along I am exactly. I mean, I can make an educated guess, but I'm not sure. I can't tell my sister about this. I want to, but she's dealt with enough of my issues. Her life is finally turning around for the better. She has a new love on the horizon. Ben's happier than ever. I know I can't tell my mother. That's out. Greg wouldn't understand any more than Mother would. Even if he did, I don't want him to know something like that about me. I like him, and it matters to me what he thinks. And Evan . . ."

"Ain't this a bitch," Nora whispered. "Have you been to a doctor?" Nora set her drink on the fireplace.

"No. I don't have a doctor here yet. I took a pregnancy test a little more than two weeks ago. Clear Blue Easy," she said laughing bitterly.

"How can you be sure, Camille? Those store-bought tests aren't always accurate."

"I haven't had a period since August. First, I chalked it up as stress. But my body is changing. I went on-line to find out what the symptoms are, other than the big two: an MIA period and morning sickness, of which I have both. My breasts are tender, and I'm craving all kinds of crazy stuff. I have never in my life liked canned grapefruit. Now I can't get enough of it. Can you believe it? I've been with Evan seven years, haven't been pregnant once. Leave him, and I'm pregnant."

"And you've known all this time? Why didn't you tell me as soon as you found out?"

"The timing didn't seem right. I didn't know if I should keep this baby or not. I had been leaning toward not having it. I still don't know, but now . . ."

"Evan calls earlier and knocks you further off-balance."

Camille nodded. "That's exactly it. Evan calls, and now I'm not so sure I can just close the door on our baby like that. I'm not sure about anything."

"You could do this yourself, you know. Women are doing it every day. Raising children on their own."

"I see what Mel goes through. Ben is a sweetheart, but he's so much work. He's almost a full-time job. And even if I want to do this by myself, Evan knows how to find me now. He can show up at the office whenever he feels like it, and if he knows about this baby, he might make me go back."

Nora raised her glass. "Here's to excuses that we allow to

keep us from making sound choices. Now what is this business about Evan making you go back? Why do you believe he has that kind of power over you? You aren't a runaway child, Camille. Do you want to go back?"

"No. Sometimes. I don't know. I know it's better for me to be here . . ."

"But . . ."

"But there are so many things I miss. I miss being needed. I miss being in a relationship. I miss his love. All the things I didn't have as a child."

Camille looked over at Nora. Nora looked devastated, and Camille was ashamed of herself. She suddenly remembered that Nora must feel neglected herself right now.

"I'm sorry, Nora. I'm sorry for what happened to you. It's not fair. I wish there was something I could say to help, but to be honest, my personal opinion on the matter isn't going to give you warm fuzzies."

"That's exactly what I need right now. Honesty."

"If I were you, I would kick both of them out on their butts."

"You ever heard of Mathis Communications?"

"Everybody has. They're almost as big as Viacom. Mathis . . . Mathis . . . That's—"

Understanding hit Camille when she remembered Will's austere father and she said, "Wait. Are you saying—"

"William's family. I'm a figurehead, Camille. Just like Wally Amos became. You recall Famous Amos cookies?"

"You don't own your company?"

"Not since the early eighties. Back in '81 Reinventing suffered some huge losses. I started an untested program that failed miserably. I was in trouble. The company was foundering, and I didn't know what to do. MC swallowed us up and put me on contract. William was the irresponsible one in the family. Their black sheep. He was thirty-two at the time with two divorces under his belt, no children, no accomplishments to speak of. Every last one of his six siblings has done something newsworthy or at least noteworthy. The Mathis clan is known for winning awards and setting a standard."

"William's father, Harold, wanted Reinventing to be William's proving ground. Harold pumped a whole lot of money into the operation, brought people in to help me to design better program formulas, put me out in front of the public as much as possible, and now they're making a killing off my back. Welcome to modern-day slavery."

"So, in essence, you can't get rid of William."

"William can get rid of me if he wants to. My contract is always negotiated on a three-year spin. It's up for renegotiation at the end of the year."

"Okay, fine, but Nora, you *are* Reinventing the Woman. The company would be nowhere without you. People buy the product because you're the guarantor. People run to these events and speaking engagements because of you."

"Don't be so naive, Camille. Self-actualization specialists like me come a dime a dozen these days. I think Dawn's try-

ing to rattle the cage and groom herself after me so she can replace me."

"Nora, that's crazy. She could never replace you. Anybody
can see she doesn't have what it takes. Complete Woman
would fall on its face entirely, and Reinventing would die. She
knows about as much as I do about how to finesse the public."

"Don't underestimate Dawn. She's got a good case for replacing me. She's attractive, she knows the spiel, and she's
humping my ex–future husband."

"I don't know a lot about life, but I will tell you this, I know
something about human nature. William's a smooth character,
but he's not stupid. Just weak with women apparently. I'm
positive he knows you're an integral part of this movement. If
he didn't, he wouldn't have wanted you to be his wife to secure you the same way they've acquired the company."

"Makes me feel like I've just been auctioned off at
Sotheby's."

Camille ignored the bad joke. "I'm pretty good at reading
people sometimes. Not always, but sometimes," she said,
thinking of Evan. She'd had no clue that he would turn out to
be such a disappointment.

"I used to think I was too. Now I need some time to work
this out and figure out what I'm going to do. Damn, this bottle is almost empty, and I don't have another. But back to more
important matters. Do you want to keep this baby?"

Camille was silent for a minute, thinking back. "A short
time ago, I wanted Evan's baby so much. I wanted to be his

wife. He kept telling me the time wasn't right. I used to wonder what it would feel like having our child growing inside me. Someone who would be mine to take care of and teach. I used to crave it. Now that it's happened, I'm so confused."

"Are you saying you want to get rid of it?"

"If I don't, I might not be able to move forward the way I need to. I have a lot of growing to do."

"Dr. Culbert," Nora said.

"Who?"

"I can get you an appointment for as soon as Wednesday. I'll go with you for a consultation. Then we can schedule to have the procedure done."

"Nora, thanks, but you have enough to deal with. I've already found some places in the Yellow Pages. You and Mel can't bail me out of my messes every time. I have to do this alone."

"Camille, I can help, darling. In my personal opinion, I think you should keep the child, but if you don't want to, I can at least offer the best medical care there is."

Camille was growing tired. The sofa had the same firm comfort of her bed. Not to mention that it was probably somewhere around five A.M. by now. Already weak gray streaks of light were climbing in through the window.

"What will you do about Will?" Camille said, half asleep.

"Wait. At least for a time."

"For what?" Her shoes had already been shed. She plucked her coat from the arm of the sofa to cover up with it. It was so nice and warm underneath the coat. There was no way she could drive home. She closed her eyes a final time.

"Until I figure out what I should do. There is an old saying I live by: Patience is key to a solution."

"That's too hard in this case. How will you be able to act like you don't know about them?" Camille murmured.

"I'd rather make a smart move than a quick one, Camille."

"I still say William needs you just as much as you need him."

"That may be true, but until I'm sure one way or the other what I'm going to do, this has to stay between the two of us."

Camille took a line from an old Seinfeld episode. She'd watched that show faithfully back in New York. "It's in the vault," she said.

"All right, darling. You get some sleep. And remember to stay as far away from the two of them as possible. I'll be in the other room if you need anything at all."

The last thing Camille felt or knew was Nora humming a tender melody and her dainty hand stroking her hair. It soothed Camille and paved her a smooth transition into a peaceful, satisfying sleep.

8

*R*EINVENTING RULE EIGHT: *Get quiet and listen to yourself. Your heart will tell you what to do.*

WHEN SHE'D CALLED TO MAKE the appointment, the nurse had told Camille over the phone that once the procedure was done, she couldn't drive herself home. Someone had to be there to help her. The following Saturday morning, Camille waited for Mel to go to work, said she had to go into the office for awhile, then faked car trouble for Catherine's benefit so questions wouldn't be asked. She caught a cab to take her to the clinic for her appointment.

Sitting in the back seat, Camille stared out of its filmy window that didn't look as bad behind her black glare-proof sunshades. Earlier in the week had been cold, but today it would reach sixty-five according to meteorologist Topper Shut. The sun had that splashy, heavy Day-Glo yellow glaze it took on in the fall. The leaves were drifting off the trees in droves. The sky was a superb, immutable-looking cornflower blue with clouds that rivaled those she'd seen in Florida when she'd accompanied Nora to Miami following their trip to New York.

Though Camille acknowledged the nice weather, it was a day that she could not appreciate. For one thing, morning sickness had come at 5:00 A.M., so she was tired. And there was the hard blue leather from the cab's back seat molding itself to her. It was uncomfortable under her right thigh, where the leather had split wide and the yellowish foam bulged. She too felt ripped apart.

She glanced at the simple brown leather Timex fastened to her wrist, thinking she was going to miss her appointment if the driver continued this way. With his jet-black, wavy-haired head lolling from side to side to Madonna's "Take a Bow," he drove so slowly that she wished she'd gone ahead and driven her own car.

As they rode silently, getting closer to the clinic, Camille nervously fiddled with the tiny heart-shaped sapphire ring Evan had given her last Christmas while she continued to stare out the window across the scarcely trafficked lanes of the smooth road. She made herself focus on the scenery. She looked out at tall office buildings with glassy black windows, surrounded by empty parking lots. Then there were groups of long-legged trees, deleafed and bony, stretching from freshly manicured grass.

They rode on past an old-looking whitewashed middle school sandwiched between more trees and a sprawling shopping mall with a wide, white multilevel parking garage shooting out of the very center of it. It was early. They stopped at a long red light. Camille became engrossed in her assessment of the mall and its many stores boasted on the colorful marquee. She didn't notice that they'd arrived at the clinic until she heard the tick-tock of the cabby's turn signal. She gripped the flexible blue strap on the side of the car door to keep from sliding across the back seat further as the driver swung quickly into a left-hand turn.

The cabby changed the radio station and maneuvered into a parking space in front of a frugal beige building that looked more like someone's house than a clinic. Camille wrinkled her brow and said, "This is it?" to the cab driver, hoping he was mistaken.

He turned, gesturing toward the building's clear black numbering and said back to her in an Indian accent, "Thirty-one-o-six," as he nodded. "That will be nine dollars and twenty cents."

Still gripping the car door strap, she couldn't force herself to move. Her heart was rising into her throat. She wasn't positive, but she didn't think she was breathing too well either because in her ears it sounded like wheezing.

"Miss?" the driver said.

Camille looked at him weakly. She scanned his long pecan-tinted face, his blade-thin lips, and then his wide brown eyes

253

that were impatient, and she could tell they were calling her crazy. His outstretched hand rested against the seat near her face asking for the money, but she still couldn't move, until a knock on the back window made her jump.

Camille looked over to see an ultra-dark-red-lipsticked face peering at her.

"Oh. Oh," she said, coming back to herself and clearing her throat. She lifted her purse from the floor of the car and rifled through it a second, then handed the cabby a ten before opening the car door despite the woman standing next to it. Whoever she was, she was at least courteous enough to move to allow Camille to get out. Camille slammed the door.

"Please don't do this!" The woman sounded desperate. She was very tall, reed skinny, but graceful like an Alvin Ailey dancer. She was the shade of a very ripe plum and regal. She carried herself with an air of confidence that Camille knew she lacked. Her face was full of pleading, and her fingers were curled around a wooden stick connected to a big white sign that said, *Save the Babies: Stop Murdering Our Future.* Camille blinked, not speaking.

"Don't make this mistake," the woman said. "Please, lady."

Camille cringed. A group of picketers were at her back voicing their protests in unison. Fear gripped her. What if they grew violent? Camille walked on quickly. She was relieved when she stepped inside a singular swinging glass door into a calm room full of air-conditioned breeze. Five women who looked more like young girls flipped restlessly through magazines and glanced now and again at a closed white door. Camille was instantly sorry for them. She took in their faces on the sly as she signed her name on the sign-in sheet in a loopy blue-inked cursive. As instructed, she gave the sample she'd brought with her to the nurse behind the counter.

There was one woman she couldn't help but stare at because her stomach was a large melon curve. Camille said to herself that there was no way she could be *that* pregnant and do this thing. This horrible, horrible thing. But she couldn't let herself think about it. She had to remain detached if she was going to go through with it.

Camille smiled hello to a freckled girl with short red hair whom she sat next to on the short sofa. The girl was reading an article in *People* magazine about Will Smith. Camille looked over the girl's shoulder, thinking how attractive Will Smith was and was instantly ashamed that she'd had such a thought about a man at a time like this. She grabbed a copy of *New Woman* and pretended to read it while she checked out the rest of the room. It was claustrophobic and colorless. Sterile. Everything was either beige or white. Then she realized why she couldn't cry. It was surely the kind of place where no feeling existed. And she was part of it. All human emotion was being used up outside the front door because she could still hear the picketers shouting. That scared Camille even more. The last thing she needed right now was to be the victim of a bomb-happy picketer.

"Marsha Garris." A hard-voiced nurse had appeared in the

doorway. Her unsmiling painted lips were bright pink. Gray streaks marked her black hair. During the uncomfortable silence, the overly pregnant woman struggled upward and slung her purse onto her shoulder.

Freckle face finally broke the silence. "Your first?" She pointed at Camille's currently flat tummy.

Camille nodded over the top of her magazine.

"Hmm. My third," she said, like it was her claim to fame.

"You too?" A wide-hipped blonde girl in a jean jumper threw in, and the girl with freckles nodded with a slight smile.

"I don't know why this keeps happening to me," the girl with freckles said. Camille wanted to remind her about birth control, but wasn't in any position to make that comment.

"I know," the blonde said. "All of these women out here dying to have babies and can't and here I am . . ."

"I know what you mean. Seems like I'm pregnant every time I even look at a guy cross-eyed."

"That's the truth. But this is the last time. I'm never going through this again. I wish they would shut the hell up!"

A Mexican girl joined in then. She looked as if she had been waiting for a chance to speak up, so she said, "Who? Those picketers? It's amazing. They try so hard to convince you to keep a baby they aren't offering to take care of. It's all I can do to take care of myself. Where would I get money to keep a baby fed and clothed for eighteen years?"

The circle of girls nodded.

"That's exactly what I say," the girl with freckles offered.

"Stacy Ball."

The nurse was back. The girl in the jumper sighed and shrugged. "The last time," she said. "I mean it." She disappeared behind the door with the nurse, and the door closed firmly.

A half-hour passed before the nurse called Camille. In the meantime silent, sick-faced women passed now and again headed toward the front door, leaning on a boyfriend, a friend, or whoever had brought them. It made Camille feel worse because she didn't have anybody with her. Nobody but the baby she was about to betray.

"Camille Foster."

Camille let out an audible breath. It was a relief to hear her name called, but she was scared too. A new woman who had arrived moments before wished Camille luck, but she barely acknowledged her as she walked toward the door. Camille was more interested to know what was in that back room. She met the nurse in the doorway and thought she might faint when the door closed behind her, but all that waited on the other side of the door was a larger waiting room with a television perched on a wall playing the morning news.

"Okay, hon, the test was positive. You are pregnant."

Camille gave her an I-told-you-so look.

"I have here some paperwork I'll need you to fill out while you're waiting, and then once that's complete, we'll need you to participate in a brief counseling session."

That brought Camille's eyebrows up. No one had said anything about counseling over the phone. "Counseling?" she said.

The nurse nodded. "A short formality, but most women find it very helpful. Once you've completed your session if you still wish it, you will be examined by the doctor to see how far along you are. Then we will continue on to the procedure. If you have any questions, let either me or Nurse Goldman know. You may have a seat over there and start filling out your forms."

This part went swiftly. There was no long wait after the counseling session was over. Camille was called into a room and asked to remove her clothes. When the doctor entered, she already lay on the patient table with her feet in the hard palms of the shiny steel stirrups. The nurse had draped a sheet across Camille's middle. She wore a paper gown that tied at the back.

Camille could barely understand what the doctor was saying. For one thing, his accent was overly thick. His "r's" rolled violently. So she simply stared at the sterile wall with its purple posters depicting gestation periods while the doctor probed her matter-of-factly and murmured something that made him chuckle. She forced herself to breathe evenly. Until the noise began.

The clicking disturbed her so much that she gripped the side of the table. She looked up at the ceiling to concentrate on the pattern of its tiles. But the noise kept coming. It brought to mind thoughts she'd so far been able to resist. *I don't want to do this. I don't want to do this.* The thought kept building like thunder until it became a scream in her head. *I don't want to do this.* She wasn't sure when she started saying it aloud, but it happened. Her lips were moving. She was whispering it. Chanting it.

She began shaking so hard her teeth chattered. In the dark recesses of her mind, a clear image formed. The picketer's drawn, plum face. Lips bright with color and disapproving. The pleading expression sunk in the palm of her scant onyx eyes, and seemingly there was pleading even in her hand (the one that wasn't holding the picket sign) the way she held it up in the air as if she asked for something to be placed in it.

More images came. The young girls in the waiting room whose faces were awash with sick fear. Hopeless girls. Camille had seen faces like that on a business trip to Bangkok years ago. They couldn't have been more than teenagers, but were already veterans in this . . . this thing. Camille squeezed her eyes shut to block out the images, but it didn't help. They came to her, collages of them, in radiant flashes like shooting stars. She was not one of them. She was a grown woman with a good job. And maybe this was a sign that she should try harder to put to rest the memories from New York and her need for Evan. What else could explain how, after all this time, she had become pregnant without even trying? She'd finally begun a new life, and crouched in her womb was a new life just beginning to take its shape. Maybe this was a sign that leaving Evan really had been for the best.

The procedure had not yet begun, but the nurse reached out to hold Camille's hand when she sensed her deep anxiety. To Camille it was as if a lifeline were being thrown out to save her, and she took that too as a sign. It was the only invitation she needed. The doctor was just about to start when Camille, tugging the nurse's hand and then taking hold of the nurse's forearm with her free hand, lifted herself from the table to sit up on its side. The brittle paper spread over the table crinkled and tore beneath her.

"Sweetie," the nurse was saying like she was warning a disobedient little girl. She tried to pull away, but Camille wouldn't let go of the nurse's sturdy hand. The doctor looked up questioningly.

"I don't want to do this," she sobbed in the nurse's direction, bowing her head. The awful vacuum noise ended. Camille didn't wait for a directive. In a fog, she was able to gather her clothes and put them on. When she walked out of the dim little clinic, the sunlight blasted her with a shocking glare that caused her to cup her brow. She flicked a glance at the yelling protesters, then walked toward the service station next door to call a cab to take her home. After placing the call, she stood next to the pay phone waiting for her ride and watching the protesters pack up their things.

A thought came to her with the same boldness of the sun. What she'd lacked when she'd left Evan was a sense of purpose. That was why it had been so hard to give up on loving a man she knew deep down that she hated with all her heart.

For a brief second, the plum-faced protester held her gaze. Camille smiled gently, caressing her middle. If all she'd needed all along was purpose, she had it now. She had it in droves and droves.

⚜

A YEAR AGO, SARAH BEATON, a woman in Camille's department at Braxton Enterprises, had quit working there when she decided to stay at home with her new baby, Sabrina. One afternoon Sarah brought her newborn to the office for a visit. Camille had never been in close quarters with a baby. All she'd experienced of Ben was a paper-framed picture that Mel had sent her that was his hospital photograph. It portrayed a broad-faced, hairy infant with splotchy skin and miniature dry lips that could have been ready for a kiss.

Camille didn't know Sarah well, but with prodding from her boss, Valerie, she had walked down the corridor to the reception area where a handful of women gathered to oooh and aaah over the baby in her animal-print carrier, wrapped up in a voluminous peach blanket with a tiny arm in the air. Ruth Wister had offered her finger for the baby to hold. Camille stood back against a wall watching.

At some point one of the women just had to hold the baby. Then another said, "Let me see her," in a high-pitched cooing songy voice. And then there was an assembly line occurrence. Baby Sabrina was being passed around from hand to hand. She came last to Camille, who was too shy to try to hold the

261

child, but Valerie didn't take no for an answer. She instructed Camille which way to position her arms: "Hold her head; support her back." She looked away, embarrassed, when Valerie was arranging Sabrina. Something as commonplace as holding a baby was something that every woman should know. But then the warm weight was comforting. In the crook of her arm was this grapefruit-round little head with its sheen of midnight, feathery hair. A pair of guileless eyes in milk chocolate studied her face. Her cheeks were generous, and there were two chins. The fingers of Sabrina's hands were that of a porcelain doll. And Camille made the mistake of smelling her. Nothing smelled exactly like a clean baby. It was a combination of smells. It was ocean breezes, vanilla candles, and if warmth had a smell, it was curiously that too.

Camille had gone home that night to talk with Evan about babies and about marriage. He'd said the timing was wrong. Camille's hopes were dashed, and she was depressed for days. Funny, now that she was gone, he was asking to be her husband over the telephone. Well, it wouldn't work. She would have her baby after all, and Evan wouldn't know. His antiquated Peugeot would never make it to Maryland, nor would he have the money or nerve to come search her out. He would stay put in New York. She counted on that.

When she got to the house, Ben and Marlon were on the Hicks's front lawn in puffy coats, running in circles like puppies around a lifeless dogwood tree. They stopped periodically to belly-flop into a pillow of leaves Aaron had raked the day before. Camille noticed the boys as she got out of the cab after paying the driver his fare and smiled, thinking *someday*, before winding her way up the driveway once the cab driver backed out. In the yard, Catherine was planting winter flowers behind a neat shin-high white hedge she'd propped in the ground. Deep into her work, she only glanced when Camille came up the walk. Her hands were filled with earth, and her skirt was hiked up above her knees. She packed the dirt around a frail flower and massaged the soil into place.

"Camille, we should—"

"Not now, Mother." Camille stepped over a bag of mulch and glanced toward the Johnson house, squinting from the bright sunrays.

Catherine wasn't the only one out working in the yard. It was midafternoon, and since it was a nice day, many neighbors were out raking up great multitudes of crunchy brown leaves for the leaf collector. Not Mr. Johnson next door, though. He'd bought a leaf blower to hose piles of them from his pristine lawn toward the curb. The whoosh of the blower reminded Camille of where she'd just been. Instinctively, she pressed her hand against her stomach. She'd almost made a big mistake. She shook the thought quickly. There was no reason to dwell on it. As Nora would tell her, an unmade mistake is nothing but a disregarded choice. And she could not remember being as happy as she was right now. This was the right thing to do. Somehow she would have to tell Mel about it. But for now the baby would be her secret. She smiled as she opened the screen door.

Camille entered the house. First she stopped off in the family room to check her voice messages from work. There was one she couldn't figure out from Harold Mathis, but she didn't take time to think about it because she was hungry. Her stomach was rumbling like crazy, and she had a taste for a steak. She remembered the lean porterhouse she'd bought from Giant that she would cook with red onions. In the kitchen Mel was playing some old Stevie Wonder and sitting at the table addressing Thanksgiving Day cards.

"Hey," Camille said, moving toward the refrigerator.

"Hi, Cam," Mel answered thoughtfully. "Why is it," Mel asked, "that there isn't a holiday for dogs. Dog Day."

"What?" Camille said it tiredly. Mel was embarking on another one of her tangents.

Camille took the steak out of the freezer to defrost it in the microwave. In the downtime, she figured she would get her preparation items ready. The red onion, salt, pepper, season salt, steak sauce. She reached into the cabinets for each item. She would have a salad too. Though she didn't care for tomatoes, those sounded good right now. She pulled them out of the crisper. Her mouth watered.

"For dogs."

Camille screwed up her face. "You don't own a pet," she said.

"No, not animals. But picture this . . ." Mel moved a hand across the air to make an invisible marquee. "A federal holiday, right? The end of the year, you turn in a list of any men who have done anything bad to you. Liars, cheaters, abusers, deadbeat dads like Jeff. Then on Dog Day they're rounded up, the government gives you three big National Guardsmen to hold them down, and you get to beat the hell out of them. Dog Day."

"Sounds violent."

"But wouldn't it be the bomb?"

"Yeah. Whatever. What would be the bomb is if your mother went back down South. Why is she still here?"

Mel shrugged. "She said she wants to spend some time with us. Why do you care? She's not bothering you. Can you believe that dumb Jeff is complaining about buying Ben a coat? Doesn't give me a dime for his son otherwise, but complains about a coat. And the man makes good money."

"As long as he buys the coat, don't worry about it. But your mother. That woman is . . . I don't know. She looks at me funny. And every time we're alone, she keeps asking me to go out to dinner with her."

"Well, dummy, maybe she just wants to spend some time with you. Ever since she found out about Evan, she's felt guilty."

Camille sliced off the end of a cucumber, salted the sea-green pulp, and bit into it.

"Guilty?" She crunched. "I'm sure that's not in Catherine's vocabulary."

"Let's not start up that road again. I'm so sick of Jeff I don't know what to do."

"Mel, she's been here since September. All her stuff is in Florence, but here she is taking over your bedroom while you sleep in the guest room. You don't mind that?"

"It's Mama, Cam. Not some stranger. The woman hasn't seen you in seven years and hasn't seen me in about a year. She doesn't have any obligations in South C., she has plenty of income, so what's the big deal? If she wants to hang out with her daughters for awhile, she's allowed."

Camille peeped out into the hallway to make sure Catherine hadn't come inside. "You make it sound as if the three of us are having one big party in here. Tell me the truth. You don't think it's at all strange that she just pops into town and then practically moves in?"

Mel paused long enough to make Camille suspicious.

"All I know is she's a big help with Ben, and I can use all of *that* I can get my hands on."

Camille rolled her eyes. Mel had always been president of the Catherine Foster Fan Club. She sliced up the rest of the cucumber and started on the tomato.

"What are you guys having for dinner?"

Mel gave an envelope a liberal lick before sealing it shut.

"Aaron's over at his house now making some crawfish dish, girl. He insisted."

Camille noticed that Mel screwed up her face. She guessed the gourmet routine had gotten old.

"Sounds . . . interesting. You want one of these steaks?" Camille laid the steak in a bed of hot oil.

"That's not the question of the day. The question is, Are you sure you're ready to be a mother?"

Camille froze. Was it in her face? They said that pregnant women had a special glow. Was it visible in the way she walked? This morning, standing naked in the mirror after her bath, she looked as skinny as she'd ever been. There was a slight pouch that resembled water weight gain, but that was all. So how could Mel know?

"Shall we talk about it now, while Mama and Ben are outside? Or do you want to wait for another time?" Mel asked.

A sudden nausea overcame Camille that had nothing to do with her pregnancy.

"Cam, you should probably turn the heat down on the stove. You're gonna burn it."

Camille looked down at her sizzling steak. On autopilot, she cut down the heat and used a fork to turn over the meat and prod it.

"How did you know?" she asked finally. She went to bite her nails, but the french manicure made it impossible.

"Planned Parenthood called. Seems you forgot to get your payment for the cancelled procedure. They wanted to find out if you would be coming back to pick it up or if you preferred that they mail you a check. I told the woman you'd call her back."

"Don't tell Mother."

She could have kicked herself for putting her home phone number on the form. When she'd been filling it out, she'd hesitated over whether she should leave it blank. Apparently she'd made the wrong choice, and now it was too late.

"Does Greg know?"

Camille turned. Mel had set aside her project and was looking at her.

"Greg?"

"Do you love him? I guess you do since Evan's the only other man you've slept with. Personally I think it's too soon for this, and if I were you, I'd probably opt not to have the baby, but—you should have been using something, Cam."

"What are you talking about?"

Mel blinked twice. "It is Greg's baby, isn't it?"

"I'm a little more than three months, Mel."

Mel stood up, obviously shaken.

"Mel, please don't tell Mother. She'll only make it worse."

"Oh, my God. No. Okay. Okay. I'll take Monday off. We'll go back up there and get it over with."

"I'm keeping my baby."

The fire alarm sounded. Mel grabbed a section of newspaper and fanned furiously.

"You're burning the steak," she said. "Cam, don't do this to yourself."

Camille removed the pan from the stove. Her appetite was fading with each second. "I've already made my decision."

"You'll be tied to Evan forever. Always. Just like I am with Jeff. Is that what you want?"

"Evan is not an issue at this point. My baby can't . . ."

"You said yourself that now that he knows where you work, he can show up at any time. Mark my words. If that man finds out you are having his baby, he will do a number on you that'll make your head spin. Next thing you know, you'll find yourself right back in New York living in hell. And this time you won't be able just to pick up and run away in the night. Not with a baby."

Camille leaned against the counter, her face à map of pain. "Mel, what do you think? That I'm completely stupid? Up to this point, I've been on the fence. I know that. I admit that. But up until this point, I didn't have . . . I have this baby to think about now, and if I don't do anything else, I can't let Evan be a part of our lives. This baby deserves a chance. I would think you'd understand that."

"No, I don't. What I understand is what I see. You came here, and you were determined. But then every five minutes, you were changing your mind about going back. One minute you're glad you're away from him. Then you're not. It's like watching you ride a seesaw. Since I've been through it, I know a baby is serious business. You can't bring a baby into this world when you're as shaky as you are."

"Shaky? Mel, I'm a twenty-nine-year-old woman. I'll be thirty by the time the baby arrives. You were twenty-four when you had Ben. Still in school and everything. I've made up my mind about Evan and I'm doing this. I want this baby."

Mel sat down and said, "Oh, God. It hasn't been a dull moment with you, sis. Never a dull moment."

"Don't think I'm out hunting up trouble."

"What about your job?"

Camille finished topping off the salad and said, "Nora knows."

"She all right with it?"

"She thought I was terminating today."

"You'll still be able to keep your job?"

"Mel, what dark ages are you in? Women have been working and having babies for a long time now."

"Come here."

"What?"

"Come here." Mel stood and held out her arms. "You look like you could use a hug," she said.

9

*R*EINVENTING RULE NINE: *Remember that life's best compass is your own heart, with God as your needle.*

AFTER DRIVING OVER TO KING to get their Starbucks Monday morning (it was too cold to walk that far), Camille and Nora walked a different way. They trudged up Montgomery away from the river, this time without Kismet. The sun was out in full force again, but the wind was high. It stirred up dead leaves on the sidewalks, it ruffled the brightly colored awnings atop doorways, it sent Nora's trailing scarf fluttering out behind her.

Arm in arm, they worked their way up the sidewalk. On this side of town, there were only buildings to gaze at and a tennis court that was not much used. An ABC store stood apart from a neighborhood grocery store nestled in an ample parking lot with signs that threatened to tow any car that was parked there more than two hours. They walked and drank their coffee in silence while Nora took time to process what Camille had told her in the car.

"So you say you got all the way there," Nora said finally, then sipped at her coffee, "got on the table, and then changed your mind. What made you change your mind?"

Camille noticed that the Liz Taylor rock was conspicuously back on Nora's finger.

"Nora, I can do this. I know it."

"There is no need to convince me of it. It's your decision as a woman. My question is, What about Evan?"

"He won't come here." Camille had talked herself into believing that this was true. But Nora moved her arm from where it was tucked into Camille's and waved a hand at her.

"Don't be a fool, child. The Scouts said it best when they said be prepared. I suggest that you try to get him to see you sooner rather than," Nora looked down in the area of Camille's stomach draped in her heavy, lined wool coat, "later."

"See him? I don't want to see him again. Ever. I did the right thing that night, Nora, when I left. Now I have this precious little baby inside me. I have to protect this baby."

"See him. Call him. Whatever you need to do. As long as you tell him in no uncertain terms that you will never go back. Take legal action if you have to, but act now. Let's look at the facts. You ran out on him in the night and left everything you owned."

Camille was confused. She hadn't remembered telling Nora that part. But then she'd told Nora so many things, she could have easily mentioned it.

"The boy was left high and dry. No word from you. No money to help pay the bills."

"My mother took care of the rent on the house for the remainder of the lease." Two joggers whizzed by them in matching gray Navy sweats with bands decorating their foreheads.

"Yes, well. The fact remains that you ran out on him and left him. You have to make him understand that you won't go back to him, Camille, or he will show up to surprise you, and you won't know how to handle it. At least for now, he doesn't know where you live, and since our building is secure, he won't be able to get upstairs, but who's to say that he won't be hanging around waiting for you to come out of the building for lunch one afternoon? A man like that will be more determined than you believe he will."

"Nora, I know Evan. If he had a way to get to me, he would have by now. He wouldn't have called. He'd have shown up. Believe me. Obviously he can't get away or find the money to get to me. The holiday season is almost in full force, so he definitely won't be able to get off from work for awhile."

"All right, then, when the season is over. Then what? By then you'll be four months and counting. What's the plan then? How will you avoid him?"

Camille stopped walking. She hadn't worked out those details yet. She couldn't admit that she didn't have a plan. She only knew that she would protect this child no matter what.

"Camille?"

"What about Will?" Camille asked. She didn't want to think about Evan anymore. It only overwhelmed her. And that couldn't be good for the baby.

"What about him?"

"Have you figured out what you're going to do?"

Nora gave her a distracted look. "Not yet."

"Mmm."

Camille threw her emptied coffee container into a public trash bin, then started on her poppy seed muffin. Noticing a few pigeons scurrying nearby, she threw them a few crumbs.

"Speaking of Will," she said, "you have any idea why his father would call me?"

Nora stood stock still. "Harold called? You? Why would he do that?"

Camille shrugged. "He called the other day."

"The other day. When?"

"I don't know. Last week sometime."

"And did you phone him back?"

"Not yet. I can't imagine what he'd want with me."

Nora grasped Camille's arm. "Why are you just now telling me?"

Camille was confused. Nora looked so concerned. She didn't answer.

"What exactly did Harold say? In his message."

"Nothing, really. Just his name and that he wanted me to call him."

"How does Harold know who you are? Were you introduced?"

Camille recalled their meeting in her office. She'd been everything but considerate to the man before she'd found out who he was. Even then she hadn't known that his company held Reinventing.

"He was using my telephone the day he came to the office."

Camille stared at Nora. None of this made sense.

"Did he say anything then?"

"Just hello."

"What was he doing?"

"Nora, what is this about?"

"I can't say that I know. But I do find it strange that Harold would take time out of his schedule to place a call to you."

"Should I call him back?"

"Darling, the man is very powerful, and he owns the company. You don't have a choice. Besides, I'd be terribly interested in finding out what he's after."

The wind swept past them with a sharp whistle. For a moment, the sunlight was smothered in clouds, and Nora shivered. "Let's head back." She stopped briefly to check for oncoming cars, then jaywalked across.

"Why do you seem so upset about this?" Camille asked, taking a bite from her muffin. She trailed behind Nora crossing the street and had to rush to get out of the way of a white Taurus.

"Oh, I'm just experiencing stress, darling. I have another New Millennium Woman conference ahead and then this thing with William."

"Oh. Are you sure there's nothing else?"

"I would think that's enough, darling. Don't fret. I just have a lot on my mind, Camille. A multitude of priorities to contend with."

"I understand," Camille said. But she didn't. Although Nora had tried to hide it, Camille could tell that for some reason Nora was deathly afraid of Harold Mathis. Camille wanted to reassure her.

"I'm on your side," she said. "No matter what Mr. Mathis wants, I'm loyal to you."

"Of course, darling," Nora said casually. "I would never doubt that."

Nora was walking faster. Camille had to increase her speed to keep up. How Nora ever managed to cover so much ground in the spiky heels she wore was amazing.

"You're sure I should call him back?"

"Camille, as I said, Harold owns Reinventing. He's not a man you'd want to ignore."

"And what should I say?"

"Hear him out. Listen to what he has to say."

"And then what?"

"And then tell me what it is he's after."

They dodged a large, suited man in sunshades talking loudly into his cell phone. Camille thought about the report she'd seen on the dangers of cell phones.

"What he's after. You make it sound sinister."

"He's no saint. I've known Harold a number of years now," Nora said, "and I'll be honest with you. The man's a snake. There is always a trick or two up his sleeve."

Camille was almost speechless.

"Then what could he want with me? I don't want any part of his trickery," she squeaked out.

"You don't have to do a thing, Camille. Just find out what he wants and report back to me."

Not watching where she was going, Camille stumbled on a raised brick in the sidewalk.

"Careful, darling," Nora said, her hand at Camille's elbow to steady her. Nora slowed her pace.

"As I live and breathe!" A large, smiling woman blocked their path. She was red-faced and wearing an outdated brown wool coat with a small cape. Strands of her wind-blown, shaggy blonde hair frizzed out of the amateur bun in the middle of her head. Her porcine eyes flashed excitedly.

"Imagine. A glamorous lady like you strolling along drinking Starbucks, for goodness sake. How do. I'm Emma Sample."

Nora smiled brightly. "Good morning," she said and stuck out a hand, which the woman shook a little too vigorously. Camille smiled and she turned her head so Emma wouldn't notice.

"I was just talking about you, I swear, the other day. My best girlfriend, Diana, and I are taking your seminar and I says, Dee—that's what we call her, Dee, because she simply hates Diana. I tried calling her Di for a time, but then that sweet princess from Wales was so suddenly and violently taken from us, poor thing. I cried like a newborn baby, and for days and days I watched all the news reports. I was obsessed. I couldn't do a thing but sit glued to the TV and my husband, Herbert—we call him Bert—Bert says, 'Honey, you've got to stop this. You cannot stay holed up in this house like a couch potato.' Well, I gave Bert a good piece of my mind! I was just shaking I was so angry. I said, 'I'll have you know, that poor woman was cut down in the prime of her life. The prime. And if I want to take a few days to recognize that she lived, I will do it by God.' Well, Bert let me be after that I tell you. He'd never seen his wife let go like that. Except when our son James went joyriding in the neighbor's car once. But that's another story."

Emma paused, and Camille looked at Nora, who appeared frozen and close to withering away on the sidewalk.

"Now what was I saying?" Emma said. She tilted her head and looked toward the clouds as if the answer was written there.

"Oh yes. I told Dee, 'Dee, we have been stagnant for too long. It's high time we do something about it!' And Dee, she says to me, 'You know, Em'—that's what she calls me, Em. She says, 'You know, Em, I've been thinking the same thing, and I've got

278

just the thing to bring us out of this rut!' And out she pulls a New Millennium Woman brochure. And I look it over and I know it's just what we need. And I tell Dee I'm so impressed with your work because I saw your infomercial, and a couple years ago, I read one of your books, I can't call it out off the top of my head, but I love your work. So anyways, Dee and I will be there front and center at your seminar, and I can't wait!"

"How flattering," Nora said graciously. "I'll look forward to seeing you there, darling."

"Darling! Wonderful. Just like you say on the infomercial. Oh, Dee is going to be green. Just green. May I have your autograph, Ms. Jordan?"

"Call me Nora, please."

Camille smirked and recited silently that the only Ms. Jordan was Nora's mother and she was in a nursing home in New Orleans.

"Nora," Emma said slowly, trying the name out as she dug into her shoulder bag with fervor. She produced a pen and a blank page in the back of her address book.

"I apologize. This is the only thing I have to write on."

"No problem, my dear. This will do just nicely."

Nora whipped the pen across the tiny page, then handed it back.

"Oh, thank you. Thank you, Nora. I'll cherish it."

"And I will see you and your friend in two weeks."

"Have a lovely day," Emma said and beamed. She stood aside to let them pass.

As they got closer to the building, Nora said, "Camille, a bit of advice. Don't ever lose your anonymity."

"I hear you," Camille said, "and I wholeheartedly agree."

⁂

ON FRIDAY MORNING A COLD RAIN came gushing from the blue-tinged charcoal sky, lasting the entire day. It was steady and hard, falling in big splotches. The biting wind that had kept up all week finally abated, but the rain accompanied by a thirty-five-degree temperature proved more than enough to chill, but not freeze.

By midmorning it was messy out. The roads were glistening and slick, standing water in places spiraling up and out like spray from lawn sprinklers when disturbed by moving cars. It made for a terrible evening rush-hour commute.

Camille sat in bumper-to-bumper traffic, inching forward bit by bit. What was normally a ten-minute jaunt to get to the beltway from the office drew out into a lengthy journey. A half hour had gone by, and she still hadn't reached her exit. Her driving foot ached from the effort. Brake. Tap the gas. Brake. Tap the gas. What was most maddening was getting to an intersection and trying to guess whether she should stay put at the light (even though it was green) or move forward and take a chance of getting stuck in the intersection in the way of coming traffic. When you made a wrong guess and moved forward, you'd find yourself caught, unable to move out of the way. Approaching drivers unable to move would beep their horns wildly, frustrated that they'd have to miss their light because the intersection was blocked. She breathed a relieved sigh when she made it through her last light before the exit.

Luckily, she was in the appropriate lane and didn't have to try to find a split second to slide over like the poor rabbit-faced woman with angry red hair driving a Suburban. Camille flashed her high beams to let the woman know she would allow her to get over. The woman was rude enough not to offer Camille a thank-you wave for the consideration. Camille rolled her eyes.

She was listening to Nora's tape and practicing what she was going to say tonight. Tonight she was going to tell Greg that she was pregnant if it killed her. All week, she'd been trying to work up the nerve to do it.

"Greg, you're a wonderful man, but I'm knocked up with Evan's baby. No. That's too base," she said, laughing at her choice of words. She eased down the ramp leading to the beltway behind a Dodge Ram with Texas plates.

Adjusting her side mirror slightly so she could see to merge, she said, "Greg, you've been such a good friend to me. I appreciate having you in my life, I really do. I know we kissed that time, and it was beautiful and special, but I . . . No, too sappy."

There was a fender bender off on the shoulder of the road. Road flares were bright red beacons around the cars involved. A flatbed tow truck was positioned in front of the mess.

"Greg, I have something to tell you. I'm with child. God, that sounds like a line from a Jane Austen book. I'm with child. Dumb. Okay. How about . . ."

She couldn't think of a better way to say it. There just wasn't an easy way. She focused on merging with traffic in front of a creeping eighteen-wheeler whose lights beat against her rearview mirror with such force that she had to scrunch down in her seat so she could see where she was heading.

She was two hours later than planned when she reached Greg's door.

"Hey," he said. "I was worried about you, girl. It's rough out there." He looked relaxed in a solid walnut brown sweater, dark jeans, and bare feet.

"Yeah," she came in breathless and trembling, unbelting her trench coat and then unraveling layers of a shawl-sized green print scarf imprisoning her throat and chest.

Greg led her into the foyer and took her coat. The dripping oversized umbrella he left unopened just outside his balcony door. A breath of cold air escaped into the living room. Greg turned up the fireplace.

"Sorry I'm late. Traffic was so backed up." Camille was hugging herself tiredly.

"Well, come on, get comfortable. Put your feet up," he said. She sat in the cozy chair and put her feet on the ottoman. Greg took the liberty of removing her shoes and then covered her stocking feet with a mud-cloth blanket.

"Thank you. That's so nice."

"You're welcome. Well, can I get you some tea?"

"Please."

She was up as soon as he went to the kitchen, roaming back and forth.

"I rented two movies I think you'll like," he yelled out to her.

A mesh of clanging and cabinet door closing followed.

"What's that?"

"I said, I rented two movies. *Shawshank Redemption* and *Austin Powers.*"

"*Austin Powers?*"

"Yeah. James Bond–type spoof. Mike Myers." He did an Austin impression that was pretty good and laughed.

"Oh yeah," Camille said absently. She remembered having seen the trailers awhile back.

He brought out a tray with the tea on it, and until she saw what else was on the tray, she hadn't realized she was starving. Greg had added cheese and cracked-wheat crackers, a small dish of green and ripe olives, a cluster of grapes and some sliced strawberries, and melba toast with what turned out to be crab and artichoke dip in a glass bowl.

"Ooh. Yum."

"I thought you might want a little pick-me-up."

Her mouth was watering. Sometimes it was as if the baby growing inside her was a little tapeworm, wanting to be satisfied several times a day. She forced herself not to be greedy as she reached for one of the tiny plates and helped herself. The grapes were large red ones that she ate in pairs.

"I stopped by Sutton Place before coming home," he told her.

"Nora talks about that place all the time. I haven't been."

"It's cool."

She took the teacup by its handle.

"Careful. That's hot," he warned.

"Oh, I know," she said. Heat wafted from the mug.

A splinter of wood from the floor caught and ran her stocking along the bottom of her foot.

"Ouch," she said. A splash of tea hit the floor.

"You okay? Told you it was hot." He was smiling.

"It's not that." She set the mug on a coaster on the table, then sat on the edge of the ottoman to assess the damage. She'd paid ten dollars for the pair. The breach was small, though. She could still wear the hose with pants and enclosed shoes.

"Well, what is it?" Greg sat next to her on the ottoman. It was a wonder that they both fit. He was a husky man. Sensually, he touched the run with the tip of his finger, and then Camille saw the look. The one Greg had bestowed on her that time he'd awkwardly kissed her.

"I'm pregnant," she blurted out.

There are moments so quiet that silence seems to have just as much life as words. He stared, lost in the jumble of her simple admission. She held eye contact with the floor as if it might move. The tiptoeing sound of the rain pelted the balcony door with wet drizzling swatches.

Camille could feel him, feel his every emotion. He was so close beside her on the ottoman. Their arms touched, their hips did not, but their body heat made it seem so. The way his breathing threaded in and out so quickly, she knew he was struggling. There was more to say. There was an explanation to give. (Did she really owe him one?) She guessed she should give him something more, but what was right to say next? What did one say to follow such words when they weren't expected or wanted words? It was like giving the grand finale at the beginning of the show. And so she thought she should probably apologize for that.

"I'm sorry."

"No. No. Don't be . . ."

"I should have, uhm . . ."

She felt better pacing. It gave her something else to focus on.

"I didn't know you were seeing someone. I thought you were . . ." Greg was slumped over, his hands folded together.

Why did people keep automatically assuming she hadn't been celibate since leaving Evan? But Greg didn't know anything about Evan.

"It's my ex-boyfriend's baby. He's back in New York. I just found out. I'm three months." Her stomach still thrummed. She hadn't eaten a full meal since lunch. She plucked a handful of strawberries.

"Three." He stroked his beard thoughtfully.

She could tell what he was thinking.

He said, "So you aren't seeing anybody."

"Just you. I mean . . . ," she answered.

He studied his fingernails. "At least you have choices. What will you do?"

She could have kicked him. The jerk sounded hopeful. She couldn't tell him about the girls' faces and the protester with the loud lipstick. She couldn't repeat how the sound of the vacuum made her pray to die or that the nurse's callused hand helped her save herself. So she stopped pacing a minute and said, "I'm already doing it. I'm having my baby."

"I see. Does the father know? Is he going to—"

"He isn't a part of this, Greg. It's just me."

"Why not?"

"He isn't part of it." She said it firmly so Greg would know not to probe further. He was running his hands across his hair the way Evan did when he felt powerless.

"I'm sorry, Greg."

She stood, staring at the *Guernica* print, not wanting to see his disappointment. Her shoes were on the floor beside the chair and she walked over to retrieve them.

"What are you doing?"

"Can I have my coat, please? My umbrella?"

"Your coat . . . you're leaving? We should talk."

"Greg, I'm tired. I think I should go."

"What? Okay. Do what you want." He hefted himself up.

286

She had to get out of here. In a whirlwind, she was wrapping herself up in her scarf and coat preparing for the icy weather. She slipped black leather Isotoners over her fingers and worked at the lever on the umbrella so it would be ready to swing open once she was outside. Greg kept his hands in his pockets and mumbled to her that she should drive carefully and to call him to let him know she'd made it home safely. Camille made her escape fast. She didn't see Greg lean his forehead against the closed door once she left, nor did she hear him say, "But I love you" in the quiet foyer so softly that it was drowned out by the sound of the pouring rain.

⊰⊱

THERE WAS A MESSAGE ON HER VOICE MAIL. It said, "Honey babe. It's me. I waited for you to call me back. Camille, I miss you." She deleted it before it finished playing out and her telephone rang. She massaged her abdomen. The baby was making her seriously hungry again. She checked the caller ID screen to ensure that it wasn't a long-distance call before picking up, and said, "Hello?"

"Finally, Ms. Foster. You're a difficult one to catch."

She recognized the ground glass voice and sat up straighter, clearing her throat. "Mr. Mathis," she said.

"I expected a telephone call from you."

"Yes, sir. I was planning to try to reach you this afternoon. So much has been going on." She had really been mucking around what to say to him. Could he tell it was a lie? She took a nibble from the danish on her desk.

"I understand. In that case I won't keep you. Ms. Foster, I'm a man who gets to the point. What are your plans for next Wednesday evening?"

She was caught by surprise. "Next Wednesday?" She looked up to see Dawn and Will talking rapidly as they walked down the hall past her office. She grimaced. Those conniving dogs. She wondered how Nora stood knowing their secret.

"We can discuss a few things," Harold was saying.

"A few things," she repeated.

"Let's say seven. My assistant will e-mail you directions to the Mathis headquarters."

This was happening too fast.

"Uhm. Mr. Mathis, what is this about, if I might ask?"

"Ms. Foster, this is a confidential matter. I expect that you'll be on time and that you will tell no one. I mean, no one, especially Nora, that we've had this conversation. Do you understand?" He hung up before she could answer.

After work, Camille pulled up in the drive beside Mel's blue Amigo, which curiously had a dent in the front end. She got out of her car and examined Mel's Jeep for a second.

Walking into the house, she was hit with the strong odor of rubbing alcohol. In the family room were Mel and Desnee in front of the TV wearing sweats and moving vigorously with a bald man on the screen. The table had been put on top of the sofa.

"Mel? Everything okay?" Camille asked.

"Doing Tae Bo," Mel said. "Des ordered the tapes."

"What happened?"

"What?"

"Your car. What happened to it?"

"Oh that. Car stopped short in front of me. At a green light."

"Stopped short?"

"Some old biddy. I don't know why she still had a license. She had to be every bit of eighty. I tapped her. No damage to her ride, though. She was driving one of those old-time Lincolns. Come on, Des, keep up girl! Work it out!"

Desnee looked ready to pass out, but she mustered up enough energy to say, "Cam, you should try it too. Exercise is good for pregnant women."

"I'll pass." She picked up the *Journal* on the way upstairs to her room.

Camille needed to talk to somebody, and Greg was the most logical choice. She kicked off her shoes. All day she'd been thinking about the call from Harold Mathis, but he'd directed her not to tell anyone. That meant Greg too. Apparently he was plotting something against Nora. He'd mentioned her by name. Especially Nora, he'd said. If she told anyone and it got out, he had the power to fire her. And with a baby coming, she couldn't possibly afford to lose her livelihood. More now than ever, she needed her income. Well, she didn't have to talk to anybody in the company about it, but she could get an objective opinion. Maybe if she ran the whole thing past Mel, Mel could help her make sense of it and give her some advice on what to do.

As Camille walked downstairs calling Mel's name, the doorbell rang. She opened it, and there was Greg standing in front of her holding up yellow roses. He held them out to her, but she didn't take them. She couldn't move.

"I've been thinking," he said. "A great deal."

"Thinking?"

"I . . . Well . . . May I come in?"

"Uhm."

He eased past her and lay the bouquet on the small round foyer table. "I've been thinking, Camille."

"Yes, I heard that part." She couldn't breathe.

"Well, I've . . . Ever since that night you told me about . . . you know. Ever since, I've been. I want to . . ."

To her amazement, Greg knelt before her, taking her hand in his.

"What are you doing?" she asked.

"Oh my God," Desnee said.

Camille had not noticed that Desnee and Mel were watching. She glanced toward them. Mel's mouth was open. Desnee dabbed perspiration off her brow.

"Don't say anything. Hear me out. I'm not sure how you feel about me, but I love you, Camille. I can't stand the thought of you doing this thing alone. It's not right. I don't have a ring right now, but we'll go out whenever you say and get the most beautiful one you can pick out. I want you to be my wife, Camille. Let me take care of you. You and your baby."

Greg put his hand on her stomach.

Camille was crying. She was crying and she was laughing too. Ever since finding out about the baby, she'd lived in a constant state of fear. There were questions she'd asked herself. Could she be a good mother? Could she make it work by herself? Was she ready? Years from now, how would she explain where the father was? Now here was this beautiful man offering her his name, his protection, the world.

With Greg, it all seemed extraordinarily possible now. To be loved and cared for by such a good, handsome man and have a family was the only thing she'd ever truly wanted. She used to pray for it constantly, but since deciding to keep the baby, she'd given up hope. No other man except Evan had ever wanted her before, and with a baby, she was sure her odds were slim to none. But now . . . now God was smiling down on her in a big way. Camille didn't hesitate. She had no choice but to say yes, so she did. She said it with a huge smile. Greg took her face in his hands and kissed her with the fullness of his passion, then held her in his arms. Finally, she thought. She sagged in his arms. Camille felt a security so complete that she surrendered to it for all she was worth.

10

*R*EINVENTING RULE TEN: *A straight line takes you forward. A pattern keeps you going in circles.*

<hr/>

THERE WAS SO MUCH TO DO over the next two months. A dress (which was tricky, because she couldn't determine how big she would be by then), a reception hall, a caterer, flowers, a wedding party, a cake, a honeymoon. At least the church was nailed down. They would have the ceremony at Greg's small church in Burke.

Greg solved some of Camille's problem by hiring a wedding consultant, a Miss Sophia Denton, whose claim to fame was that she'd done the Jacob Housen wedding last year, whoever that was. Greg and Camille thought it would be rude to ask. But Sophia seemed capable. She'd met them at the office for an initial discussion to discover what Camille envisioned for her special day. After the talk, they walked Sophia to the elevator and then went back to Camille's office to trade notes.

"I love her," Camille enthused. She gazed at her beautiful pear-shaped diamond as she did a hundred times a day.

"Well. She seems to know what we want," Greg agreed, closing the door. He put his arms around Camille and gave her a strong kiss. His lips were warm and tender.

"Greg," she said, moving away. She straightened her suit jacket.

"What? I can't kiss my fiancée?"

"Somebody might come in."

"Relax. Everybody knows we're getting married. I'm sure no one would be surprised to witness our affection," he said.

"I love you," she told him. It felt strange saying that to another man.

"Kiss me again then," he commanded, and she obliged. This time it was long and incredible. She had to break away. She straightened his tie and wiped a lipstick smudge from the corner of his mouth.

"I have work to do, Mr. Emory. I promised Will a copy of the report on the responses to our revamped CW campaign." She went to stand behind her desk and said, "Hmm."

"What?" Greg asked.

"It's . . . Did you leave this here for me?" She picked up two sheets of paper from the desk.

"What?"

"This. It's a printout of my intranet picture. And one of Nora."

He moved in closer and leaned across the desk.

"You took a nice one, baby. I didn't leave it though. Maybe Randall wanted you to see how well it turned out so you would stop tripping about it."

"I wasn't tripping. I merely said I thought it was stupid."

"Well. Same difference."

"But why would he leave me Nora's?"

"I don't know. Perhaps it was an accident. He could have been carrying both and inadvertently left this one too."

She touched the speaker and dialed Randall's extension. Met with his voice mail, she left him a brief message to call her back.

"I'd better get this report to Will." She looked at her watch.

"Dinner later?"

Camille couldn't stand lying to Greg, but Harold Mathis had been clear.

"Tomorrow night, Greg. Mel promised to go look at some wedding gowns with me in Rockville tonight."

"Way out there?"

"It's an outlet. I can't see spending hundreds of dollars on something I'll only wear once."

"Well. All right," he said. He pecked her cheek.

"Pick you up for your appointment in the morning then?" he asked, referring to her doctor's visit scheduled for ten.

"Yep."

She sat in her chair preparing to pull up the report on her computer screen, but when she swiveled her chair, her eyes fell on a yellow sticky lying on the floor to the side of her desk. She could see that there was writing on it. Something in thin red marker. She pushed her chair back and leaned forward to retrieve it.

You can try to hide it, but I know, it said.

Camille tossed it in the trash, hoping she had enough time to get the report to William before her deadline.

⟡

CAMILLE HAD SEEN GRAND BUILDINGS in New York—the Chrysler, the Museum of Modern Art, the U.N., St. Peter's Cathedral—but there was something almost fictional about the Mathis headquarters. It was so large and assuming. An architectural dream that would make Mel melt to see it. The building and grounds had the feel of a community to it. There were courtyards outside and inside it, and during the day sunlight spilled in from almost every angle. To get to it, you had to pass through a wispy country road leading up as it would to a private estate, where you were met by arched gates manned by serious-faced guards to whom you had to provide a numbered password to gain entry. And then you were escorted by a nondescript car that moved slowly ahead of you toward the main entrance of the building itself.

There were acres and acres of grounds like a plantation

might have, with gazebos and small man-made lakes, and even a lighted golf course that caused Camille to stop a moment to watch a man in casual plaid tee off. This was unbelievable for two reasons. It was cold outside and dark, and this was a place of business. She had never heard of a golf course at an office. Her stomach was full of butterflies. She'd heard of wealth before, but this was a world all its own. Yet again she wondered why a man who could own all of this would want to speak to her.

Camille was met at the front door by a very short bejeweled woman with large, protruding teeth that gave her warm smile a comical quality. But her carriage was above reproach. She held herself at her full height (not over five feet) and spoke with the most soothing voice Camille had ever heard when she introduced herself as Ms. Steele and offered Camille a seat in the lobby. As Ms. Steele walked, her glasses, threaded with a gold chain, bounced against her bosom.

Camille sat on one of the many couches in the cavernous lobby and thought that there was nothing steely about this lady. She was warm and plump and genuinely kind. Camille stared at a white marble fireplace that spanned an entire wall. In fact, the whole wall up to the ceiling was marble.

"May I get you something? A fruit tea? Water? It is after hours, so I can offer you a glass of wine to warm you. Or sherry perhaps. And we have plenty of delectables I'm sure will interest your taste buds."

For once, the baby was not demanding sustenance. Camille was way too nervous, but she held onto a glimmer of confidence since she looked nice and professional. She'd worn her best suit, which she'd bought last month on sale. It was a grape Versace pantsuit infused with blue undertones. The way the jacket was made, a little loose and long, she didn't look as if she'd gained any baby weight.

"I'll have water, thank you," she said.

"Bereneice here will take you to Mr. Mathis's rooms. Your water will be brought to you there."

His rooms? Camille turned. She hadn't heard the tall, slinky Bereneice tiptoe up behind them. Camille eyed her suspiciously. She was a model type. Her cheekbones were so pronounced she looked undernourished. An abundance of hair done up in cascading tar black curls was pushed off her anorexic, creamily made-up face and crept down her back like a horse's mane. Fake lashes dripped from her eyelids. A fat gold handcuff of a bracelet was attached to her bony wrist and went well with her sheath dress, though inappropriate for winter. But her coloring, an incredibly deep golden brown like she'd been cooked in olive oil, was rich and glowing.

"Follow me," she said. There was a slight accent Camille couldn't place.

They lurched swiftly in a petite glassed-in elevator to the top floor. Bereneice led the way through a carpeted maze of patterned flowers. Lighted hallways and turns and more turns approached. Camille looked around wildly. She would never find her way out of this place. She wished for a moment she'd told Greg where she was going.

"How much further?" she asked timidly.

"Not much."

At the end of a hallway was a set of double doors.

The air smelled of something sweet, and Camille knew why when Bereneice reached out a shackled hand to open one of the doors. Harold Mathis leaned back in a chair behind an enormous desk in an opulent office the size of a penthouse, smoking a pipe he held clenched between his nubby teeth. Coltrane played softly on a chrome Bose CD player at his desk.

"Ms. Foster. Come in. Have a seat. Thank you, Bereneice." His voice was as hard and gritty as she remembered.

Bereneice nodded and exited, leaving her alone with this terrifying enigma. Before she'd known who he was, his presence hadn't affected her, but now she was fairly shaking.

She glanced around. Behind her was the same type of marble fireplace she'd seen downstairs with a stand-alone world globe beside it. He noticed where she looked and said, "Marvelous, isn't it?"

It took Camille a few seconds to notice that a bottle of water and a glass of ice were on the table beside where she sat with a sampling of what Ms. Steele had called delectables. There were scones, shrimp puffs, some type of cucumber construction, and something unidentifiable that Camille refused to touch. She nearly dropped the bottled water in her lap as she poured.

"Congratulations." He removed his pipe. His smile was a grimace.

"Pardon?"

"Your engagement. I hear you've accepted a proposal from Mr. Emory."

"Yes, sir." She assumed Will or Nora had told him.

"I was surprised, but congratulations," he repeated.

"Thank you." Camille sipped her water. Harold Mathis stared at her beneath his heavy lids as if to size her up.

"Anyone know you're here?"

She wanted to lie and say yes.

"I've kept our meeting confidential," she said and was surprised at her own boldness.

"I would ask you a question, Ms. Foster."

"A question?"

"What do you think of our headquarters?"

"It's lovely. Very nice."

"We have offices all over the world. When I was a young man starting out in the 1930s, never did it occur to me that I would be master of such an entity. I am pleased to say that I surpassed even my father's dreams for me."

Camille blinked. Was this old man hitting on her by telling her his accomplishments? Was that why he asked her here after hours? And that Ms. Steele offering out wine and sherry like a madam. This was too much.

"Do you enjoy your job at RTW?"

"Very much."

"Tell me," he relit his pipe. "What is it you like most?"

She wished she'd brought a recorder. She wouldn't have proof of harassment otherwise.

"There's satisfaction and fulfillment in helping other women."

"Go on."

"The staff is friendly." Silently she said, *Some too friendly*, thinking of Dawn and Will.

"Especially Nora. She's been a wonderful mentor to me."

"And then there's Mr. Emory."

"Yes, well, Greg." Camille blushed and spilled water on her hand.

"Ms. Foster, as I told you over the telephone, I am a man who likes to get to the point. As I don't have a great deal of time, I'm sure you won't mind if I get to it. I've asked you here for a purpose. Following the Christmas holidays, the director of programming for the MathCom Cable network will be moving to London. The vice president, Carol Barbieri, up to this point has not been able to locate a suitable candidate to take on the position. Ms. Barbieri is seeking raw talent, you see. Someone she can mentor, if you will, and mold into a successful television executive. I am aware of your background in demographics, which will be essential to the position, and so many at Reinventing have been impressed with your contributions to Reinventing as well as your fresh ideas. We think you could possibly bring something new and exciting to the table at MCN."

"A job? You're offering me a—"

"Your salary would more than double. You would have to relocate to San Diego; however, your moving expenses would be covered. You would receive a company car, an expense account, and a three-bedroom oceanfront condominium that I'm certain would be sufficient for your needs."

"You're offering me a job."

"From what I understand, the schedule is far more flexible than the one you have now."

Camille's mind was reeling. She was having trouble digesting this. She sipped more water to keep from choking.

"Mr. Mathis, with all due respect, why me?"

"As I said, no one else has come close to fitting the position. In fact, it may just be tailor-made for you." For some reason, he smiled wickedly and lifted his brows.

"For me. Mr. Mathis, I'm getting married this February 14. I have a child coming."

"I'm fully aware of your circumstances." She wasn't sure who'd told him about the baby. It had to be Nora.

"Then why would you want me?"

"Reproduction is a fact of life, Ms. Foster. I am certain it won't place your performance at a disadvantage. I was somewhat surprised when I learned about your impending marriage. The fact remains, I'm convinced you're the one for the job, and it's not difficult to find something for Mr. Emory as well if we must," he said dryly.

"At Reinventing, you are welcomed, Ms. Foster, but not necessary. On the contrary, at MCN, you may just make a profound difference."

His eyes seemed to be weighing her character again.

"This is all . . . very overwhelming," Camille responded. She wanted to leave. Coming here, she hadn't known what to expect. But the last thing she assumed was that she'd be asked to take a job by one of the most powerful businessmen in the country. Something about that didn't fit. A man like Mathis offering her what amounted to the world for a job she was well aware that she had neither worked for nor was qualified for. She would have paid real money to know what he was up to. She didn't have the courage to come out and ask him. This whole evening felt out of control. If she said yes now, she wasn't sure what she'd say yes to. If she said no, the insult might make him retaliate. He'd said she wasn't necessary at Reinventing. What would Nora do? she wondered.

"Mr. Mathis, let me have some time to think about this, please. There's a lot to consider."

"I understand. Bereneice, show Ms. Foster out."

Once again, she had mysteriously appeared, an emaciated walking statue.

"This way," she said. Camille thought that maybe Bereneice knew very few English phrases. Mainly "follow me" and "this way." Camille stood and shook Harold Mathis's outstretched hand firmly though she felt weak enough to lie down.

"My assistant will be in touch with you prior to the new year. I am confident you'll have an answer at that time."

"Yes, sir."

"Oh. And be sure that you do not mention our meeting to anyone. It wouldn't make me happy if you did. Not a word to Nora or your future husband. No one. You may speak with Mr. Emory about this only if you make the decision to take the job. I expect your full cooperation."

"Of course, sir."

Once Camille left the room following close behind Bereneice, a woman came out of the shadows. Harold Mathis turned, filling his pipe with more sweet tobacco.

"You heard?" he asked, his mind partly on his task.

"Not all. The music . . ." She gestured toward the disk player.

"Is it done?" the woman asked hopefully.

"Not exactly," he answered. "But it's only a matter of time. She won't refuse. Not with what you've planned."

The woman laid an affectionate hand on his shoulder and said, "Thank you. You didn't have to do it, and I—"

For a change Harold's eyes softened. He placed his hand on hers, looked up, and said, "Nonsense. No need for appreciation. You're one of the few who never attempts to take advantage. You know I would do just about anything for you."

The woman smiled and kissed the top of his balding head.

❧❦❧

CAMILLE DROVE AROUND FOR HOURS trying to get a handle on her thoughts. She was numb. A job. Not just any job, but a dream job. Three months ago she would have jumped at it. But three months ago, she wasn't comfortable in a job she loved surrounded by people who cared about her. But with a salary like what Harold Mathis offered, she could get everything the baby would need, including a full-time nanny. And San Diego was such a beautiful place to bring up a child. Pleasant weather all year round. No humidity to affect the baby's respiratory system with allergies and infections.

Camille pictured her and Greg taking the baby out for walks along the beach with the wind in their hair as they admired gray seals sunning themselves in lazy heaps beneath the crystal sky. How funny the way life threw such curveballs. For years, all she'd wanted to do was survive. Take one day at a time and get through it without breaking. Now here she was being given a chance actually to live. To live. She'd been at the outskirts of her own life ever since she could remember.

But there were cons. Leaving meant being away from Nora. Why wouldn't Harold Mathis want Nora to know about this? Leaving meant not being there with Mel. It meant walking away from Reinventing the Woman, and she needed that place. Inside those walls, she was becoming something. Every good thing that had happened to her this far had begun with Reinventing the Woman. Even back as far as that audiotape,

The Pursuit of Hope, that had opened her eyes and helped her know she had choices. Reinventing was her foundation, but Harold Mathis could not know that. He couldn't know what he was asking her to do.

Camille sat in the visitors' parking lot in front of the Reinventing building, wanting to feel its atmosphere. Wanting to feel some emotion that would help her make sense of how this powerful man could so arbitrarily offer this opportunity. It was late. After ten. Unfortunately, the office wasn't alive with people to give her what she craved right now. A sense of reality. A sense of belonging. She started her car and left.

An hour later, she was pounding on Greg's door, which he opened wearing a confused expression and a dark robe.

"Cam? Baby, what are you doing out at this time of night? What's wrong?"

She walked in shaking her head and said, "I need you. I need to be touched. I need to feel."

He closed the door.

"Okay. Calm down."

He put his arms around her, but she said, "No. Not like that, Greg. I need . . ."

Camille began to cry and press butterfly kisses all over his face, taking off her coat, his robe. "Like this," she said. She quickly unbuttoned her suit jacket, unashamed about exposing her body.

Understanding ignited him to action. His hands on her skin

were a balm. She wanted them everywhere, it felt so good. But he was patient. Molding her shoulder while his mouth brought a special kind of heat to her throat. Then his fingers searched her spine and moved on. She was so weak, he had to help her climb the stairs to the loft where he slept in a motion-less waterbed.

There was no thought of Evan when Greg moved inside her. No thought of her past. Not an inkling of fear. There was only a feeling. A light being formed. A craving being quenched. She could not yet grasp what she thought about this job that she had been offered. Knowing for sure the right thing to do was like trying to fit a cloud in her fist, but oh, there was this. This man inside her, arching to her will, his dusk, silk skin a savor beneath her palms. And as joy began to tremble within her, she could think of only one thing: Harold Mathis may be a powerful man, but at this time, in this place, she held the power. She held the power.

The morning stretched itself out like an easy yawn first across his bed from the skylight above them. Camille stirred. Greg was wide awake, lying on his back with his arms flung out, one of which Camille was using for a pillow. He stared up and out at the sky, remembering the night before. Wondering about it.

"Well. Feel like coffee?" he asked. He could tell by her breathing that Camille was awake too.

"Sounds good," she said, still not opening her eyes. She was thinking of Evan and whether he had done this with someone else too. A part of her hoped he hadn't, and she hated herself for hoping that.

Greg eased his arm out from under her head.

"I'm going to shower first. You feel okay?"

"Mmmhmm."

"Not nauseous?" He stroked her cheek.

"Nope. That doesn't happen often anymore, thank the lord."

She turned over in the same position he'd been in and squinted up at the skylight.

He left the bathroom door open. The water was loud and the air misty. He was singing something she hadn't heard before. She scrunched down beneath the down comforter. He had a good voice. It was a comfortable song. Everything about him was comfortable. And secure. It was nice finally to have this. She leaned over to smell the scent of his cologne drowned in the bedsheets. Out of the corner of her eye, she caught a fluttering something.

"Greg, look!"

He came rushing out of the shower, his body soaking wet and soapy.

"What?"

"Look." Camille pointed toward the skylight and said, "Snow."

He sighed.

Last night, she hadn't been able to see him fully. She hadn't imagined that he would be this perfect.

"Baby, that's flurries. That's not real snow. Can I finish my shower now?"

"Yes. Fine."

"I have a better idea, though. Why don't you come join me."

"Greg, no."

He pulled her out of bed anyway while she laughed and screamed.

Over coffee, afterward, they talked at the kitchen table.

"Find a dress?"

"Hunh?"

"A dress. You and your sister."

"No. I'm going to look some more."

"What was up last night, Cam?"

She looked up from her coffee.

"The way you were. What happened between us."

"Making love."

"Well. Not just making love. You were . . . It was like you were tortured or something. The way you came at me."

"Came at you?" She was embarrassed now.

"Maybe that's a poor choice of words, but you were pretty aggressive."

"I didn't mean to be."

"Well. No. I liked it. I've never seen you like that. That was different. A side of you I didn't expect."

"Oh." She couldn't tell him the truth. That her feelings of weakness led her to act out as she had.

"There anything you want to tell me?" He rubbed the middle of her back.

"No."

"Well. It doesn't take a psychiatrist to tell that something's bothering you."

"I trust you, Greg," she said suddenly.

"I trust you too."

"Okay. If you do, then you have to trust that everything is okay. I have some stuff I need to think about that I can't share with you just yet, and this baby keeps me tired, but honestly, I'm just fine."

"Sure. I won't invade your privacy," he said. He poured himself more coffee.

"I'm going to go upstairs and get dressed so we can get to my appointment on time. Okay?"

"Of course, baby," he said. "Of course."

11

*R*EINVENTING RULE ELEVEN: *Strength comes with knowledge, and knowledge by experience.*

ON THANKSGIVING DAY, Catherine drove up in front of the house in a second-hand Volvo with paper tags. She beeped the horn several times.

"What in the world?" Mel said. "What is all that noise?"

Ben looked out the window. "Mom, Nana's got a car."

"A car?" She joined Ben in the window and said, "Oh, my goodness."

Then a key was turning the lock. The door swung open, and Catherine swept into the house carrying a grocery bag hooked on her arm. She took off her sunglasses, smiling.

"I thought you might forget the cranberry sauce, so I picked some up. And some sparkling cider. I know how much ya'll like that. Hi, Desnee," and gave her a friendly peck.

"That's not all you picked up," Mel said.

"What? Is there something on me?" Catherine swiped imaginary dust from the sleeve of her blouse and readjusted the bag to hand it off to Desnee.

"The car, Mama."

"Oh, that," Catherine said. She began humming.

"Yeah, oh that. Where'd you get a car from?"

"Like most people do, I bought it. You've heard of this concept, sweetheart?"

Camille was in the kitchen with Greg basting the turkey for a final time. The smell from Aaron's nasty jambalaya was getting to her, so she covered it with Saran Wrap.

"Listen to you. What are you doing going out buying a car? You didn't mention to me you were buying a car."

"I'm grown, Melanie. I don't have to run my decisions by you."

"I don't approve, Mama."

"I'll keep that in mind. Is supper ready yet? Hello, everybody." She rubbed Aaron's shoulder fondly, then pecked Ben and Marlon. They were building a Lego castle in the middle of the family room floor.

"Well. How are you, Ms. Cathy?" Greg kissed her cheek.

"Gregory, it's so nice to see you, son. Everything smells so good. You girls outdid yourselves. Desnee, baby, pour me a healthy glass of that sparkling cider. Put the cranberry sauce on the counter."

Camille nearly dropped the baster. She couldn't remember a time when Catherine had complimented her for anything.

"You're in a great mood, Ms. Cathy," Desnee said, handing her a glass.

"It's Thanksgiving. Cheers." Cathy toasted them with her glass, then took a sip.

"How's the turkey?" Mel asked Camille. She had just finished setting the dining room table with a centerpiece of orange and white carnations flowing out of a horn of plenty.

Camille transferred the fourteen-pound bird to a serving platter and said, "Ready."

The boys cheered and left their construction work.

"Here, baby, let me help you with that." Greg took the serving platter and brought it to the table.

"Did you see it?" Mel asked Camille.

"What?"

"That car."

"Why is that a big deal?"

"It's not just a car. It's a Volvo."

"A used Volvo, Melanie," Catherine threw in. "It has over fifty thousand miles on it. And I can drive it back to Florence when I go."

"Whenever that is," Camille muttered, as she filled a water glass.

Aaron looked around the room and asked, "Is there something I can help with?" but was ignored. He leaned awkwardly against the wall. Too much confusion was taking place. First, Desnee was loudly complaining to no one in particular about how dinner would ruin her diet while she munched on a potato roll. Catherine set the can opener on the cranberry sauce, but that noise she drowned out by singing a Christmas song into a fork. Mel was shepherding the boys out of the dining room, saying, "No. Come out. You two are eating in the kitchen."

"Aw." They showed their disappointment by stomping back into the kitchen.

Camille and Greg had put into action a tag team effort to set pans and dishes of food on the buffet.

"But, Mom, we're hungry," Ben said.

"It's coming up. Mama, could you please stop singing. I'm getting a headache," Mel said.

"Fine."

Cathy topped off her song and concentrated on slicing the cranberry sauce.

Camille slowed her pace. Almost all of the food had been passed off to the dining room. She was winding down now. She'd been up since five. She sat on a stool and asked Greg to get the potato salad out of the refrigerator.

Desnee yelled in despair, "Oh, no! How am I supposed to say no to Ms. Cathy's potato salad? I'm putting on pounds by looking at this spread."

"Girl, please," Mel said. "You're putting on pounds by eating that bread in your hand."

Camille laughed at that and reflected on the last seven years and how different it had been from this year. Having over Evan's dismal mama and stepfather who complained throughout the meal every year. And sometimes having to entertain his brother Daniel, who always managed to steal something (she and Evan's mother would hide their purses among the pots and pans). Without fail, Evan would drink too much and lose his temper. Now she didn't have to worry about that. This year was so stress free. She didn't have to be afraid anymore. She had Mel and Ben and this precious baby and Greg. Aaron and Desnee were such good people.

Camille took her place beside Greg at the table when all was ready.

"You boys come in here for this part. Before we pray over this wonderful food," Mel said, "I think we should individually give thanks. We've all been so blessed. I think we should go around the table and everybody say what they are thankful for."

"What a good idea, Melanie," Catherine told her.

"I agree," Aaron said.

Starting out with the boys, each of them spoke a few words. Camille's turn came last. Her heart was so full that tears gathered in her eyes so she bowed her head.

"I am thankful," she began, but somehow she couldn't capture what she felt with mere words. "I'm thankful," she tried again, "for this."

She looked at their faces, even Catherine's, and knew that they understood what she was trying to say.

❧

"I HAVE THIS SEMINAR COMING UP, the biggest one of my career. My fiancé is romancing my closest friend. I can't eat these days, I can't sleep half the time. And now you're turning on me too. The only real friend I thought I had."

Nora puffed on a cigarette.

"Turning on you?" Camille said. "What do you mean? I'm not turning on you."

"Why are you being so mysterious about Harold?"

"What mysterious? I told you what happened."

"Tell me again," Nora said. Tracy buzzed, but she ignored it.

"What do you want me to say? I told you all there was to know."

Nora shook her head and said, "Doesn't sound like Harold. But you're telling me that he called, asked you a few questions about your job and how you like it, and that was it."

"That was it," Camille said. Her stomach churned. Even the baby seemed upset about her lies.

"He wants something. He didn't ask you to meet with him?"

"No."

"Didn't ask you to do anything?"

"No."

Nora sectioned an orange on a paper towel. "What did you say to him?" The shrewd eyes were like fire torches.

"I asked him why he wanted to know."

"And what did he say?"

"Said he was curious, that's all."

"*Curious.* That's not a word Harold uses. *Curious.*"

"Okay, well, maybe I'm paraphrasing. I can't remember what he said verbatim. Maybe he said something like he just wanted to know. I heard it as *curious,* though."

"Harold never does or says anything out of curiosity. His most innocent questions have a reason behind them. Always. There's something he wants or something he's planning, but it doesn't make sense. Why would he come to you? Have you been talking to William?"

"No. Nothing other than work. I stay as far away from him and Dawn as possible."

"Good. Because those two are up to no good. I just know that Dawn is sweet-talking William into replacing me."

Someone knocked on the door. It was Tracy. She stuck her head in.

"Oh, hi, Camille. I didn't know you were in here. Sorry. Nora, it's Carmen Graham on the phone. I thought you might want to take it."

"Yes, of course. Tell her I'll be with her in just a moment. Thank you, Tracy."

Then to Camille she said, "I have to take this call. But Camille, I need you on my side. You know that I do."

"I am on your side, Nora. Nothing has changed that."

"You hear from Harold again, let me know." Nora removed one of her clip-on earrings.

"I will. I'll keep you abreast of everything that's going on."

Nora picked up the phone and put on her happy, confident voice, saying *darling* as if she didn't have a problem in the world.

Camille left Nora's office feeling dejected and tired. All these lies had to stop. Harold Mathis was a horrible old man, asking her to keep secrets. In a few weeks she would have to give him her decision. Well, she'd already made it. She wasn't going anywhere. She was getting married, buying a house with Greg, and having her baby right here as planned. Let him find somebody else for his perfect job. She was comfortable right here. All she had to do now was get motivated to start planning this wedding. With this job business weighing on her mind, she'd been dodging Sophia Denton's calls.

She picked up some of the tasteless, industrial coffee from the staff lounge on her way into her office, then sat down at her computer to check her e-mail. There was one from Connie Steele, Harold Mathis's assistant. Camille opened it and gasped. It was an e-ticket, one way to San Diego in her name, dated December 26.

For several minutes she couldn't think. She was in a panic. She read the e-mail over and over, not wanting to believe it.

They were trying to push her out. Nora said Harold was planning something, but why would she have to be gotten out of the way? It just didn't jibe. Camille picked up the telephone on the first ring.

"Camille Foster," she answered.

"What the hell are you doing to me? Hunh? I've called and called you. You never return my messages. I have been patient with you. I've bent over backward for your ass. I want you home now, Camille. You understand me? You bring your ass back to New York, and I'm not playing with you this time."

"Evan, stop it. I don't want to hear your stupid threats."

"You be careful what you say, Camille. One of these days you may look up and see my face."

"Good," she challenged. "My fiancé would love to see your face."

Dead silence. Then, "Your . . . Your what?"

"That's right, my fiancé. And he would love to get his hands on you." Why hadn't she seen before what a coward he was?

"So you got big talk now that you hiding behind some dude. It won't work, Camille. You're my woman. You will never belong to anyone but—"

She hung up and pressed the Send Calls button so that her calls would go to voice mail. She thought she felt the baby flutter. At least one good thing had come out of the toxic hell she'd left behind.

"Hey there."

"Greg. Good morning."

"You look like you could use a massage."

Before he reached her desk, she minimized her Outlook mailbox, paranoid that he'd see Connie Steele's e-mail. He probably didn't know who she was, but she couldn't be too careful.

"I sure could."

He began working the kinks out of her shoulders.

"Well. Time's going by pretty quick."

"Yeah." She didn't have an idea what he was talking about.

"We should really get moving on these plans, don't you think?"

"Oh, the wedding. Uhm."

"We've got so much to decide on. Have you gone out again to look for a dress?"

"Not lately." More like not at all. The lies were getting too easy.

"I rented my tux."

"Already?"

"There was a special, so I thought why not. Will and I both."

"Does he have to be your best man?"

"Camille, we already discussed this. Will is a good friend. What do you have against him?"

"I just don't know him that well, Greg."

"There's no rule that says *you* have to know him well for him to be *my* best man. That's my choice. I don't know your sister well, and I have no objection to her standing up with us. It matters that she's important to you."

"You're right."

"Why don't you come see me tonight. I'll cook something nice."

She was irritable and tired. She wished he'd stop kneading her shoulders, but didn't want to hurt his feelings by telling him.

"I need some rest, Greg." She straightened a length of garland on her desk.

"Rest at my house. We both know my bed's big enough for two."

"I can't. Maybe tomorrow night. I'm exhausted. I might even go home early and just veg out in my room in front of the television."

"Suit yourself. Are we going to . . ." He stopped, then said, "Never mind."

"Are we going to what?"

"Nothing."

"Greg."

"Well. I don't want to sound impatient. But I've been wondering if you wanted to wait until we're married before we make love again. Or until after the baby is born."

"Oh, God."

Camille sagged in her chair. She didn't want to think about that. There was this wedding to plan, Nora accusing her of being a Benedict Arnold, Evan calling with threats, Catherine running around being nice all of a sudden, and this job hanging over her head. Her body was turning into the Goodyear blimp by the second. She would be in maternity clothes within another month. Who could think about having sex at a time like this?

Her hormones were racing. Her first inclination was to punch Greg in the mouth for mentioning sex. The thought of violence scared her. She took a few deep breaths.

"I'm sorry, Greg. I don't mean to be . . . this way. I'm just so tired."

"I understand, baby."

"I know you do. Can we talk about this another time?"

"Whenever you're ready."

"Thanks."

He seemed to get the hint because he backed off from the shoulder massage and said, "I'm going to go wrap some things up. I have a lunch meeting with one of the vendors this afternoon. You need anything?"

"No, Greg. I'm sorry."

"It's fine, baby. It's cool. I love you."

"I'll see you later on."

It was the stupid job making her crazy. It was causing her to tell lies. It was causing her to lash out at Greg. It was time to put an end to this. She pulled up Connie Steele's e-mail again. An e-ticket. How presumptuous Harold Mathis was to take for granted what her answer would be. Well, he would see that she wasn't one of his puppets. She clicked on the Reply button within Connie's e-mail, then fired off a message: *Please inform Mr. Mathis that I appreciate the offer,* she wrote. *But I will not need this ticket, as I have decided to remain employed as program manager here at Reinventing the Woman.*

She clicked the Send button. There. It was done. She was now out of whatever his game was. Now she could focus her attention on planning her wedding. But why did she have a sinking feeling that there was more to it than a simple e-mail refusal?

✑✒

TWO WEEKS LATER, SOMETHING HAPPENED. To use the word that Nora said Harold never used, Camille found something curious in the master bedroom that her mother had been using since she'd arrived. A button had come off the gray cardigan she'd wanted to wear to the movies with Greg, so she went into the bedroom that was actually Mel's to search the night table drawer where Mel kept her needles and thread. There they were on top in an unmarked manila envelope: photocopies of checks for large amounts written out to Catherine by Nora with receipts attached to them.

Camille counted them. Fifteen copies and deposit receipts. Her heart throbbed in her chest. No one was home to ask. Catherine had gone out hours before. Mel and Aaron had taken the boys to Dave and Buster's. The doorbell rang, and Camille thrust the material back into the envelope and carried it downstairs with her.

"Brr. It's freezing out. Hey, baby." Greg kissed her forehead when she opened the door.

323

"Greg, I found the strangest thing."

"What?"

She handed Greg the envelope. He looked at her, then took out the contents.

"Why would Nora be writing my mother these checks?"

"She's a wealthy woman. Always helping people. Maybe your mother went to her for financial help. You said they were good friends."

"Good friends is one thing, Greg, but fifteen checks? And look. They're all for thousands of dollars. Look at this one. Ten thousand dollars. I don't get it."

"Where's your mom now?"

"I don't know. She's been gone awhile."

"Okay. We have some time before the movie. Why don't you give Nora a call?"

"I think I will. Come on."

They went into the family room, and she picked up the cordless and punched the numbers to Nora's house.

"Hello?"

Will answered.

"Is Nora there?"

"Who's this? Camille?"

"Yes. Is she there?"

"That Will?" Greg asked, and Camille nodded.

"How are you, Camille?" Will was saying. "All ready to walk down that aisle with my man?"

"Tell Will I said hello," Greg whispered.

"Of course. Nora in?" she said impatiently.

"She's off shopping somewhere or something. Shall I tell her to call you?"

"Yes, please. Greg says hello."

"Oh, he's there?"

"Yeah."

"Let me holler at him a minute."

She handed Greg the telephone, and he proceeded to laugh loudly into the telephone, saying, "Man, what's up?" Camille took the envelope out of his hand to look at the copies again. She was going to get to the bottom of this mess.

Camille sent Greg home with a promise to call him later. She fixed herself a light meal of chicken soup with a salad. Around a quarter of seven, she heard a car pull into the drive. A few seconds later, Catherine came in.

Camille marched out to greet her. "What are these?"

For a split second, Catherine looked afraid. She took the envelope. She looked at the envelope, then through it, as if she had never seen it before. She looked up at Camille.

"You've been searching my things?" Catherine said, lifting her chin.

"I have better things to do than to rummage through your stuff. Try innocently looking for a needle and thread to sew a button, and what do you know? I come across these check copies adding up to a good eighty thousand dollars."

"So what?"

Camille folded her arms. "I want an explanation, Mother. Why would Nora give you so much money?"

"They're nothing. She's helping me out."

"Helping you. Why would she help you this much? That how you got yourself that expensive car outside?"

"It's used."

"It's a Volvo, and it's two years old."

"I'm not going to fight with you, Camille." Catherine tried to climb the stairs, but Camille blocked her path.

"I'm not going to fight with you either. But I will have an explanation."

"There's nothing to talk about. There were debts that mounted from your father's illness. Nora is a good friend. She helped me pay things off."

"All of these checks have recent dates. You mean to tell me that you just now asked her for help? Daddy's been gone all this time."

"It's not easy to ask someone for that kind of money. Least of all a friend."

"All right. I'll buy that."

"There's nothing to buy, Camille. I asked for help, Nora gave it, and that's all there is to it. Now if you'll excuse me, I've been out all day, and I would like to have a good soak."

Camille moved aside to let Catherine pass. Catherine snatched the envelope.

"The next time you go looking for something," she said, "I suggest you leave other people's personal items alone."

◈

MONDAY MORNING IT REALLY DID SNOW. The air was calm and still as it fell like puffs of cotton, coating bare tree limbs, streets, sidewalks, cars. Scattered patches of grass peeked out from beneath it. It was supposed to snow like this all day, and by then there would be nothing untouched by it. And it looked as if it was sticking pretty well. Camille was glad Greg had gotten her car winterized. She drove slowly up the beltway on her way to work. It took two hours to get there.

When Camille reached her office, she booted up her computer and after she logged on, she put Sade's *Love Deluxe* into the CD-ROM. She looked at the computer clock. It was almost eleven. She still hadn't heard back from Nora over the weekend. Mel and Catherine made it seem so casual that Nora would just give Catherine eighty thousand dollars. She couldn't let it go, not until she heard the same story from Nora.

She opened her e-mail. Like Greg said, Nora was a generous woman. She'd bought Dawn a quarter-of-a-million-dollar home. She made probably a couple of million a year. It was possible.

Camille's voice-mail light was lit. She checked it, hoping that Evan hadn't called again. She'd had five messages from him

327

over the weekend. But it wasn't him at all. It was Harold Mathis. She felt weak. She closed her eyes and leaned forward. Sade's haunting voice on "Like a Tattoo" rang in her ears. This was not going to be a good day. Harold Mathis had not asked for a return call, but had ordered her to appear in his office Wednesday evening. Again with the Wednesday nights. She looked at her wall calendar. A week before Christmas. Clever. Maybe it was time to tell Nora the truth and ask for her help.

Camille picked up the phone and dialed Nora's extension.

"Yes?" She was on speaker.

"Nora, may I come in to see you a minute?"

"Hi, Camille. Listen, let me come to you. One of Rob's technicians is making magic on my computer. I'll be down in a second."

"Thanks."

Camille looked at e-mail while she waited. Harold Mathis didn't let up. A detailed e-mail from Ms. Steele giving complete travel instructions was there. Why was he trying to get her out of the way? She would soon find out.

Nora strolled in wearing a long, straight wig reminiscent of the sixties. She had a terrific sense of style. The hair coordinated perfectly with a burgundy pin-striped suit and high-heeled black boots. She brought with her a cup of french roast and a grapefruit half peeled.

"Everything's in order for the New Millennium Woman conference," she said.

"Seems so. Last count was nineteen hundred, and that was

yesterday. Greg says he thinks there'll be a last-minute surge. It won't stop there. I agree."

"Leave a final count on my voice mail. I'm leaving this afternoon for Dallas and won't be back until next week."

"A lecture?"

"Something of that nature." She smiled, pointing above Camille's desk. "Mistletoe."

"Greg brought that in here last week. Crazy man." Nora eyed the many decorations.

"You must really have the Christmas spirit. How was your weekend?"

"Different." Camille turned off the music.

"How so?" Nora started peeling the grapefruit on the edge of the desk once she settled in a chair. The acrid smell enveloped the room.

"For one thing, I don't understand why you would give my mother eighty thousand dollars."

Nora didn't once look up from her fruit.

"I do that all the time. Somebody close to me asks me for something, and if it's somebody I trust who I know needs it, I'll let them have it. I have a giving heart, Camille. It's that plain. Any further word from Harold?"

She looked disinterested, but Camille could tell she was dying to know if there was more news. Camille opened her middle desk drawer for the e-ticket printout to show Nora, but something else was on top of it. Those intranet images again. This time the pictures were on the same page. They'd been cut out and glued together, side by side. Camille stared at it. She pulled it out of the drawer. She read the note that was attached. Her skin crawled. How could it possibly be true when there was no resemblance? But all of a sudden so much made sense. Camille looked up at Nora, blinking. Her face was hot. She didn't want to pass out. She focused on the diamond on Nora's finger, glinting beneath the lights as she worked the skin off her fruit.

"Darling, you all right?"

Nora halved her grapefruit while Camille struggled to breathe. She concentrated on it. Inhale. Exhale. Then she hit her stride with it, breathing deeply to bring in more air. She was finally able to stand up.

"You look unwell, Camille. Is it the baby? Are you hurting?"

"I have to . . ." Camille couldn't get the rest out. She had to get to the house. She left Nora standing in the doorway calling her name.

❧

It had never taken Camille such a short time to get home before. She was there in 45 minutes, having sped up the beltway in a fury that got her a ticket when a trooper pulled her over for it. She made up some story about being sick due to her pregnancy. The officer wrote her a lesser ticket than he would have normally and tipped his hat, telling her to drive more safely since the wet snow was coming fast.

When Camille reached the house, she found Catherine

330

cleaning collard greens in the kitchen sink. She looked up, surprised, and was about to ask Camille what she was doing
home, but Camille came in and slapped her hard. All of the
anger, all of the pain she'd experienced from the past was an
ingredient in that slap. Catherine let out a wail and held her
cheek. She sputtered.

"What . . ." Catherine's expression finished asking the question for her. Water from the faucet overflowed the bowl of
greens in the sink.

"What is this?" Camille said. "Answer me. Hunh? What is
this?" Camille threw the page with the pictures toward the
counter. It drifted to the floor.

Without looking at it, Catherine knew what this was about.
She wiped the blood from her mouth with a clean dish towel
she'd used for her hands. Catherine reached for the telephone,
but Camille knocked the receiver out of her hand. She stood
nose to nose with Catherine, pointing a finger.

"You tell me the truth, and you tell me right now."

"Not like this. Let me call Nora first." Catherine glanced at
the paper on the floor.

"Whatever there is to tell, I want to hear it from you. My
mother."

Catherine backed away from Camille, tears splashing her
face, and she said, "I'm not your mother."

She'd known it. She'd known it sitting in her office looking
at the paper with its glued pictures. She'd known walking
quickly to the garage in a fog. She'd known starting her car.

Driving it out of the gate. Accelerating across the Wilson Bridge. She'd known, but she hadn't admitted to herself that she knew. Like a woman with clues that her husband is unfaithful distorts the truth of her own understanding so that she can still go on. The whole ride home, Camille had wanted some other excuse for the evidence of what she'd seen. And because she was desperate, if Catherine had chosen to lie, she'd have held onto it. The truth had been voiced now. Catherine had given it a stamp of reality. Camille's first instinct was to shout *Liar!* just for the sake of reacting against the thing she hadn't wanted to hear.

Her knees were weak. Camille made herself pull out one of the kitchen chairs and sat at the table. A migraine was starting. She laid her head on the table.

"She didn't want me to tell you," Catherine said. Her red eyes were glossed with tears.

"The money?" Camille massaged her temples.

"For me to stay quiet."

"Blackmail money. Dirty money."

"I needed that money. There were debts and . . . Wade made me promise I would tell you about Nora. Before he died, he made me swear I would if I got the chance. He wanted to tell you himself, but you didn't come. When Mel told me you were here—"

"Mel told you I was here?" She felt nauseous. The lies would not end.

"That's why I came. I had to come. She heard your father

make me swear to him. She asked me to come and do what was right. But then Nora didn't want you to know. She knew I had outstanding bills. You were so broken, Camille. I felt guilty. I knew it was partly my fault you turned out like . . . I made Nora give you a job, and we agreed to a lump sum to pay my debts. But then Mel was upset that I'd agreed not to tell you. I went back to Nora and told her I had to keep my promise to Wade. She gave me more money. Then she kept regularly giving me checks without my asking. She asked me to have brunch with her Thanksgiving, and she showed up with the car."

"A Volvo. Ha. I don't believe this. All this time she pretended to be my friend," Camille said, "and now you're telling me that was a lie. She paid off the rent on the house in New York."

"I'm sorry, Camille. It's the way she is."

"How in hell is she my mother? Tell me that."

Catherine sighed. Her voice shook as she spoke.

"She'd wanted your father since high school. I wasn't like Nora. I was a good girl. Plain really. Nora was always part of the fast crowd. She could dance. She had . . . a way about her. The boys were after her hard, but the very one she wanted, your father, wouldn't have her. He liked her well enough, but he was *my* high school sweetheart."

She said this proudly, as if it was her greatest accomplishment.

"We married after college, me and Wade. We had Melanie a

year later. Everything was going along just fine. We were young, and we were in love. A friend of your father's, much older man, Yuri Brooks, owned a club downtown called the Nite Spot. Your father went there often. Bunch of our folks from the old gang hung out at Yuri's place. It was extra special for your daddy because he played the saxophone on weekends, and sometimes he'd sit in and jam with the band. He was so good."

Camille faintly remembered him polishing the brass on an instrument he'd take out of an old case from high up on the entertainment center. He'd never play it, but looked at it and shined it for hours, then put it back again.

"Before Melanie came along, I would go with him. After I had her, I didn't go out as much. One night we had a big blow-up over something silly. He picked up his sax and slammed out of the house on his way to Yuri's place. Nora was there that night. They drank too much. I didn't see Wade until the next morning. He kept quiet for weeks about what happened, and it tore me apart when he finally told me. I almost left him. But I loved him so, I couldn't do it. I didn't want to.

"Not much after that, Nora came around saying she was pregnant. She thought she was going to take Wade away from me, his wife. He didn't want her. Wade told me later she begged him to be with her, but he refused. She told Wade she knew a doctor who would take care of things, but he talked her out of it. She didn't want to raise a child. She wanted her

334

career. Her life was too fast for a baby. He told Nora to have you and said that we would raise you as ours. I didn't want to do it, but I loved him more than I love my life. That's a lot to swallow for any woman, to see the product of her husband's infidelity. But he wouldn't give you up for adoption. It wasn't easy back then for black babies to get a good home. So he brought you here."

"And treated me like an outsider."

"I was bitter sometimes. I kept wondering why I had to live with your father's mistake."

"Why did I have to be treated as a mistake? I was a child. Innocent."

"I tried. My heart couldn't take it. Every time I looked at you, I saw her."

"You turned him against me, too."

"Poor Wade was warring within himself. He didn't know how to handle it."

It was time to leave. Camille could feel the pull. She couldn't look at Catherine anymore. Ever. Couldn't be in the same room with her. The same house. She went for the door.

"Where are you going, Camille? Melanie's going to be so . . . Where are you going?"

"Do you realize," Camille said, "that all these years I tolerated an abusive man and allowed myself to believe he was what I deserved? I figured if my own family didn't love me, then maybe I wasn't worthy. Now I find out it wasn't me at all who wasn't worthy. It was all of you."

She walked out of the kitchen, stepping on the yellow note that had detached from the page with her and Nora's pictures. It said, *Nepotism.*

12

*R*EINVENTING RULE TWELVE: *Love yourself first and best.*

THE SECOND TIME EVAN HIT CAMILLE it was over football tickets. She'd gotten free Giants tickets for winning a contest at work. Camille hated football and had given the tickets to Art Benson in the accounting office. That night she'd made the mistake of mentioning it to Evan. Evan was a basketball fan. But she'd given tickets to a man, so he believed there was something going on between Camille and fifty-eight-year-old Art.

Evan beat her that night with whatever he picked up. First it was the remote control. The batteries came flying out of it. He dumped a plastic cup filled with ice water on her, then hit her repeatedly with the cup. It kept slipping out of his hand.

He rolled up a copy of *Newsweek* and continued. There were kicks in between. Blows to her head. A deck of cards he'd been teaching her to play Spades with thrown at her.

At the end of his nightmarish tirade, Evan broke into tears. He dropped to his knees and pulled Camille up, battered and bleeding, into his lap to hold her. She was barely coherent, but she remembered thinking maybe she deserved it. She thought that maybe Evan saw in her some flaw that he was trying to beat out, and that once he did, she would be lovable. She thought there was something innate that was visible to all those around her, and that was why she was mistreated. How wrong she had been.

On the outside Camille was a zombie because she was still in shock, but inside she grieved. She felt a pain greater than any she'd ever known for the sad girl in the pages of that old journal. This was too much. She had to process Nora's part and Catherine's, Wade's and Mel's. It could take forever. For months she'd doggedly tried to put Evan behind her. Something bigger than Evan had loomed on the horizon. How could she ever trust again?

There was nowhere to go, really, but Greg's. That would be better than sitting alone in a hotel room. By the time he came home, she would probably be ready to talk. The snow was sticking, so she drove carefully to his place. She checked the clock on the dash. By now, Nora was probably in the air on her way to Dallas. Camille didn't want to see her ever again.

She found a parking space close to Greg's door and skidded

into it, thumping the curb. The snow was piling up fast. It came diagonally from the perfectly gray sky because of the steady wind. Paper-thin flakes wet her cheeks and lashes, making her squint. Its wetness was the unsalted tears she couldn't let out. Her lace-up brown leather boots sank into the snow on the slippery ground to make intricate foot patterns as she reached Greg's door and found the key to go in. Warm heat swirled in the doorway.

To her surprise, lights were on. Greg looked up from the newspaper, sitting very still.

"Camille."

He gave her a nervous kind of look, like a doctor might give a mental patient he was unsure of. Her head still throbbed. She touched her temple and sighed, frowning, and he laid the paper on the table and went to her.

"I knew you'd come sooner or later. I was worried about your driving around in this weather."

"What are you doing home from work so early?" Camille asked, stamping snow out of the crevices of her boots onto the mat in front of the door.

"Baby, I'm so sorry. Your mother called me at work. She told me . . ."

"Which one?"

" . . . what happened. She was concerned."

"Ha. Right."

"Camille. Baby." His eyes were sympathetic.

"They all lied to me. My whole life is one big lie." She let her coat drape across the back of the sofa and leaning in the window, folded her arms to watch the snow and a man crossing the parking lot with the flaps of a furry hat snug over his ears.

"I can't believe they did that to you."

"I came from New York to find my peace. My life. There never was a life, Greg. Only an illusion."

"I wish I could say something to make this easier for you. But we'll get through it together."

"I knew something was strange when Moth—Catherine came all the way from South Carolina out of the blue. Then she stayed and she stayed. I kept asking Mel, Why is she here? Why is she staying so long? Mel knew the whole time. And then Nora . . ."

"Can I get you anything?" Greg asked. Slowly he walked up behind her placing a hand on each arm. Camille shrugged him away. She went to the sofa to unlace her boots, then went to the window.

"She was supposed to be my friend. The great Nora Jordan. Helping hundreds of women learn how to respect themselves. Take care of themselves first and become whole. Wonder what they'd think if they found out she's a big fat phony? Chasing my father down long enough to get pregnant, then dumping me off when she found out she couldn't have him."

"Well. I think she was what she *could be* to you, Camille."

She turned away from the window.

340

"How could you say that? How can you think she did right by me? It was all a lie. Why would you take her side?"

Greg lifted a hand.

"Hold on. I'm not saying that. Honey, you have to calm down. This can't be good for the baby."

"Then what are you saying?"

"What did you think? She would just tell you: 'Hi, I'm your mother'? You wouldn't have received her like that."

"I won't receive her as anything ever again. Her and that blackmailing bitch Catherine can rot in hell." She began to pace in circles.

"Camille."

"I see the way you're looking at me, Greg. You had two parents who loved you. You haven't lived my life. You don't know a thing about what I've gone through."

"That's because you won't let me in."

She stopped in her tracks. "Can't you see that I don't know how? I don't know how to let you in, Greg. I don't know how to open up. I don't even know what exists inside of me."

She sank to the floor in a heap, her hand covering her mouth to silence her sobs.

"Oh, baby. Baby. I don't know how to help you. I only want to love you, Camille." Greg was crying too. He came to her on his knees to cradle her head in his lap. The emotion swept over her in a tidal wave and was gone. Years with Evan taught her how to suppress such outbursts.

"I know," she said. "I know. Me too. That's why we have to take the jobs."

He stopped caressing her hair.

"The job?"

She sniffed, then rose to her knees beside him.

"Harold Mathis."

"What are you saying?"

"He offered us jobs."

Greg stood up. "Us?"

"Couple weeks ago. He called me."

"Why didn't you tell me?"

"He wanted me to come down to his office for a meeting. He was real mysterious about it."

"Why are you just now telling me?"

"He ordered me not to. Unless I decided to accept the job."

It was Greg's turn to pace. "I'm not following you, Camille. What job?"

"Director's position with their cable network."

"Why would a man like that offer you a job? That job?"

"He said you'll have a job too. I've pieced it together. Nora's behind it."

"Hunh?"

"I know she is. Catherine kept threatening to tell her secret, so she pays her off, then tidies it up by asking Mr. Mathis to arrange a job for me on the West Coast. Knowing how I felt about Catherine, she knew I wouldn't be in touch. She'd be safe from the truth. And she'd still play the friendship card."

"I don't believe this. This a damn soap opera," Greg said. Then he thought for a moment.

"Wait a minute," he said. "Did you say West Coast?"

"San Diego," Camille confirmed.

"San Diego? Man. We should talk more about this, baby." He went to the minibar to pour himself a drink. In quick strides, Camille was beside him, hanging onto his arm.

"Greg, you *have* to come with me. I can't do this by myself."

"San Diego, baby. I love *my* job. You love *your* job. We were gonna buy a house and raise the baby here." Greg drank deeply from his glass.

"Come on, Greg. I can't stay at Reinventing knowing what I know. I can't believe in her anymore."

"What makes you think Mr. Mathis won't rescind the offer now that you know the truth?" She didn't tell him that she'd declined the offer.

"I don't know for sure. They sent me a ticket. The plane leaves two days after Christmas. He's asked to see me next Wednesday. Please say you'll take a job with me. We can have a fresh start there, Greg. I know it. I can't stay here the way things are. You will come won't you?"

"There is a bright spot to all of this," Greg said.

"What's that?" She was afraid he was going to turn her down.

"Us. We've got each other."

He hadn't come out and said no, so she took that as a yes and hugged him.

⁂

CAMILLE HUNG UP ON MEL for the fourth time, and Greg turned the phone off when the ringing didn't stop. Greg did everything he could to help divert Camille's thoughts. He talked to her about work, tried to interest her in playing Tekken on his Play Station, and gave her a foot massage with baby oil. Finally he'd trudged across the street in the mounting snow to the shopping center for rented videos from an off-brand rental store and Chinese food from the Golden Pearl carry-out restaurant where they'd preordered the beef and broccoli and fried wonton that Camille had a craving for.

Camille had wanted to go with him to give herself something to do. But what if she fell, he asked her, and hurt the baby? Or got herself sick with a miserable cold? She'd regret it. He made her stay inside, and knowing she loved history, left a book in her hand on the fall of the Incas that she threw on the bed when she heard him go out.

While he was gone, Camille sat in the window seat in his bedroom that faced the parking lot, looking out for his return and massaging the baby. It was getting on three o'clock, but the sky was so lifeless it could have been five. Unwanted thoughts crept back to her. Before she could stop them, she was starting to cry. She had fooled herself. Ever since she'd left

Evan, she was sure that she was moving forward. The changes she saw each time she looked in the mirror had said so. She wasn't the same girl in glasses too shy to talk. Her new look had given her confidence she had never possessed. Inside, who was she really? She was just as undefined now as she had been as a child.

Some school kids who'd been let out early were chasing each other throwing weak snowballs and shrieking. Camille shook her head. Too many thoughts lay out like shards of straw in front of her. But she kept coming back to that little girl she felt so sorry for. *Go find something constructive to do.* It was Catherine's battle cry. Fall and winter, she had school all day. In summer, she went out into the neighborhood right after breakfast and played in the grass alone until the Johnson girls joined her. The evenings, she came inside only after the streetlights were already on, and unlike Mel, she told herself that she was special because she was allowed to eat in her room.

She tried to be quiet when she was inside so Catherine wouldn't notice her or become upset. She made sure she did her chores first: kept her room neat, swept off the porch, and cleaned the windows and sliding glass doors with Windex. Her favorite indoor activity was to look at the pictures in the encyclopedia books. When she tired of that, she made imaginary tea for her Barbie dolls and the stuffed animals she stacked side by side on her bed. Then she'd sneak around the house, hiding in closets, under beds, wherever she could spy on Catherine and Mel. She'd take notes in her journal until her

favorite line-up of sit-coms came on. She thought what she'd
said in the journal, her question that had taken fifteen years to
answer: *Why does Mommy hate me so much?*

How long had she prayed for a mother like Nora? A woman
who understood life and what being a woman was about. A
woman she'd spent mornings walking with arm in arm, giving her snatches of stories about herself. They'd had fun together. She'd watched in the wings while Nora made fiery
presentations to hurting women. She'd been proud. She'd
wanted to be like her. Looked up to her. And yet Nora had
confided in her and let Camille see her at a vulnerable point
that made Camille believe they were friends. Friends. The
pain seemed to slice her open, and more tears came.

She couldn't do this. She couldn't sit around thinking about
this. The burden was too heavy. It was better to move around.
Greg was taking too long anyway and the baby was hungry.
She padded down the spiral staircase to make some tea and a
snack, when Greg came in shaking off snow like a wet puppy.

"You're back. Just in time. I'm about to make us some tea.
Was it brrr out there?"

She reached the bottom step and knew immediately that
something was wrong.

"I, uhm . . ."

Nora came in behind him, wrapped in yards of fur starting
with her hat.

Camille seethed. She sat on the stairs and couldn't take her
eyes away. For the first time, she was seeing Nora for what she

346

really was. A little, aging woman trying to hide behind a persona she'd created that was all smoke and mirrors.

Nora walked her cool, no-nonsense walk. Despite the snow Nora still wore her high-heel boots. The teardrop pearl earrings she'd worn earlier quivered like tiny pendulums as she brushed snowflakes off her coat.

"She was waiting in the parking lot," Greg explained. He didn't meet Camille's eyes.

"Greg."

"Camille, you have to." That was all he said, and she wasn't prepared to debate with him because she knew he was right. The odor of broccoli filled her nostrils when Greg walked by to get to the kitchen. She wished she could erase the details of this day, sate her appetite, and hibernate in bed the rest of the week.

"My flight was cancelled," Nora said, as if that would explain everything. She unbuttoned her coat and casually laid it across a low bookcase.

"I have to check back in the morning to see if I can get out. They say the snow's supposed to end later tonight."

"What do you want?"

"I spoke with Catherine."

"Your accomplice?"

"Camille, you have every right to be angry. May I smoke here? But hear me out, please. I promise you I won't stay long." She took out a cigarette.

"No, you cannot smoke, and further I don't need your permission to be angry when you stand there knowing everything you've done is unforgivable."

"Are you going to sit there throwing fireballs at me, or can we talk to each other like adult women? I didn't come here for your approval or disapproval about what happened. But I thought I owed you an explanation."

Camille rolled her eyes. "Why, so you can sleep at night?" she asked.

"No," Nora said defiantly, "so *you* can. I'm sure you have unanswered questions."

"Then you'll be pleased to know your dirty work's been done. Catherine gave me the story already. You were hot in the pants for my father, you screwed him to try and trap him, but the joke was on you. I was the inconvenience that came out of all of that, and you had no qualms about throwing your mistake off on a bitter woman and my poor father who never lived down his shame."

"It wasn't like that."

"Oh, I can't wait to hear this. What was it like, Mommy Dearest? Do tell."

"It was not a one-night stand. That's what Wade told her, and I agreed to it. We didn't want to hurt her. I admit that I cared for him. You can't be intimate with somebody that long and not feel something. But Wade and I were not a casual affair. We had a chemistry between us, but he was smart enough to know I wasn't the domestic kind, and I was smart enough to know that that was the type of woman he needed in his life. Wade was the kind of man who had to have a center. A foundation. I had goals that were too big. I wasn't cut out for having babies and cooking and cleaning. That was Cathy's thing. So he did what was best for him, and he married her. We should have stopped then, but we couldn't seem to stay away from one another. When I found out I was pregnant, Wade wanted me to have you, and he wanted to raise you. What was I going to do with a baby, Camille? I was twenty-four. My sister had overdosed. I was on fire to make my mark. So I did what we both thought was best."

"That woman treated me like dirt. Like less than dirt. You had to know she would. As much as she loved my father."

"I couldn't know she'd treat you differently. Cathy was such a kind-hearted woman. Such a good mother. I had no doubt in my mind that she would care for you properly. Over the years she became . . . The whole thing was too much for her."

Camille looked her up and down.

"You give all you have to so many, yet you've taken everything from me. You've done nothing but take and lie. You do it every day with those poor women who think you're so special, and you did it with me. No wonder Will is screwing Dawn. She may not be as crafty as you, but at least she's real. There's no filler with her. Why did you even want me to work there when all you had to do was get me a job with Mathis like you're doing now?"

349

"A job with Mathis? What do you mean a job with Mathis?"

"Nora, please don't play any more games. I can't take it."

"Harold offered you a job?"

"Don't act as if you don't know." Camille took a closer look at Nora's shocked stare and said, "You *didn't* know."

"What job did he offer you? When was this?"

Camille remembered Harold Mathis's warning.

"This conversation stops now. I'd like you to leave."

"I'm not going anywhere until you tell me what Harold said to you."

Greg said, "You've had your say, Nora. It's time to go." He got her coat and held it out for her.

"Greg, please. Camille, I need to know what Harold said."

"Nora, I agreed to let you explain. You've done that. Now please leave," Greg said calmly.

He opened the door to bring his point home. Falling flakes found their way inside. Nora opened her mouth to say something else, but thought better of it. Greg closed the door behind her when she left.

"You did good, baby. I'm proud of you."

"There's nothing to be proud of, Greg. It didn't change anything one bit. She has no remorse about what she did to me. And, really, neither does Catherine."

"But that's their choice, honey. You're a better woman than they could ever be. You'll be a better mother too. Starting right here." He placed his hand on her stomach.

"But you did say something curious, though," Greg said as an afterthought.

"Curious? What?"

"I know you didn't know they were related because it's pretty hush-hush. But what gave you the idea that Will was having an affair with Dawn?"

"Nora. She said she hired a private eye."

Greg shook his head tiredly. "Baby," he said, "I'm sorry to tell you that she lied to you again."

"Why would you say that? The night she told me she was a complete mess."

"Baby, she lied to you. Dawn is Will's sister. Not his . . . I'm sorry."

Camille was stone-faced. She remembered Nora sitting on the floor of the bare apartment, drinking the entire bottle of wine. She remembered Nora throwing the ring across the room. No one was that good an actress. She'd been upset about something. But to tell a lie like that . . . The day had brought too much and Camille couldn't take anymore.

"Think I've lost my appetite. I'm going upstairs to take a bath," she said.

She tramped up the steps.

"Camille."

She turned. "I don't want to talk, Greg. Why is it that nobody else knows? Or is it that I'm the last to know? Again."

"Baby, Dawn is a private person. She didn't want anybody

351

else to know. But Nora knows perfectly well who she is. I can't believe she told you that."

"But Dawn. When she introduced me to Mr. Mathis, she called him Will's father. She said Mr. Mathis. That's what she said: 'Have you met Mr. Mathis?'"

"I'm sorry, baby."

"*I'm sorry, baby. I'm sorry, baby.* Don't keep telling me that! I . . . I'm going to take my bath."

That night she dreamed she swallowed an oak and held a thousand candles in the palm of her hand. She lit them all and smiled, proud that she could hold onto them. Nora appeared in the form of a breeze and blew out each candle one by one until Camille took the last one left flickering, tore open her own chest, and buried the flame in the base of the tree.

༄

THE FOLLOWING WEDNESDAY EVENING, Camille sat in Harold Mathis's luxuriant office, the wall of fire in the cavernous fireplace behind her as she sipped warm cider from a company mug.

"Ms. Steele received your decision via e-mail, and I wanted to discuss it."

"I do too. Some things have happened and I've changed my mind."

Harold Mathis leaned his elbows on the desk and made a steeple with his hands. He considered her above them.

"Things?"

She waved a hand in the air hoping to make it seem frivolous when she said, "Personal things."

"I see."

"I'll be ready to leave immediately. Greg won't be able to move for a few months. He has to get some things situated before he can come out. Would that be all right?"

"Not a problem in the least. I'm pleased you made the appropriate decision."

"I need to know something, Mr. Mathis."

He leaned back in his chair. Now that she'd accepted, he had relaxed and was fingering his pipe. "Yes?"

"Why me?"

He stared into the flames behind her.

"I asked you a few weeks ago, but your answer didn't fit. Why would a man like you take a pregnant woman and her fiancé, give them jobs, and move them across the country? There's got to be a reason behind it, Mr. Mathis."

"Ms. Foster, I do things for various reasons. Not always necessarily out of kindness, but there are times when I am asked something by someone I respect. Let's just say it was no accident that we met."

She couldn't think of who else might ask this for her and she said, "Nora?"

His sardonic smile gave her a chill. The cider had cooled, but she sipped it still.

"Know one thing: Nora Jordan is a woman who can think of

no one but herself. She would sell your soul if she could. She will cross you and court you at the same time. I've known her long enough to know. Why my son insists on allying himself with her is a mystery. Ms. Foster, I will share one thing with you. At this precise moment, Nora is on her way back from Dallas, where she believes she's made a deal with Bjorn Industries to form a new company. You see, at the end of business, December 31, her current contract with my company runs out. She has paranoid ideas regarding my plans for the future of Reinventing the Woman. What she doesn't know is that months ago, she renewed her contract to continue as Reinventing's spokesperson. She'll soon know."

Camille was ashamed that this same woman he'd described was her mother.

"Oh," she said. Her heart was broken.

"So. You will be ready to leave?" He gestured and she noticed that the silent Bereneice was waiting by the door.

"I'll be ready, Mr. Mathis. Thank you." She set the mug down and was escorted out of the room.

As before when Camille left, Dawn came out from the alcove that led to Harold Mathis's private bedroom. Harold turned to face his youngest, favorite child.

"Thanks, Daddy," she said.

"No need. I'm glad it worked out the way you hoped. Although I do not understand why this was so very important to you. I could have done better."

"I told you, Daddy. I owed it to her, but it had to be my way."

"I believe you should have told her the truth, my dear," Harold said blandly.

"I lost Yuri after one foolish night with Wade because of Nora."

Dawn thought back to how a jealous Nora had gone to Yuri with the truth.

"It was only right that she agreed to pay the price for it all this time. She wouldn't have gotten anywhere without your help with her company. She'll always need you behind her. She knows you can squash her career in a heartbeat. And I never would have survived if she hadn't pretended all these years to be my Camille's mother."

"I don't understand why you made Nora pay the wife to protect what you've allowed as the truth, yet you provide Camille clues that point her in a direction of deducing that Nora is her mother."

"Daddy, I couldn't help it. Seeing her out walking with my baby every day. Watching the two of them get closer. I couldn't help it. And Nora made sure I was around to see it. She purposely formed a cozy relationship with my daughter. Her little act had to come to an end. That's why I had to get Camille out of here. That snake would have found some way to hurt my baby to get back at me. She didn't deserve that. She's a beautiful girl, Daddy."

"That she is, Dawn. But to think Nora is her flesh and blood . . . I wouldn't wish that on one of my enemies. I only wish that you would allow me to do more for the girl."

"More? You've bought everything she's ever needed. Put her through college. She's to be married now, and she's off to a dream job you created just for her. Greg is such a good man. She'll be fine. Pretty soon she'll be a mother herself, and the rest won't matter. Nora's too afraid of you to do anything but go along with it."

"Won't matter?" Harold said.

Tears welled up in Dawn's eyes. She turned away.

"I have to tell myself that, Daddy. I made my decision a long time ago, and that's all there is. Do me a favor. Let me lie to myself if I have to."

She walked toward the windows overlooking a garden covered in minor patches of leftover snow and gazed up at the blackened sky.

⋙⋘

WAKING UP IN THE MORNING on the day she was scheduled to leave, Camille checked the clock. It was barely six and drizzling out. She performed her ritual of watching the sky change through the skylight and talking to the baby for a time. She was heartbroken over Nora, but she pushed it from her thoughts and tried to remember if she'd packed everything she needed to take with her. Greg sighed in his sleep. She looked over at him. He lay on his side, his handsome face void of expression. For as long as she was with Evan, she loved to watch him sleep. She could watch him for hours. Why didn't she feel that same pull with Greg?

Because you don't love him. The thought came to her before she could stop it, and she knew what she had to do. She got out of bed quietly and took a long shower, then dressed in warm clothes and called a cab from downstairs.

"Why didn't you wake me?" Greg came down to join Camille on the sofa where she sat, drinking coffee with tears in her eyes. Her luggage was beside the door.

"What's wrong?" he asked.

"You can't go with me." She bowed her head and crossed her hands in her lap. He sat with her and cupped her chin.

"Only three months, baby. That'll be fast. You'll be settled and we'll—"

"No, Greg. You can't go with me. I have to give you this." She held up the ring and put it in his palm. His other hand dropped from her face. She couldn't stand the stunned look in his eyes. The hurt.

"Take this back," he said, holding the ring out. "You're confused right now. I understand. A lot's happened. You have three whole months to think things through."

She wouldn't take it.

"My cab'll be here any minute," she said, as if once she left, he would be fine.

"Why, Camille? Why are you doing this?"

"This is hard, Greg. But it's the right thing."

The ring fell. He buried his face in his hands. The wind blew so hard the window panes rattled. She went to put a hand on his leg to comfort him, but he jerked away.

"I'm sorry, Greg, but I can't. There's been too much of this."

"You push away the one person who really loves you. That makes a lot of sense."

She was crying hard now. "Stop this, Greg."

He stood, gritting his teeth and pointed a finger at her. His eyes were red fire.

"All my life," he said, "I've fixed things. I'm good at it. When my dad died, my mom needed somebody to take care of her. I was sixteen, but I did it. I worked two jobs. I helped raise my little brother. I put myself through college. I take care of things. That's what I do. And then I met you. Damn, Camille, you were so shy and warm and sweet. You needed somebody. You needed something to help you. And I watched you. You started pulling it together, and you were hanging tight with Nora, and you were struggling to get on top, and every day I would feel your courage. And I loved it. I loved your courage. I started loving you for your courage. And I kept saying to myself, This girl can do this only if she gets a little push. A little help. I kept telling myself, This girl needs me. And I loved that you needed me 'cause nobody's really needed me for a long time, so how can you sit there telling me you don't? What's changed, dammit? Make me understand why you're throwing us away."

She held her hands beneath her chin as if she was praying,

and the tears squeezed out of her closed eyes. A car horn beeped. She knew it was the cab. She wiped her eyes with the heel of her hand.

"I can't let you go like this." He stood in front of the door.

"I told myself that I needed you, Greg. When I was a girl, I told myself I needed my—the woman I thought was my mother. I told myself I needed my dad. I told myself I needed Mel, and the kids at school, and then Evan, and Nora. All this time I've been running behind everybody else's love but mine. After all that's happened, I know the only person I really need is me."

She put her hand to her chest. The horn beeped again, insistently.

"Me, Greg. God knows why, but Mr. Mathis gave me this opportunity, and I have to use it to find out who I truly am and what I really want. Me and my baby. Now if you love me the way you say you do, you'll let me go, because even though it hurts, you know I have to do this on my own. You know."

"You don't love me." He said it as if all the life had deflated from him. He hung his head and moved away from the door.

"Don't you get it, Greg? Don't you see? This is about loving me. I'd better go. But I'll be in touch."

"I can't watch you go like this."

He walked back toward the kitchen while she opened the front door and motioned to the cab driver to come for her bags. Once she was loaded into the car, she leaned her head against the glass. So much had happened that she was too

359

weak to process it right now. She had time. She had an entire future ahead of her. Out of the corner of her eye, she saw Greg standing in the upstairs window. She was sad that it had ended like this. He was right. He had been the only man who ever really loved her. But that didn't matter now. What mattered was this baby and that blank canvas.

The driver took off slowly through the snowy lot. She held Greg's gaze and watched as long as she could until the cab turned the corner and she faced forward. One thing was certain. She had learned a great deal over these past months. She wiped tears from her eyes, telling herself that she wasn't running away from something this time. This was different. For the first time in her life, she was running toward herself.

ABOUT THE AUTHOR

Patty Rice is cofounder of My Sister Writers, a writers' group for African-American women. A poet as well, she has published a chapbook, *Manmade Heartbreak*. Ms. Rice resides with her two daughters in Maryland, where she is working on her next novel.